# THE
# ANARCHISTS

# THE
# ANARCHISTS

BRIAN THOMPSON

Copyright © 2012 by Brian Thompson

Great Nation Publishing
3828 Salem Road #56
Covington, GA 30016

www.greatnationpublishing.com
email: info@greatnationpublishing.com

This book is a work of fiction. Names, characters, places, and incidents are products of the author's imagination. The names Stan Witmore, Mason Conway, Justin Rochester, Harper Charlotte Lowe, Samantha Wright, Wynter Dawn, Yvette Sloan, Crystal Cantrell, Madison Marie Coley, Ramsey Mateo, Ellis Murtaugh, and Kelly Roshenburger were provided by the "Name a Character" contest winners and released for use with all legal rights. Any resemblance to actual events or persons, living or dead, is purely coincidental.

Printed in the United States of America

ISBN: 978-0-615-60214-1

Library of Control Congress Number: 2012932879

# ACKNOWLEDGEMENTS

To: My Lord and Savior, Jesus Christ, whose life continues to inspire and shape mine.

My "number one" Heather: a special thank you for this story's framework and your personal sacrifices and my parents, Bradley Harley, Sr. and Barbara Thompson for their undying support!

Everyone who provided invaluable input, especially: Reggie Alford, Stacey Bancroft, Adrienne Boisson, Martha Brown, Nakia Brown, Samedia R. Bryant, Debra Franks, Michelle Hover, Jeff Ransom, Jackie Rodriguez, Jenna Tress, and Susan Williamson.

All my former teachers who continue to inspire me: Tim Askew, Cindy Lutenbacher, Sandi Delp-Naso, Sue Posch, Toni Salaam-Butz, Kathy Walsh, and Linda Zatlin. I appreciate you more than you know.

Steven Manchester, my friend, and brother-in-Christ. Thank you.

The "Name a Character" contest winners (in alphabetical order): Rosa Batchan, Nick Carita, Carolyn Davis, Lauren Ellington, Jesse Epps, Kristi Lambert, LaKesha Mills, Barbara Shelton, April Ragland, Lisa Sinnock, Valerie Strawmier, and Jean Williamson. Thank you for your unique contributions.

My student virtual assistants: Maryann Key, Alex Oshifodunrin, and Lynae Bogues. Thanks!

Also, to my "Superfriends" Tyora Moody of Tywebbin Book Tours, Tia McCollors, Kemya Scott, Maria Joyner, Starr Hall, and Jonathan Brown/Definitive Visions, LLC. You are appreciated.

To my pastor Bishop Eddie L. Long: thank you for teaching me how to withstand adversity.

Watch for the sequel to The Revelation Gate, *Gates of Kuzimu,* coming in 2013.

*This work is dedicated to those struggling to make things right in the world.*

# PROLOGUE

Bound at the feet and hands, Noor straightened his posture. A crooked smile crept across his mouth as his eyes met those of his judge's heir. "I dared to overthrow your righteous kingdom and take *his* place," he spat with contempt. "There, I admit it. End this joke of a trial and suffer me to die."

EL's voice filled the chamber. "So be it."

Noor flinched, as blue winds whipped about his body. The floor vanished into darkness. He looked away, bracing himself for the worst. Swept into the air, he dropped down. . . *down* – faster and farther than any flight he had ever known. As he plummeted, those who supported the coup joined him – nearly half of EL's finest. To his surprise, the number included his five, most trusted lieutenants and secret co-conspirators.

Together, they rebelled against the command to serve. And together, they would perish for it.

The convicted crossed realms. From their origin in the third, to the second among the heavenly bodies, and into the last – that of the mortals. The skies cracked with thunder and lightning. Stars tethered themselves to each of the beings, giving the brilliant appearance of a billion falling flames, and the pungency of brimstone filled the air. The collisions flattened the mountains, raising valleys into new, higher precipices. Geysers of hot water spurted up through the fissures in the ground and formed boiling pools around the incinerated plant life.

Noor rolled over to his knees. Indeed, his essence had changed into that of a mortal female about the age of 20. He was alone, and retained several of his unnatural abilities.

But this body's sensations startled him. Small bumps appeared on its skin, but the flickering yellow bursts nearby abated them. He approached one of them until the fire overwhelmed him and he jumped backwards onto a jagged stone.

He winced, for the rock pierced the heel of his right foot and drew blood. Marvel and fascination over the pain excited him. EL forbade His servants to see blood, for it represented suffering to the mortals. It also possessed an ancient secret that only humans could choose to understand. Pursuit of that mystery for himself led to his capture and subsequent dismissal.

Why had EL exiled him and changed his gender? What purpose did that serve?

After the fire dissipated, a pile of neatly-folded clothes appeared in its place. Scorning the mercy, he dressed anyway. A few attempts passed before he appropriately wore them. Surveying the area, Noor recognized the city on the horizon – he had visited this particular peninsula several times before – and admired it for its lack of social restriction. Thus, he'd adopt its moniker as his forename and keep Noor as a surname.

In the remote distance, the smoldering horizon beckoned to be explored. Noor remembered the divine decrees, which indicated the lifespan a mortal would not exceed 120 years. He could not locate his trusted soldiers in that time, not if EL had changed their appearance, as He had to Noor. No, he must recruit five humans and find them in a century's time.

"If I cannot rule in EL's realm," he resolved, "then I will conquer this one."

# CHAPTER ONE

## MICAH AND HARPER

*New Year's Eve morning, 2049*

Prior to committing what some considered murder, Micah Darrion James held a high resolution photo of his family. Meanwhile, Harper Lowe, his always punctual girlfriend, changed from a fire engine red, v-neck sweater shirt and grey dress slacks into a knitted top and jeans.

Harper was a slender and leggy Caucasian, with shoulder-length blonde hair she ponytailed and obsessively dyed black to mask the premature gray. For the picture, she let it down at Micah's urging. Christian, then six months old, had been propped up between his father's thick legs, a smile squeezing from his fat cheeks. Two-year-old Gabrielle, his ebony-skinned daughter from a previous relationship, held a plush toy. Still tanned from the vacation, Micah laughed. His natural curls were cut low. It was his 38th birthday, about a year-and-a-half ago.

Last night, he happened to coerce his mother into entertaining her grandchildren for a few hours on New Year's Eve morning. He and Harper needed "couple time." Otherwise, the former scientist would question her son into the ground about their doings, asking "where are you going?" and "why can't the family go with you?" A two-time divorcée, Laverne James heavily scrutinized the relationships of both her sons — especially this interracial one. She informed him that Harper's enlarged breasts signaled pregnancy. He explained it as the effects of a push-up bra and hoped she left it at that.

Micah and Harper did not speak en route to the facility. It was their least expensive option, shoddy in more than a few ways, and situated in a dangerous location. Words had been previously exchanged on the subject, but nothing constructive. Harper was "irresponsible" and "forgetful." Micah, who had gotten downsized months ago, was "jobless" to his face and "basically worthless" behind his back. Because of their collective gross inadequacies, they agreed to end it. A third-party's involvement meant neither had to dirty their hands in the deed. The decision itself would remain a joint one.

Their transport rattled, halting at a traffic intersection where it moved no more. Micah cursed and authorized the ignition again, but the engine failed. Jupiter, an American auto giant, specialized in practical vehicles, but this one passed its prime 50,000 miles ago.

Harper started the vehicle's warning lights and expectantly looked at her boyfriend of three years. *We should have traded it in years ago, like I told him we should do.*

"I've got it." He cursed again before entering the pouring rain without Harper's umbrella, protected by his stained, black leather coat. Beneath the hood, his patchwork had not held: a critical hose hissed steam from a tiny split. Wrapping the crack to the best of his ability, he reconnected the hose. This time, the hydroelectric engine sparked alive.

"Piece of junk," she snidely remarked. "We're going to be so late."

Completely drenched, Micah cranked the heat to high and cut his eyes at her. "At least we own it. We'll get there in time."

"These people don't wait. It's not a drive-through window, Micah. You can't just get there when you get there and expect a D&C like a Happy Meal."

*I'm not the one who changed outfits.* "It's New Year's Eve. We'll be waiting anyway."

Micah tuned the satellite radio to something he could listen to and drown her out. When the station played a classical song he liked, Harper shut it off.

"Do you have to be like that, Harp?"

She crossed her arms. "I love the sound of falling rain, and I can't hear it over that."

He knew that but did not care. Silence forced him to dwell on his lingering drowsiness. Micah lit a cigarette and took a long drag.

"Really?" Harper shook her tousled hair, which showed hints of gray and blonde at the roots. "Of all the things you can think of to do. . ."

Micah exhaled smoke. "You shut off the satellite, I'm soaked, and you want to piss and moan about a cigarette? Listen to your rain and leave me alone."

Harper's hands cupped the bottom of her growing belly. Micah noticed it. "It's not a 'him' or a 'her' yet," he said, his voice trailing off. "It doesn't matter. . .not now."

"It's a boy," she ventured. "I know it, and it matters to me. You would too if. . ."

"C'mon."

She turned in her seat. "Your great-grandfather. . ."

"It didn't happen. And you can't have faith just because someone in your family did. That's part of why church is so fake now. . ."

*Here we go.* "There were articles, pictures, eyewitnesses. . . what about all the people he healed?"

". . .and you've got people pretending to love God, or even know him, or her, or it. People get leadership roles because they know how to work crowds. They put together shows with God slapped on them somewhere. I don't understand how you can believe in that. It's a con. I won't even get into the money thing."

"My faith lets me sleep at night," she shot back, "and I know that even after we do what we're about to do, God will still love us. Faith isn't a scientific thing, Mike."

The allusion to his insomnia irritated him. "God will forgive you, if you know it's wrong and you do it anyway? That's weak."

"That's love and mercy."

They said no more on the subject until Micah stopped at the clinic. Despite the rain, a line of silent but hostile-looking protesters blocked the entrance. A pang of fear hit his stomach. "These wackos make me nervous. Wait for me at the curb. I'll walk you in."

"Why, so we can be even later?" Harper opened the door, umbrella in hand. "Just park. I don't care where those people post up our pictures. We had a nine o' clock and it's 9:11. After 20 minutes, they cancel you, and I'm not going into the New Year without ending this."

"Ending what exactly. . .us, or the pregnancy?" He suspected the answer. "Just wait."

She departed without responding. Micah watched the canary yellow oval approach the gathering dressed in all black. If he abandoned the Jupiter in the unloading area and it got towed, that would be another financial burden. And then they would not have a way home.

Harper tried to circle the line, but a gaunt woman with a face painted like a skull blocked into her path. "Consider your options carefully," she warned.

The irony of options humored Harper. "Snap a picture and get out of my way."

"Give it up for adoption. Let a relative raise her. Take responsibility and raise her yourself. This isn't just about you and how you live your life."

Harper cursed Skull Face. "Then, who's it about: my unemployed boyfriend? The bills we can't pay? What do you even know about anything?"

"I know women like you use abortion like an eraser. Murder's a sin!"

"Do you have children? Have you even had sex before?"

The brazen woman's lip quivered a bit.

"Do you adopt? Take in foster kids? Show me one scripture that says 'tell someone what to do, but don't help them.' That's a sin. Tell me! We'll turn around and go figure this thing out."

"You could have prevented it." Skull Face reloaded on rhetoric. "Contraceptives work almost all of the time unless you don't know what you're doing."

Harper raised her fist to strike but a clinician kept her from doing so by restraining the expectant mother's wrist.

"That's enough." The woman had forced her way through the crowd. "The ban goes into effect tomorrow. Give this young lady the opportunity to exercise her right to choose today."

"Choosing death is not God's will!" said Skull Face.

"Maybe not," said the clinician. "But what about free will?"

At that, the doors shut behind them at 9:19.

Inside the whitewashed and sterile waiting room, Micah imagined the programmers responsible for the trippy music had been lobotomized. Four magazines later, the power cell of his holographic phone, or "holophone," had reduced to emergency levels, severely limiting his entertainment options. The spectacled nurse looked wroth and unwilling to change the HTV channel from the forum talk show airing. This type of holographic programming irked him even more than the judgmental assembly outside. He pushed his way through the ranks like a linebacker.

Irritated, Micah redirected his attention to the show, which, at a low volume, sounded like fighting turkeys. It featured five women of different walks of life analyzing and debating issues. Far stage right, a conservative pundit on the panel had a fashion sense as buttoned-up as her viewpoints. Next to her sat a wisecracking, middle-aged businesswoman. At center, Kareza Noor, a beautiful, middle-aged local executive, acted as guest moderator. To her left, a popular liberal provoked arguments to rankle the right-winger. Last on the panel, an Asian woman folded her hands and rarely spoke her mind.

The topic swung from trivial gossip to the changes in abortion legislation. The front desk attendant turned up the volume. Micah leaned forward and cocked his head. Though the James/Lowe family's finances were in disarray, this one thing went their way. The law would not go into effect until midnight tomorrow. Had Harper's boss Jackie not advanced them the monetary units, they would have had this child. Thinking about the diapers, formula, and healthcare expenses alone made his nights restless.

"Some of these peaceful demonstrations have turned violent, especially in Florida, and New York City – which has the highest number of legally-induced abortions. It's not about 'put-my-picture-on-a-website-so-everyone-knows-my-shame' anymore. People are getting killed," said Kareza with definition.

"Well, abortion – it's murder. Period. Point-blank." The conservative crossed her arms. "The legislation squares with existing laws. Kill a pregnant woman? You're charged with double murder." She flipped her hand. "Can't call it alive when on one hand, and deny it's alive on the other!"

"Murder is illegal," said the finger-pointing liberal. "But abortion shouldn't be. I'll put it out there. I own an Ordnance."

The funny one ducked, drawing nervous laughs from the live audience. "You brought it here, on the set? Take her purse! Pat her down or something."

"That's my Second Amendment right. How I use it is my choice. This new law takes freedom of choice away and enforces a system of beliefs on all women. That's unconstitutional. That's the decision handed down 80 years ago, Roe. Vs. Wade, and it should stand."

"So, let me get this straight: citizens should have the choice to shoot someone or kill babies?" the conservative barked. "Why even open your mouth and say something so stupid?"

"Stupid? Free will is stupid? What do you do about the poor and impoverished without access to free contraception and educational services because our conservative president cut funding to it? Tell them not to have sex? We were all teenagers once. Trust me: 'just don't do it' doesn't work."

Micah found interest in the topic, though his views were simple. They couldn't afford it. Laverne couldn't stand to help, and Harper's affluent mother wouldn't. A couple thousand monetary units now were better than the millions they may spend in the years to come. Their answer was simple, even now, as he imagined his son or daughter being destroyed. *My son.* He wanted another boy, but not now. Not like this.

Kareza crossed her shapely legs. "So, playing devil's advocate, should abortion be legal in 'certain situations' – like rape, incest, molestation, and the like?"

The funny one laughed. "Guest moderator for one day and you're trying to start a fight?"

"We're trying to get to pick at the heart of the issue," Kareza replied.

The Asian woman perked up. "The Center for Disease Control reports that pregnancies from rape, incest and molestation make up a small fraction of the three million abortions performed last year – less than one percent. Almost 80 percent say they aborted because of finances, unplanned pregnancy, or inconvenience."

"It's a sad state of humanity when bringing a life into the world becomes 'inconvenient'," said the conservative, drawing a small pocket of applause.

"Let me point out," said the liberal, "those numbers are documented cases of incest, rape, and molestations. It happens off the record all the time. How does a 12-year-old girl report that her stepfather or mother's boyfriend impregnated her and get someone to believe her story? This law forces her to keep a daily reminder of a sick act or seek a dangerous and illegal alternative."

Micah became so engrossed in the conversation that he failed to notice his name being called. A different nurse tried to mute the HTV in vain.

"Mister James, by now your wife should be in recovery."

"That was quick." Micah rose and quietly approached her. "Is she alright?"

"She's still under anesthesia. She will need you to fill a prescription."

"Any idea of how much this'll cost?"

"Not sure. I can't access that information at this time. Probably 300 units or so."

Micah's eyes bulged. "Generic?"

"That's the generic version."

He would have to pay a fraction of the utilities again and pray that they did not get cut off until Harper's next paycheck. Thankfully, her position as a psychiatrist paid reasonably well. But with the cost of living, the note on her transport, and their burdensome student loan debt, 1.2 million units a year did not go far.

"Here," she said, handing him a thumb segment-sized, blood red disk. "I know Kareza Noor, the woman on the HTV. She'll be able to help you with whatever you need. Be back at a quarter 'til one to pick her up."

Hands in pockets, Micah started the half-mile trek back to the free parking lot. "It was our decision," he told himself, though he knew that he pushed for it more than she did. He regretted forcing her to do anything and hoped she did not resent him for it.

More than halfway there, he checked the time. Ten minutes past noon. He stopped inside a busy Dunkin' Donuts on the next corner. Harper had not eaten breakfast, so a bran muffin and a shot of hazelnut-flavored caffeine might do her some good.

Fifteen minutes later, he ordered and paid, hustling the rest of the way. With all green lights, he'd still be on time – barely.

He docked his phone to charge it, placed the coffee in the cup holder, the muffin on the passenger seat, and started the Jupiter's engine, which turned over without reservation.

The sun broke through the clouds and shined on him. Thinking it a sign of good things to come, he turned on the radio. One of his favorite classical pieces, "Mars," played. He smiled, backed out of his space, and turned onto the street. When Harper got in, he would turn it off, and they would peaceably talk.

Since his layoff from the structural design firm, they had been under financial pressure. Harper's pay didn't cover the bills, so budgeting became a complicated balancing act. Unexpected expenses meant begging or borrowing to make it work. Micah's job search had been so unsuccessful that he even applied for menial jobs that preferred humans over droids. "Too educated" for those, and "not educated enough" for high-level mathematics positions, he was stuck. But, with this pregnancy out of the way, he felt better about their future.

Micah braked at the light a block away from the clinic. The song continued to build and he pretended to conduct the strings. Up the street, the protesters had vacated the property. Almost half of the tune had played before Micah realized the light still had not changed. His holophone lit up and projected an image of Harper in front of him. "Mike, where are you?"

"I know you've been waiting. I'm sorry. I'm stuck at the light out front. Be there as soon as it changes. And I have a little surprise for you."

Harper spotted the Jupiter from a café across the street. "Can you see me?" She waved behind the front window. "Baby, I didn't. . ."

"Plus," he interrupted, "I think I've got a lead on something good!" The signal turned green. Micah accelerated and pulled over 30 feet from the entrance. *We can finally afford to talk marriage!* "Do you know Kareza Noor? Is she in your department? Never mind. Tell them to wheel you out. I'm on time for once. And, we need to talk about. . ."

"Mike, listen, I'm across the street. I told them to stop. . ."

Suddenly, a raucous explosion blasted through the clinic, turning the Jupiter over and upside down. The suicide doors swung open, but the vehicle's collapsed dashboard pinned Micah into his seat. Shards of window glass jutted out from his face. He struggled to breathe.

"Harp. . ." Micah could not finish her name without coughing out the blood pooling in his mouth. He hoped someone heard his pleas.

# CHAPTER TWO

## DAMARIO AND MADISON

*New Year's Eve night, 2049*

The short-haired brunette at the bar winked.

Damario Coley – dark-skinned, dreadlocked, and terribly bored – gazed back at the archetypal beauty. Healthy and tan-skinned, she wore her curly chestnut hair in a school-boy haircut. Her slender waist sloped up to full breasts and down to a thick set of hips. In truth, she did not outshine Madison by much, but his wife considered curves "the Devil." She modified her diet, exercised, and dropped a dress size or two. Now, Madison was built like a well-toned rail.

Unwilling to be caught window-shopping, Damario whipped out his holophone and manipulated its displays. Drawn by the flickering blue lights, Madison elbowed him in the ribs.

"We're supposed to be spending New Year's Eve together. It's a Friday night, for God's sake." She smoothed her silver dress. "Put that thing away; I didn't plan this party for nothing."

"Just let me. . .finish. . .this. . ." Damario's fingers roamed across the glass surface, which projected a number of pictures and words above his palm. "I'm behind on the analysis impact...for the currency deal. Checking a few figures, Maddie."

Madison sighed with disgust. "If you're going to ignore me the whole time, I might as well let the others run the show and we can leave. Let's talk and not go into the New Year fighting."

"Now? You want to talk now?" Damario stifled his irritation. "I'll get you something to drink. After that, we can talk about whatever."

Madison's face softened. "Alright."

Damario crossed the room to the bar, where a bartender mixed drinks. "Pomegranate martini, up with a twist, two olives, and Macallan 18, neat."

"Sorry, Mister Coley, we've got Justerini and Brooks, but no Macallan."

Damario gritted his teeth. Since the barkeep referred to him by name, Madison must have briefed him as to her husband's liquor preferences. He offered to spring for the expensive stuff, but she said she'd "handle it," which apparently meant purchasing the cheap stuff to spite him. She'd mock him through its smoky aroma, as if to say their marital strife canceled his right to drink anything classy or vintage. "Fine, make it on the rocks."

From order to fulfillment, the process wasted barely three minutes, and now he faced returning to Madison. They would make small talk, and then argue more over something stupid. He did not want to mingle with the attendees: agents from Shenk Real Estate and their spouses. Employees of the development empire incessantly talked shop.

With any luck, the kiss between them at the dropping of the ball would be a smidge passionate and not an awkward peck. After that, the return drive home may even be civil. That would be a welcome change, and possibly improve the remote chance of them being intimate – but not dramatically.

It had been three months since she had openly undressed in front of him and six since they had touched one another in a loving fashion. It had been so long that Madison closed herself off to all of his indecent proposals. A massive financial project at work involving the federal government occupied his mind for the most part, but lately, even that did not help. Neither did practice at the gun range or the gym. Two months ago, he found out how she had managed her loneliness and found himself fighting similar temptations.

After he received his order and authorized payment with his fingerprint, a soft hand rested on his forearm. "Hi," she said with a foreign accent, European from its lilt. "I saw you across the room and I wanted to tell you that I love your locks."

"Thanks," he shrugged, heartbeat racing. "I. . ."

"Scotch neat, huh? That bad of a party?"

*Absolutely.* "I kind of hate New Year's parties."

"Me, too. Partiers are much more entertaining to watch from a distance." She viewed the two very different drinks in his hands. "You're here with someone."

He glanced over at Madison, who waved him over. He held up an impatient finger and mouthed *wait a minute.* "Over there, in the silver dress with the black heels. That's my wife."

She giggled at his morose tone. "It figures you would be taken. I'm Kareza Noor, and I'm terrible at flirting. It's like I haven't had a decent date in 20 years."

"Damario Coley," he said with aplomb, as they shook hands. "Flirting's easy, especially for women. Anyone could walk you through it."

"So you'll do it? I'm game for a lesson. But you better take that to her first. I'll be here when you get back."

Damario slowed his pace back to the loveseat, but his unsteady hand spilled a little of the drink onto the floor. "He had pomegranate juice after all."

"Half of which you spilled on the floor. What's wrong with you? Forget it! Just sit down."

"Look, I get it: I screwed up. The bartender's busy. But just give me a bit. I'll bring you another one and I won't spill it. I'll even have him throw on an extra olive."

"Alright," she assented. "But after that, we talk. No convenient disappearances."

He wondered what the "emergency situation" could be. She'd never tell him the truth, but always found the time to bother him with minutiae.

Damario returned to his post and drank from his glass. Another man had engaged Kareza in small talk directly in Madison's sight line. He positioned himself close, tapped the small of her exposed back, and then excused himself to the back edge of the bar. Kareza ended the conversation and met Damario.

"Thank you for saving me. One 'don't I know you from somewhere?' and a drink and he thinks he owns me dead to rights. Maybe he's the one who needs the flirt lesson, and not me?" She jiggled the dissolving ice in her glass. "I hoped you'd make it back. What's first?"

"We exchange names," he lazily said. *I wonder what Madison wants to say?* he wondered, while letting a swallow of scotch settle in his mouth. *A confession perhaps?*

"Did that, remember? Me, Kareza. . .you, Damario. Are you okay?"

"Yeah. Oh. . .no, I'm fine. Right, we did exchange names. Now, I say something like, 'Kareza? That's a lovely name.' Then, you tell me. . ."

". . .what it means? It's Italian. I'm half-Arabic, so that's where my last name comes from, but your opinion of me might change if I tell you what Kareza means."

He raised an eyebrow. "That's world-class flirtation right there, but I consider myself pretty open-minded. Give me a shot."

Kareza edged close, leaned into his ear, and explained her

name's origins in a few sordid phrases. The sensation of her breath against his ear, the percussion of her sultry accent on certain syllables, and the aroma of her perfume warmed the length of his body.

She drew back and smiled at the red flush washing over his face. "It's the name of an Italian city, too. My mother heard it and thought it was pretty, but swears she didn't know its meaning when she named me. So, I don't tell many men. They usually say all types of freaky things to me."

"'Freaky'? Definitely not a word you want to use in the first conversation. . .unless that's the kind of company you want. Keep it simple."

She parted her purple-glossed lips with a devilish grin. "Who says I don't want it? I need a good match, and I can't remember the last time I had good sex. Maybe that's who I need to attract."

"Suit yourself." He placed the empty whisky glass onto the bar and ordered another. "But why tell me all this?"

"Because you're off-the-market and it's easy to talk to strangers," she smiled, while readjusting the falling strap of her dress. "Every attractive person at this party is taken. And you volunteered to show me the ropes – which I appreciate, by the way. Who knows – I might meet someone after all."

"You're welcome." He smiled. "So you think I'm attractive?"

"Does it matter?" her voice trailed off. "You're married. Some married men have actually tried regardless of that. For some reason, I think I can trust you."

The label of "trustworthy" disappointed him. "You think you can trust me, but you don't even know me? I could be like every other person you've met."

"No, you can't be. It's just your personality, and it's nothing to get all riled up about. Believe me, I'm not great at flirting, but I am a great judge of character. I never miss."

Thankfully, a former client-turned-friend – the talkative, southern divorcée named "Sloan" – had engaged Madison in a lively conversation. After ordering his wife another drink, he decided to call Kareza's bluff. "Prove it."

"You're the type who allows the woman to make the decisions, not because you want her to, but because you want to keep the peace. Your wife probably finds you too passive and when you exert yourself, too aggressive. If you can't find a balance, you drift to whichever fits the situation."

Damario nursed his drink, taking in a little to avoid making direct eye contact. Kareza's assessment had stripped him naked and highlighted his vulnerable points. "How did you come to that conclusion?"

"I do high level work for the Genesis Institute, but I'm a psychiatrist by trade. I start out by reading into whatever my clients aren't telling me. Most communication happens on a nonverbal level. It looks like you are the aggressor when she wants you to be."

"Genesis Institute," he mused. "That a non-profit?"

"For profit. I'm overseeing an advertising campaign that kicks off in the next week or so. What do you do?"

"Financial analysis for G.R. Cooper, a little trading here and there."

"Aren't you involved in the congressional push for the new currency?"

"Yeah." His enthusiasm pushed his voice up an octave. "But if you ask me, the mark will never pass the House, or in the other nine countries where they're pushing it. Too much opposition."

She smiled, her top lip mischievously curled. "I don't know. You might be surprised."

The passionate charge behind her question forced him to safer conversation. "And you're a psychiatrist...you counsel married couples?"

"Nope. Don't believe in marriage. Lifetime monogamy is a ridiculous, contrived concept. I counsel singles, do a little grief, and I sometimes advise the newly-divorced on how to rebound."

"Be honest," he joked. "Tell me how you really feel."

"Think about it, Damario." She licked her lips and grabbed his right hand with her left. She traced his wrist veins with the pads of her index and middle fingers. "We're two, able-bodied human beings – an attractive man and woman. There's something between us that's electric, and you know it. But you're willing to give up what could be for what shouldn't be."

"Who's making the freaky proposals now?" Kareza had lied. She knew how to flirt well. Damario thrust his hands into his slack's pockets. How many other people in this room has she offered the same thing? "This cannot happen."

"Yes, it can. You could have me," she said with allure. "Your devotion to an antique concept stands in the way of something beautiful and passionate. Think of kings, David and Solomon. They knew this and were considered to be great leaders."

Damario jerked back. "Why bring up the Bible?"

Kareza touched a spot just below her throat where the emblem of his platinum chain fell. "I assumed that you aren't wearing that for decoration's sake?"

He dropped the object beneath his undershirt. "I love my wife and respect her." He paid once more and cradled the nearly-full glass. "Pleasure meeting you, Kareza."

Damario disappeared into the throng of people surrounding the HTV's three-dimensional images. By the time he reached Madison, her eyes had glazed over with boredom. This time, he softly walked until reaching them.

"Why, hello, Damario!" The audacious southern twang assaulted his eardrums. "Beginnin' to think you were gonna leave Shenk here all alone, while you chatted up that pretty Hispanic gal. Gosh, I just loved her dress, but I'd never be able to pull off something cut that low in the front without a lotta help, if you know what I'm sayin'?"

Madison cocked her head. "That's what you were doing over there?"

"She's not Hispanic," he argued. "She's European and Middle Eastern."

"Whatever."

"Well," said the southern belle. "Ya'll g'head and talk. Shenk, you and I. . .we'll conference first thing Monday."

*Please go away.* "Will do, Yvette."

"Tell my assistant if she don't put you through right then, I'll have her on the unemployment line."

"Right."

"I'll do it! Tout de suite! Happy New Year's, ya'll."

"Happy New Year," they said in droll unison. Damario reclaimed his seat and downed his scotch at once, while his wife continued to silently stare him down. How dare he! "So, you were talking to another woman, but you won't talk to me?"

"What if I did? You talk at me, Madison, not to me. You yell, nag, complain. But, if you want to talk, then let's talk. Why's Sloan calling you Shenk and not Coley anyway?"

"Stop being so loud," she admonished. "Her name is Yvette, by the way. Sloan's her last name. Get our coats. We'll talk more in the Cougar."

"Fine." After two glasses of scotch on an empty stomach, he probably was too boisterous.

Since Madison had no intention of doing so, Damario left her for the bedroom designated as a coat room. It would be rude to leave without first announcing so to her guests, but doing so to the throng of revelers on the bottom level meant delaying the inevitable.

Madison never audibly mentioned the word "divorce." It resided in her thoughts; his, too. Six years ago, both swore before God they would not be "that couple"; upper class blacks whose busyness broke the cords of matrimony. His parents were 33-year marriage veterans, but the Shenks and each of their four children – except Madison – had divorced, remarried, and divorced again. If Gene and Hilary had stayed together, Damario figured she and her sisters would be slower to pull the separation trigger.

He wandered through the elaborate home's lengthy hallway, found a bedroom on the right with an open door, and entered.

"Lights dim," commanded a female voice.

Under the faint glow, Damario recognized Kareza, who had shed her dress to the floor. In a revealing coral bra and matching panties, she closed the door and thrust herself onto him.

"What're you doing?" The scotch placed a time delay on Damario's responses. He knew he should have pried Kareza's body from his and left the room. However, he had yet to move as her body slithered across his.

"This was meant to be," she said, smooching the exposed part of his chest above his cashmere v-neck sweater. "And yet, you continue to fight it. Don't you believe in destiny?"

"Madison," he said, attempting to move his leaden limbs.

"Ever think she wasn't 'the one'? What if there's someone else and you settled for second best?" Kareza stopped short of kissing Damario's lips and planted his hand on her breast. "You tried to make your marriage work," she said, breathing onto his lips. "You failed. Find glory in that attempt. Let the moment be the moment."

Damario succumbed to temptation and kissed Kareza. He

released all the pent-up excitement and fervor upon her mouth and at his hands, which roamed across her body. The pair breathlessly paused. Kareza reached behind her back to unhook her brassiere and backed towards the coat-covered bed. Damario stopped moving, sensing a presence behind him. He turned to see Madison trembling in the open doorway.

Unsure of how much she had witnessed, but certain she saw the topless vixen lying on the bed, he opened his mouth to explain. In one motion, she approached and slapped him. Kareza moved to the opposite side of the bed and gathered her clothes.

"Don't!" She pointed a finger in his face and cursed him. "It's exactly what I think, exactly what it looks like, and don't tell me it doesn't mean anything!"

Damario wiped the eggplant-colored lipstick from his mouth. Madison slapped him again and again until he gathered enough coordination to block her next attempt. At that, the couple stormed out, one after the other, into the chilly night air. By the time she had composed herself enough to authorize her entry to the Cougar, Damario positioned himself behind her.

"Were you going to sleep with her to get back at me?" She turned to him, her eyes bulging with rage. Kareza slinked unnoticed past the fighting couple. "That's the plan – embarrass me in front of my subordinates?"

"There's no plan. It just. . .happened. And you, I know that you. . ."

"You do things for reasons." She huffed and cursed him again. "They don't just happen. There's planning, thought, logic. What were you thinking?"

"You haven't touched me since June," he exploded. "You get a period a week at a time. What about the other 20 weeks I've been waiting?"

"So, it's the lack of sex. It's my fault you can't control yourself? That's lame, Damario."

The partygoers inside the house started counting down from sixty.

"Oh, so, I'm lame? And I can't control myself?"

"Can't you hear? What do you call a drunken hook up with the first woman you see? Let me break this down for you. Remember what Yvette does for a living? She's a divorce lawyer. Monday morning, I'm making it official. This marriage is over. And for the record, I've always been Shenk. I won't be Coley much longer."

Damario shook his head and pounded his fists into the Cougar's aluminum alloy shell. "You checked out on me a year ago when you started sleeping around behind my back."

Cheers of "Happy New Year" rang from the house, followed by noisemakers and fireworks overhead. Her husband's accusation halted her rebuttals and shook her insides. She retched pink spit onto the ground. *What does he know?*

"Does Yvette know you're sleeping with her ex? Is Justin here, too? Is he inside? And that one at the hotel where we spent our anniversary? Who else?"

Madison cried uncontrollably. "I didn't. . ."

"How many?" He had to know. "You laid the guilt on real thick for me, and we didn't even do anything but kiss. How many guys, Shenk? Don't lie to me."

She sniffled and tucked her bottom lip in, as if to pronounce the letter F. *Four, 14, 40, 400, it doesn't matter. It's too many.*

Damario pushed Madison away, entered the Cougar, started it, and gunned the engine. She ran to the passenger side, but her husband locked the butterfly door and she could not steady her hand on the panel. As she finally held it still, the sports vehicle unevenly sped off down the road, swerving every dozen feet. Her heart skipped when he ran the stop sign on the residential road. Thankfully, no one in cross traffic hit him.

Alarmed, she dug through her pocketbook for her holophone. She yelled into it. "Emergency! My husband. . .he's been drinking and. . ."

"Ma'am, what's your location?"asked the human-sounding droid.

"It's a '51 platinum Cougar, license plate BMN-157," she answered.

"Locating license plate Bravo-Mike-November 1-5-7 now."

A couple of blocks away, a tremendous pop of twisting metal and shattered glass erupted.

Madison covered her mouth. Soon, a few exiting partiers surrounded her.

She dropped her Zara Hristoff handbag, kicked off her matching high heels, and ran barefoot down the street. *God, just let him live*, she thought: the closest thing to a prayer she had uttered since asking for breasts during puberty. Madison crossed the street without looking. *I didn't apologize. Would it have done any good? God, don't let him be dead.* She turned the corner. *I'll tell him everything.* The accident scene came into focus. *I should've gotten the door open. God, don't let him be dead. . .The one time I needed it. . . I should have been there. . .I could have stopped him. God, don't let him be dead.*

She skirted the pools of broken glass and spilled fluids. "Damario!" He did not respond, and she could not see him through the broken door window. "Damario!"

The front of the Cougar had been wedged between a utility pole and the stone facing of a partial wall. The residents of the adjacent home remained on their porch but watched the events unfold with equal parts disgust and interest. Desperate to help him, she stepped onto the shattered glass and pulled the handle up with all her might. No amount of normal human effort on her part was going to open it. She tried until a man stepped forward and yanked the door up but not enough to untangle Damario's unconscious body.

Madison reached in and placed two fingers at Damario's neck. He has a pulse! The fingers she withdrew dripped with his blood.

Eternity passed between then and the emergency personnel arriving.

Medical droids freed him. But, while the Cougar's safety measures had preserved his life, they maimed him in the process.

# CHAPTER THREE

## QUINNE

*New Year's Eve night, 2049*

When the music abruptly paused at midnight, Quinne Ruiz heard nothing but the memories. The first two shots of Jameson did not vanquish them, nor did the following four. She vomited, buying herself five minutes of relief before the images resumed. A red-faced, 19-year-old Puerto Rican girl with blurred makeup and pouty lips intently stared at Quinne. She cursed the girl until snickers and titters alerted her to the fact that she did not recognize her own profane reflection. After readjusting her white peasant blouse and refreshing the taste in her mouth with water, she rearranged her flattened dark brown bangs and stumbled back into the club.

"Easy." Outside the bathroom, Crystal Cantrell, or "Cee Cee," a perky blonde taller and heavier than the 5'4" Quinne, lent her a steady arm. "I should've flagged you before we even got here. You're done. We're leaving."

*Done?* Her face screwed with displeasure in slow motion. "I'm good, Cee."

"How many shots have you had since we got here, with your fake-ID-having self? Tell me the right number and I'll buy the next round."

The pounding heaviness in Quinne's brain prevented clear thought. "Eight?"

"Six. Let's go."

"I wanna shot!" Quinne belched. "Before I take shots. . .for real."

Cee Cee draped Quinne's arm over her shoulder and helped the drunkard to her feet. "You act like they'll put you on the front lines. You'll be lucky if they let you hold something sharper than a pencil."

The two stumbled through the dancing masses to the entrance adjacent to the bar. "One more," Quinne slurred. "Please? One more shot for them."

Her friend wondered about the difference between six shots of liquor versus seven, until she noticed sadness building in Quinne's eyes. "Honor Troy in a better way, Q," she gently said. "He wouldn't want to see you like this."

She'd attend basic training next week, and then likely be shipped off to whatever overseas conflict the government fought. She did not particularly believe in war or obliterating an enemy observing a political tenet that the states opposed. Nevertheless, she signed up without reservation. Nothing remained for her at home, except Anibel Ruiz; a devout Catholic, belligerent lush of a mother with a whacked out internal thermometer and a menial civil service job. Quinne's test grades were too low to garner scholarships and she had no interest in learning a trade.

"If Troilus Carter ain't want me to do this, Troilus Carter shouldn't 've died," she lamented. "So, he ain't gotta vote 'bout what I do or don't do. You ain't gotta buy me nothin'. Somebody over there will. I'll flash Saint Maria, if I got to."

Cee Cee reluctantly consented. She helped the staggering girl through the dancing couples and authorized payment before Quinne had an opportunity to expose her left breast in barter.

Quinne held up the shot and downed it. Satisfied, she wiped the back of her hand across her lips and walked outside under her own power. Her companion followed.

The outside temperature hovered around the low-40s; cold enough to see one's breath and to stab small needles of sobriety into Quinne's brain. She produced an object from her pocket and covertly sniffed from it. The sound drew the attention of her friend.

"What was that?"

"What, Cee?"

"That sound."

"What you talkin' 'bout?" She feigned ignorance. "There 're a million sounds out here."

The two women physically tussled until an empty drug container fell to the ground. Quinne did not bother to acknowledge its existence. They stared at one another until a white police Caper with interior red and blue visor lights stopped next to the sidewalk where they stood. Quinne inconspicuously hid it under the sole of her black platform boot until the traffic light changed. She then kicked it into a sewer grate.

"So you're that girl now?"

Quinne shook her head and moved close enough to her friend that they could comfortably whisper. "It's not what you think, Cee."

"So, I'm blind? Or, you're not just my girl who borrows my clothes and has a drinking problem. You're a drug addict, too?"

"Keep your voice down," said Quinne. "It's a little somethin' to stop the spinnin'. E'erybody does it a little. I only do it when I drink too much, that's all."

The girl flipped a gloved hand in response and walked away. "Wrong. Everybody doesn't do it. Goodbye, Quinne."

Quinne followed. "It ain't even that serious! Since you went back to church, you act like you ain't never did nothin'. Admit it – you've sniffed before."

Cee Cee spun around. "I drink casually Quinne, not like a fish. I don't do drugs. Never did. And I don't keep company with people who do – not anymore."

Unwilling to beg, Quinne shouted after her. "You drove! How am I supposed'ta get home?"

Cee Cee pantomimed lifting her shirt and disappeared around the corner.

Quinne sighed. They lived miles from the club. Her skin tight jeans were like tissue in this weather. With no units to pay the cover charge, she could not reenter the club. Cee Cee's suggestion might work, but enough people had seen her Saint Maria Goretti tattoo for one night.

As she lingered at the crosswalk, the Caper that stopped in front of the club circled around. Its driver stared at her through his open window. "Good evening, Ma'am. Happy New Year."

"Happy New Year."

Suddenly self-conscious, she wondered if the substance she felt ooze from her nose was mucus, blood, or the substance she just inhaled. If she turned away, he may become suspicious. If she stayed put and it was drugs, he would arrest her. Inhaling would be a temporary solution for mucus. With little recourse, she fished a tissue from her pocket and wiped her upper lip. Just snot, she discovered. Regardless, the policemen flashed their lights. An empty container had fallen out of her pocket when she got the tissue. Both men exited the Caper.

"O-Officers," she stuttered, holding her hands up in surrender. "Problem?"

"Let me guess – it's not yours? Or, you're holding it for a friend?" The driver corralled Quinne's hands in handcuffs behind her head and announced her rights, while frisking her. His partner seized the drug paraphernalia she dropped.

She rolled her eyes and reluctantly ducked into the rear of a police transport for the first time since a shoplifting charge four years ago. Unlike that offense, this one would mar her permanent record. When they arrived at the station, Quinne had no one but Cee Cee to call. Anibel would cuss her out, and Guillermo, her father, would be too busy with his nuclear family to care. Everyone else could not be bothered. She refused her rights to a phone call, instead preferring to languish inside of a common holding cell.

One by one, she watched prostitutes, junkies, and transients get summoned and released or transferred. Hours passed. By the dawning of New Year's Day, a new batch of criminals kept her company. Then, her skin started bubbling. She needed to sniff again. Though the headaches and vomiting from drunkenness lasted longer, the boils and dehydration from untreated sniffing were more severe.

Soon, without water, she'd vomit blood from her inflamed stomach lining. If she did not black out, Quinne would then wildly convulse, descend into cardiac arrest and finally die. She dragged herself to the glowing cell bars. "Help!" she managed.

The attending officer beckoned emergency personnel. "Sniffer in withdrawal."

Within a minute, a machine forced water down Quinne's throat and pumped intravenous fluid into the bend of her right arm. Not long afterward, the symptoms abated.

"Quinne Ruiz," called the attending officer. He led Quinne down a corridor to a secluded room and sat her down adjacent to her court-appointed counsel; a droid, and a foreign woman looking to be in her 30's wearing an impeccable gray pinstriped pantsuit. "Comfortable? Getting enough water?"

Quinne weakly nodded and noted the counselor's facial features were perfect. "You look like a model, or an actress. Thought you'd be older, or uglier."

"My bloodline ages well." She beckoned the droid to come closer. "Lucky for you, I'm just the kind of help you'll need today."

Quinne read the woman's clearance level. *Visitor.* "Who're you?"

"I'm Kareza Noor. I work as a non-profit court liaison and psychiatrist to youth defendants. You know, the military takes drug offenses seriously, Miss Ruiz, regardless of the soldier shortage."

"Look, I'm a chick who had a lil' too much to drink and got caught with a sniffer." The droid's vocal inactivity caught her attention. She pointed at it. "Shouldn't that be handlin' this?"

Kareza chuckled. "The fake identification didn't help either, but relax. Samantha Wright here will do enough to keep you out of jail."

Quinne looked incredulous. How?

"The sniffer you dropped had enough residue on it to get you a misdemeanor possession charge. If you plead guilty, you'll get a fine, maybe community service. You're a petty offender. Otherwise, they'd be searching your apartment right now."

"I am Samantha Wright, of the pilot legal android program. Miss Noor tells the truth," affirmed the machine in a warm human female voice. "The probability is high that you will not be assigned jail time. If you complete these terms and avoid being arrested for illegal drugs again, the charge will stay off of your record and you can still enlist."

"I ain't no addict," she argued. "Addicts repeat offend."

"Normal people don't drink themselves stupid and hit a hallucinogen chaser, especially one with these kinds of side effects. Addicts do. If you can stop is not the issue. You didn't stop. That's why you got caught. Do the treatment. Happy New Year."

Quinne returned to the cell, where she remained until her early morning arraignment. While the charges were read, Kareza smirked. "I've dealt with him before, all the time," she said, leaning over to Quinne. "Don't talk unless I tell you to."

"Miss Noor, Happy New Year. Here on behalf of the Genesis Institute, I presume?"

"Yes, your honor."

The judge eyed Kareza. "Your company does good work in the community." He addressed Samantha Wright. "Evidence has been marked, weighed. . .protocol followed. . .Counselor Wright, you've spoken with the defendant?"

"Yes, your honor," said Samantha, "and. . ."

"And," Kareza interrupted, "since her record. . ."

"Since her record is clean, Miss Noor. . .look, we've done this first offender song-and-dance before, haven't we? I know what you're going to ask. . .fine, treatment, no jail time. . .Miss Ruiz, how do you plead?" He stared at Quinne, who still had a re-hydration pack attached to her arm. She looked to the droid, and then at Kareza, who affirmed her decision.

"Guilty."

"You sniff addicts make me sick," he scorned. "Five hundred unit fine, and 120 days of drug treatment. Pay your fine, complete the program and your record will be expunged. Next case."

"Seriously!" she exclaimed. "You, and that said a fine and community service!"

Kareza snatched her by the unaffected arm. "Shut up! You'll be found in contempt and he will tack on community service. You're lucky to be alive. Reenlist later. Go to a meeting or something and get some perspective. They hold them every day downtown."

"On New Year's Day?"

"The holidays are the hardest times. Sooner you start, the sooner you finish."

Quinne made arrangements to pay the fine, picked up her belongings and hitchhiked to her apartment. She'd half expected Cee Cee to mete out more judgment when she arrived. But on Saturday afternoons, Cee Cee and her witness group canvassed the community for "lost souls."

According to the schedule she'd gotten, a counseling meeting happened in a few hours. Quinne sighed and resigned herself to go. "Channel Zero."

The HTV projected an anchorman onto the living room floor. She listened to politicians volley back and forth over a new American currency while cooking some breakfast. The smell of poached eggs, buttered toast, and sizzling pork bacon were pleasant to her nose. She cooked more than normal, as she had not eaten since lunchtime on New Year's Eve.

Quinne cleaned her plate and entered the shower, scrubbing herself clean of holding cell filth. Seven months ago, she and Troy were engaged. Today, she was a drunken sniffer.

She donned a baby pink and sky blue Nike sweatsuit and settled in to watch a movie she had seen three times. She dozed off but awoke when the door opened and Cee Cee entered.

"I see you got home in one piece."

"All mornin' in a cell, dehydration, and a misdemeanor charge, no thanks to you. Thanks for leavin' me."

"Still the victim. You look no worse for wear."

She ran her hand through her curls. "Why you gotta be so mean? I thought Christians 're supposed to be lovin'?"

"They are. . .we are. But there's so much I can take, Q. My Pop-Pop pretty much drank himself to death. So, if you're gonna kill yourself like that, I can't stick around and watch."

She sighed. They went over this every time she got drunk. "Gotta stay clean and go to meetin's, if I want to stay outta jail. There's one going on at six o' clock downtown."

"Might as well get it over with, huh?" Cee Cee scooted over on the couch and placed a hand on Quinne's. "No judgment. I'll even drive you, go with you. The streets are wild on New Year's Day, especially in that part of town. We cut our evangelizing short because of it."

Quinne clenched the hand and laughed. "Sure? I can flash good ole Saint Maria and hitch a ride."

They shared a laugh before leaving the apartment.

By 6:00 p.m., the community center percolated with excitement and meetings on each hall. Quinne pressed her thumb against a plate on the vending machine. INSUFFICIENT FUNDS FOR PURCHASE. TRY AGAIN.

"Here." Cee Cee did the same and pushed the corresponding sensors for honey glazed pretzels, popcorn and potato chips. "I know you're nervous."

Quinne grabbed them and dug into the packages. "Thanks."

"Don't be, Q." The women held hands down the hallway to the room number the court had assigned. Inside it, a middle-aged, balding white man with horn-rimmed glasses and a white turtleneck welcomed them.

"Substance abuse group?"

"Yes," said Cee Cee.

Quinne handed a thumb-sized green disk to him. "Here you go."

"Thanks. I'm Mason Conway and I'll authorize this after every class. Come as often as you like. Miss one session, and you have to make it up the same week. At the end of 120 days, if I haven't seen you enough, I'll report you. Understand?"

She clenched her teeth and inhaled. "I'll be here."

"Make yourself comfortable," Mason smiled. "We've got natural juice, water and sugar-free pastries. No coffee or tea. We don't do stimulants of any kind here."

"Don't you think that's a little strict?" Cee Cee objected.

"Maybe. People come in here with all sorts of substance addictions and the first thing they look for is to fill the void. Caffeine and calories are the first ones they try. Others fall into bed with the first person they see. Some turn to religion and find out most of them expect you to deal with your mess. This program gets addicts to focus on why they do what they do and talk about it with people who understand. You're less likely to relapse that way."

Quinne visibly shuddered. Why she got drunk and sniffed was no one's business – especially not a group of strangers. Cee Cee, her lone friend, found out why through drunken babble. "Why would I wanna talk about it?"

Without looking up, Mason handed them thumb-sized blood red disks with *Genesis Institute* imprinted on them. "You wouldn't, but you'd prefer that over another drug charge and jail, right?"

"Great," Quinne said. She inserted the disk into her holophone and viewed its contents. "Sounds like one of your Christian deals, Cee."

"No, Ma'am," Mason clicked his teeth. "The Genesis Institute and the courts keep a close eye on us and this program. If they get wind of one mention of God, Allah, Buddha, Zeus, whoever, we lose our funding."

He presented the duo with a disk on drug recovery and met

some other participants at the door. Quinne and Cee Cee sat at the bottom curve of the chairs formed to make a semicircle. Mason greeted each of the attendees with a reassuring salutation.

Quinne examined them. One appeared to be a businessman of high societal standing. She could tell by his tapered suit and highly-shined leather shoes. A new mother sat near them and reeked of baby accoutrements. An older woman who looked to be the age of Quinne's mother, a married couple, and a grungy-looking, tattooed teenager about her age followed. He smiled, first at Cee Cee, then at Quinne. She remembered those ragged teeth, but he did not recognize her, though she'd slept with him at least twice for sniff.

"Welcome!" Mason clapped his hands together. "I applaud you. You have taken the first step in reclaiming your life. I'm Mason, and you may not know it by looking at me, but I'm 12 years sober. I had it all. But, after a while, the pressure got to me and I drank. After that, you name it and I tried it. . .anything to match that first high.

"When that didn't do it for me, I sniffed. And after that, I started mixing them all. I lost everything. Went to jail a few times, and I did. . .unspeakable things. Turns out. . ." Mason choked up. "My family. . .thinks I'm crazy and should go travel the world. Being selfish for the first 45 years of my life got me this. I figure, if I help you avoid the same mistakes I made, maybe I'll get another 45."

Quinne and Cee Cee tightly clasped hands. The former blinked back tears.

"So," Mason said, composing himself. "We'll now go around the room. Introduce yourself this way: 'Hi, I'm say-your-name,' and name your addiction. Identify your enemies and fight them."

The tattooed man's addictions were sniff and marijuana. Of the married couple, the wife labeled liquor as her demon. The businessman hemmed and hawed until Mason laid a hand on his shoulder for comfort. Crack cocaine was his vice. Cee Cee introduced herself as Crystal and expressed her support for her friend.

*Great, it's my turn.* "Quinne," she said matter-of-factly. "Booze. . .sniff."

"You all need to know – this is not the end for you," said Mason. "It's the beginning of an abusive substance-free life! Let's go counter-clockwise now. New folks, now we dialogue. Talk about what's on your mind, or whatever. Be open, but please respect the privacy of others and don't discuss what you hear outside of these walls."

When it came time for Quinne to share, she gulped down some juice. The eyes in the room, particularly Mason's, did not intensify – but softened. *They pity me! Sympathy in exchange for transparency*, Quinne guessed. She preferred judgment.

Cee Cee tightened her grasp, but Quinne wrestled free and sprinted from the room. "Q!" Cee Cee started after her friend, but Mason encouraged her not to follow after her.

"Let her go," said Mason. "She'll talk when she's ready."

Outside, in the clear air, the hot tightness of the room dissipated in the overcast chill. Quinne turned the corner, jogging for blocks until pain in her side forced her to stop in an undesirable section of downtown.

After catching her breath, Quinne resumed walking, as if for an important appointment. One of the neighborhood indigents followed her at a distance close enough for her to notice. She left the community center so quickly that she did not know in which direction to return. Without breaking stride, she produced her holophone and dialed Cee Cee, who did not answer.

The device's geographical positioning system took time to load. Luckily, a public transport with a route back to her loft picked up passengers a block ahead.

Before she took another step, a dirty rag clamped over her mouth and dragged her kicking into an alleyway.

# CHAPTER FOUR

## TEANNA

*New Year's Day, 2050*

Teanna slipped from underneath the meaty arm across her midsection. Its owner, Theodore "Tiny" Mitchell, slept as if he'd been drugged.

True enough, traces of sniff lined her nightstand and sniffers were clumsily hidden inside its top drawer. After inhaling the residue, she stumbled into her nightgown and set the bottle of Hennessey on the floor close to the snoring man. When Tiny awoke, he would need it to fend off dehydration. If he was nice, she'd give him water. If not, she'd let him boil up into a ball of pus.

Lately, her unemployed lover appeared to have mellowed. It wasn't the drugs. Sniff heightened Tiny's aggression, and that put Teanna on guard. But she needed release. The craziness of her circumstances necessitated it, but she could not afford to be caught with narcotics. State officials conducted surprise visits on people they suspected of abusing the system. One slip up and her assistance would be revoked. Then, Tiny could bankroll her lifestyle, if she needed it – which tended to happen.

She'd often rung his holophone for financial aid. Most times, he did not answer, but this past Christmas, he did – showing up around 6:00 p.m. with groceries and contraband. Two hours later, both were flying high. Teanna did not remember much about the past few days, besides waking up naked. She would be 43 this November and too old to continue like this.

Outside her bedroom, she found her 17-year-old Teiji, or "Tay," and his preteen sister Meleasa in the cluttered dining room eating turkey sandwiches and barbecue potato chips. Teanna scratched her head. "Tay, you lost your mind? There's milk, cereal. . ."

Teiji eyed the clock on the kitchen wall. So did Teanna. *One in the afternoon.* "Happy New Year. I figured you wanted to sleep."

She yawned and pointed to the water faucet. Teiji filled a glass with cold water and continued doing so until Teanna held up her hand. She finished drinking and kissed him on the forehead. "Happy New Year."

Meleasa followed her lumbering mother back into the kitchen. "We go back to school on Monday, Mom. Can I go over to Mia and Tiffany's? I know I'm grounded, but just for a few hours?"

"I'll think about it. What's on your agenda Tay? Hot party?"

He sighed. "No hot party because I'll be studying. Miss Buff's pushing me for the poly-sci summer internship in D.C. with State Representative Mateo. Don't know if I want to do it."

"You got the credits to graduate now, so it ain't like you missin' anythin'. Why not?"

Meleasa sucked her teeth. "He'll miss Kelly. That's why not."

"That true?" Teanna crossed her arms.

"No." He cut his eyes at Meleasa. "Not entirely. It's my decision, isn't it, and I'll have to live with it. So, back off, Mel. Kelly's cool with whatever I do. You are too, right?"

Teanna drew a deep breath. "I ain't Kelly and I ain't 'cool' either. If you gonna be successful, can't be makin' your decisions based on a girl. See my life and the way it's turned out? I love ya'll, but I wish I'd decided some things on my own instead of considerin' your daddies."

"It's not that simple, Mom."

"Oh?" Teanna asked, feigning shock. "Un-complicate it for

me, then. Can't be that lil' piece of job you got. What we ever gonna do without that?"

Tiny appeared in the kitchen wearing boxer shorts and a tank top. "Don't play," he interrupted. "It's good money – even for him."

Though Teanna had an American Indian, Black, Filipino, and Caucasian background and Meleasa was one-quarter Dominican, Tiny held judgment for the half-Japanese boy, whom he considered effeminate.

"Not this mornin'!" Teanna crossed the room. "Babe, I told you a million times not to be out here half-dressed. At least act like you half-Christian up in here."

"Relax." He stroked Teanna's shoulders. "She's going to see it sooner or later. You probably have already, haven't you?"

Meleasa audibly gagged and crossed her arms over her breasts. If she knew. "I ain't old enough to date, Theodore."

"I didn't say you dated one. Don't be ashamed. It's natural. Admit it."

"Not gonna tell you again, go put somethin' on!"

Teiji waited for Tiny to disappear before speaking. "Mom, when's he getting out of here?"

"I don't know, later? Why? Need him to drop you off, Tay?"

"No, I mean for good. He's useful when he's working, but now? Wait a couple days and you'll be complaining about how he doesn't do whatever. Again."

Meleasa watched her mother's flush of embarrassment morph into anger.

"You 17-years-old," Teanna reminded him. "What you know? Nothin' 'bout nothin'. Wanna waste your life on some blue-eyed white girl?"

"You'd know about it," he said underneath his breath.

Teanna raised a finger to her son's face. "What'd you say?"

"Momma." Meleasa drew closer. "It's okay Momma. He ain't say nothing."

Teanna clutched Teiji by the shirt and pulled him close. "Mind your business, Meleasa. I wanna hear him say it to my face. Now, what's it you say, Tay? Say it again. . .to my face."

Teiji clammed up and dropped his head. "Nothing," he muttered.

"Come again?"

"Nothing," he repeated louder. "I didn't say anything important."

Teanna slowly backed away until her nerves relaxed. Teiji fled the room and bumped into Tiny. "Easy," he joked. "Open 'em up, slant eyes."

Meleasa trailed her brother, careful not to touch Tiny or allow him to brush up against her. Tiny stood behind Teanna, his breath tickling the hairs on her neck. "It can't be that bad."

"Yeah," she admitted. "Trouble is I ain't know how to fix it."

"You need to get away." Tiny produced two full sniff containers. "This always makes it better. Well, this and other things. Both of them are available. . .in the other room. Let's fly."

Just give me somethin' to take it all away. She followed him into her bedroom, where they indulged in a haze of copious sniff and alcohol.

Teiji's music drowned out his mother's foul mood. Lately, Meleasa joined him. It wasn't because she enjoyed his brand of music, which ranged from soft and relaxing to bubblegum to hardcore and violent. But it completely drowned out the raunchy sounds.

After a half-hour of mellow tunes, Teiji switched to a song with an upbeat, driving tempo. At its most frenetic parts, he slumped down further into his chair.

"How long you think he's staying this time?" he yelled. "It's been a week."

"That's all?" Meleasa quipped. "That's a record. He'll be out soon and then things'll be back to normal, whatever that is."

"Yeah, but when he comes back, then what? If I go to the capitol, I'll be an eight hour flight away for months. You'll be here by yourself."

Meleasa pondered that possibility. "You can't stay."

"We'll call the cops," he suggested. "Once somebody comes in here and sees what's really going on, there's no way they'll let us stay."

"They always clean up before they can get caught," she argued. "It's almost better if we just wait until he goes away again."

"Or. . ." Tay produced a fully-charged Ordnance from a bag. Meleasa stifled her surprise.

"Where'd you get that? You ain't 18."

"I'm under 90 days out. That's close enough. I got a license. Wouldn't call me 'slant eyes' or 'rice eater', if he knew I had this."

"You gonna shoot him?"

"I'm not going to part his hair with it."

"Put it away, Tay. You scarin' me."

Teiji set the Ordnance's safety. "We need some kind of help. Besides, when Mom's high, she won't protect you. Trust me on this one."

Tiny burst through the door unannounced, still in his boxers but without an undershirt. "I keep telling you kids the soundproof's out. Turn it down!" Tay's sudden movement to hide his hand drew Tiny's attention. "What you got there?"

He vaulted toward the boy, who dropped the bag, aimed at Tiny and shot him. A blue laser struck and vanished in Tiny's left arm. Tay shot him three more times in the chest. Tiny stumbled into the hallway, his hands covering the sizzling flesh.

Meleasa's screams and the sight of Tiny crawling to the living area drew Teanna to his side. "Baby. . .what's wrong? Why. . .you cryin'?"

He cursed, pointing at Tay, who aimed at Tiny's head. Teanna offered herself as a shield. "Son, this ain't the way. . .to go," she slurred. "I ain't raise. . .no killer."

"Somebody's got to look out for this family," he said coldly. "Mel, go next door." He tossed his holophone to her. "Call 9-1-1."

"Are you crazy? They'll arrest you."

"Tell them what he did. No judge would convict me." Teiji's heart rose in his throat. "You're wondering, aren't you?" He stared down at his mother. "Never once crossed your mind once before right now, did it?"

A moment of clarity hit Teanna and she moved to the side. What'd he do?

Teiji flipped the setting on the Ordnance to *kill.* "As long as he brings you what you want, you don't care what he does." His eyesight blurred with tears. "Mel, get out of here. Now!"

His sister's legs were living concrete. Teanna moved, but not enough to clear a shot. She stared at Tiny with bloodshot eyes. "What've you done?"

"Nothing," Tiny grunted. He glanced up at Teiji. "You don't have it in you."

Teiji wiped away his tears with his left hand. "Watch me, Theodore."

"I didn't do anything she didn't want," Tiny grinned. "Look at her." He eyed Meleasa. "She's sexier than you."

Visual pictures of Meleasa's account filled Teiji's mind. His finger pressed against the trigger, but not enough for the ammunition to release.

"Tay, please?" Emboldened, Meleasa moved into his line of sight and in front of Tiny to spare her brother's life.

"No!" Teiji fired around his sister until Tiny flopped face down on the hardwood floor.

Teanna trembled with fear, as she attended to Meleasa, who had been struck by a final, stray shot.

Hours later, after being whisked away in an ambulance, after the buzzing and whirring of medical droids, the rush of emergency resuscitation, the heartbeat recovered – just for a brief moment – the crashing back of reality, more emergency procedures, successes and failures; Meleasa Marianne Santana was pronounced dead. Teanna authorized the finalities, for her and Tiny, who had listed Teanna as his next-of-kin and emergency contact.

Dressed in a pair of baggy black jeans and a coffee and cream camisole blouse – the two topping a heap of her clean clothes – Teanna posted up along a wall. She wanted to leave, but her son was locked up, Meleasa and Tiny were dead, and her home had been quarantined for evidence. *Where else I gotta go?* Teanna bent over, burying her ashen face in her hands. A small hand caressed the breadth of Teanna's back. She looked up.

The counselor compassionately spoke and handed Teanna tissue. "Meleasa didn't suffer."

The grieving mother used it to clean her raw nose. "Who're you?"

"A psychiatrist from the Genesis Institute." She offered a hand, which went unshaken. "My name is Kareza Noor."

"How'd you know that?"

"Know what, exactly?"

"She ain't suffer. How you know for sure?"

Kareza eagerly pulled up the medical report on a 12-inch long holographic computer processor. "The attending medical droid from the hospital's pilot program, he. . ."

Teanna cursed her and knocked it from Kareza's hands,

shattering its projection surface. The fall triggered the device's security alert system, which rang every two seconds. Its sound resembled Ordnance fire and sent Teanna into hysterics. "Help me!" Teanna's bloodcurdling screams drew the attention of everyone within earshot – long after the signal stopped. She knelt in the broken glass; her arms bent, as if holding a limp 12-year-old's body, until she passed out.

Teanna later awoke to white desolation and a sleeve of tubes strapped to her right arm. One of the intravenous fluids was an entrancing, ice blue liquid. She sweated profusely and her heavy eyelids drooped. "What the. . ." Her wrists were chained to the bedrails.

Immediately to her left, a scowling Indian looking to be in his 50's, with *Dr. Nandor Adharma/Psychiatrics* knitted on his jacket pocket, reached over and wiped her face with a moist cloth. "Can't have you harming yourself."

"Who said I'd 'harm myself'?"

Adharma tugged on the hard plastic linking her wrist to the hospital bed. "I can't tell you how many patients have gouged out their eyes, tried to escape. . ."

"I'd never do that. Maybe escape, but not the other stuff."

"You've been through a great deal of trauma," he snickered. "We removed an eighth of a cup of glass shards from your knees. Give yourself more credit."

"Where's my son?"

"Jail, I imagine. How are you?"

"I gotta pee," she lazily responded. "How I do that?"

"Go ahead. It's totally sanitary and soundless."

"No thanks."

"Accelerated hydration means you won't be holding it long. Other than continent, how are you?"

*I wanna see Tay.* "What's this blue one called?"

He took her arm and turned the tube in question face up.

"The name is long, scientific – it'll help you regain your bearings. Now, how are you?"

Teanna remained silent. *Why's he keep askin' me that?*

"Talk is all you have." Adharma repositioned his eyeglasses. "You won't be released without my consent, and I will not consent unless you talk."

"Why you wear glasses, Nandor? Get laser surgery. What are you, Indian?"

"I like my glasses. A quarter-Indian. How are. . ."

"Pissed off, upset, irritated, sad. . .that what you want me to say?"

Adharma motioned his fingers over the computer screen projection. "It's a start. Why sniff?"

Teanna paused. "My momma traded me for a hit one night. Figured I'd see the appeal."

"Make your story more believable next time," he said without looking up.

Teanna used the bed's reclining controls to maneuver it into a more comfortable position. Usually, her lies passed muster. "Ain't know my daddy," she somberly said.

"Continue."

She paused for a moment and shifted. The doctor spoke the truth. She could no longer hold it and relieved her bladder while talking. "One night, Momma say he's comin'. Put me in my best dress – braided my hair." Teanna's reminiscing brightened her eyes. "She's tellin' me, 'Just wait, baby girl. He gonna take you out for ice cream, buy you toys'. . .do this, do that. Couple hours pass. I fall asleep in my dress watchin' TV. When I wake up, Momma's face down in sniff."

"So, why do you do it?"

Pestered by the doctor's interruption, she turned over into her pillow.

"How long do you want to be in here?"

"You waitin' on a big reveal, but there ain't one. One of Momma's men came over years later. They'd passed out and I stole some. I like the high. Makes me forget."

"Forget what exactly?" he persisted.

"Stress, bad news. Ain't much more rhyme or reason."

"The dead boyfriend, Theodore Mitchell. Did you want to forget him?"

"Not really." She shot him a warning look, but he did not relent.

"How did you two meet?"

"Church," she snapped. "Look, why don't you just leave? Ain't you got other patients? Stop botherin' me."

"I suppose that's enough for now. Command call if. . ."

"Yeah, I got it. Not a first-timer here, thanks. Bye-bye."

As soon as the door slid closed, Teanna activated the room's HTV. The local news coverage had probably exhausted the murder. Shootings were popular. She selected a comedy to watch. The most watched shows featured Blacks and Latinos. She wondered where all of the white people had gone.

After an hour, channel flipping got old. Teanna called for assistance, and a medical droid rolled into her presence. Its technical sophistication contrasted with its crude physicality. "My name is Stan Witmore, of the pilot medical android program. What can I do for you, Miss Kirkwood?"

"Wanna make a call." She hated how droids were given names from defunct soap operas to personify them.

"Outgoing calls are not permitted until your 72-hour surveillance period ends." While pleasantly toned, Stan's voice was definitive. "Do you have any family members that you would like for me to contact? The hospital permits visitors."

"No." In truth, more than half of her relatives were dead or locked up. Teanna reclined and reduced the HTV's volume to a barely audible level. She slowly and deeply breathed and closed her eyes, concentrating to forget the sounds and images to no avail. This time, she'd page Stan and ask for Adharma.

"What can I do for you, Miss Kirkwood?" Stan's voice and tone remained the same.

"Add-harm-you, whatever. . .can you get him in here?"

"Dr. Adharma is with another patient. I will alert him."

"Can you give me somethin'? Put me to sleep?"

Stan pointed to the medicine strapped to Teanna's arm. "That pouch has a sedative on a slow drip. It takes time."

Not only had the doctor done what she told him to do – go away – he did it well. "How long'll it take to work?"

Stan's exploratory lenses whirred and focused. "Based on your current weight and body chemistry, and the medicine dosage, it should take effect in an hour or two."

*An hour or two?* Teanna sprung to a sitting position. "Get me the doctor now! Get him in here now!" She screamed until her throat burned. *If actin' like a lunatic gets them to put me out, then so be it.* Teanna thrashed, growled, and drooled like a wild animal. At the point of her exhaustion, Adharma appeared.

"Has it come to this, Miss Kirkwood? Pretending to be disturbed for drugs?"

Adharma's pomposity gave her a new energy. "You ain't say nothin' about me being here for no 72 hours," she growled.

"Standard observation period."

"That's crap. It's a suicide watch. I can't sleep! Ain't you got a higher concentration for big-boned people?"

"You are not experiencing the harsher physical effects of the drugs in your system, but your body still has to be weaned from the sniff you consumed," he said in a droll monotone. "When it's complete, perhaps by then, you will be ready to talk. And, there's no such thing as being big-boned."

"Alright." Teanna laid back and tried to relax. "Ask me whatever; just promise me you'll put me out."

"The boyfriend. . ."

She stared at the ceiling. "Met on this ten-day trip to Japan I won in '33, before I went back to school."

"You were in school? For what?"

"Real estate license," she said with lament. "Tiny lived straight back then. He was a plane steward. He introduced me to Tay's daddy. Got home, found out 'bout my pregnancy. I called him, but he sent money for an abortion and never called."

"Then what?"

"I decided to keep Tay, no matter what, but I ain't finish class 'cause I got put on bed rest. Lost my job, start havin' all kinds of medical issues 'cause of my pregnancy. Got on disability. Tiny found me and start helpin' out every once in a while. We got together, broke up, then got back after Meleasa's dad left. When Tiny's around, he gives me what I need. When he ain't around, he don't."

"Why do you think they didn't like him? Did he abuse them?"

"Tiny poked fun at Tay. And Meleasa. . .cause her dad ain't around? Maybe somethin'. . .but he ain't rape her or nothin'."

Adharma looked down over his glasses. "Had she been examined?"

"Look, I just know, alright?" For a minute, the man said nothing. Teanna looked over the protective rail. "What you tryin' to say?"

"Pardon?"

"You asked if she been 'examined'? Why?"

"Unless your daughter had been examined by a doctor, a medical droid, or you constantly monitored her, you cannot know for sure."

She huffed. "Don't know the kinds of women you be examinin', but me? I know my kids, and everythin' they do."

"Did you know Teiji had an Ordnance?"

*No.* Teanna hid her quivering lips. *I never thought he'd kill.*

"Bullied children either strike in against themselves – cutting, eating disorders, and the like – or out against others. Your son chose the latter."

Pulse racing, Teanna collapsed in tears. But why kill him?

Adharma rose and attended to her medicine pouch. "Try to relax."

"I know I ain't the best mother, God knows I got problems like the rest, but I ain't think it's that bad that my son gotta go shootin' people."

Adharma used a small metallic instrument to manipulate the piston-like tube plunger, gradually increasing the dosage of the blue serum. "Breathe slowly. Count backwards from ten."

"Ten. . .nine. . ." she mumbled before dropping out of consciousness.

Teanna yawned. The heavenly bed sheets felt like threaded clouds surrounding her skin. Keeping her eyes closed, she caressed the silk and allowed it to return the favor. Bacon, eggs, cheese, vegetables, and ham – she smelled a western omelet! *Maybe there's coffee and home fries! Am I dead? Will an angel serve me? A devil? Will leavin' the bed make this go away?*

Hoping for the best, she swept her legs over the bedside to find a luxurious pair of slippers awaiting her feet. The place reminded her of a fine hotel that she'd stayed in almost a year before she had Teiji. She won a trip and trekked to Japan alone. Why did her brain choose to excavate this particular memory and interpolate it into her dreams? *And why's it so real?*

She passed through the entryway to the kitchen. Transparent curtains of sunlight draped into the breakfast nook from the large window to her left. At the stove, a man, close to six feet moved with the certainty of an expert chef – chopping, whipping and sorting with ease. He paused, blindly set a cobalt-colored mug to his right, and poured coffee into it. Teanna claimed it and dressed the drink to her liking.

"Good mornin'?"

"Good afternoon," he corrected in an Asian accent. "You like to sleep."

*Never slept in a dream before.* She forced hot coffee down her throat. *But I'd do it again.* A full pot remained, and not even two resolute human beings could drink that much in one sitting. Soon, she sipped from another cup. "For the record, the sex was great but I hate you."

"That's not why you're here, you know," he said with expectation.

"Whatever," she said with her lips at the mug's edge. "Coffee's good."

"It's not a question, Teanna. You know why you're here."

Teanna pondered the non-question. "You shoulda done right by me and your son. You know we strugglin'! See what he gone an' done?"

He slapped a western omelet and home fries onto a plate and set it before her. "What will you do to correct it?"
Teanna cursed his cold demeanor. "That ain't no choice to make."

Her former lover circled the table and covered Teanna in an embrace. The weight of her arm grew heavily around the bicep. Her feet felt bare and discomfort throbbed in her back. She blinked and opened her eyes.

Everything had disappeared.

# CHAPTER FIVE

*January 2, 2050*

Cee Cee led her bloodied best friend down the hospital corridor just past midnight. A medical droid named "Wynter Dawn" escorted them to an examination room and activated an opaque soundproof barrier behind them. "You're doing the right thing, Q."

*Right's an idea somebody more powerful pushed onto somebody weaker.* If Quinne correctly remembered it, God told Adam and Eve not to touch a certain tree. *What's right to them – eatin' and becomin' like God – is wrong to God. Weak versus the powerful.*

"Good morning. My name is Wynter Dawn, of the pilot medical program," said the imitation female voice. "I will be attending to you and examining you. Do you prefer me to be male or female? I can accommodate either selection."

"Female," Quinne indicated.

At that, a red light blinked near its metal ears. "Your head trauma indicates swelling, but you do not have a concussion, and your remaining vital signs are steady. Now, please tell me everything you can remember. Please do so in the order in which the events occurred."

Encouraged by Cee Cee, Quinne parted open her purpled lips. "Happened in an alley. . .downtown, on Market Street. Tonight. He grabbed me and. . .forced me."

"What did he 'force' you to do?"

Her eyes dropped. "Into an alley," she admitted for the first time.

"I'm sorry," Wynter pleasantly said. "Can you be more specific?"

The question sent shivers across Quinne's midsection. Cee Cee left the area. He threatened her with a knife or something sharp. He pulled her sweatsuit top over her head to keep her from identifying him. He asked how it felt, how good. He did it quickly and knocked her out with something heavy and blunt. She woke up hours later, covered in trash and with a raging headache. No one had noticed her long enough to rob her. She called Cee Cee, who picked her up and drove her straight to the hospital.

"What were you wearing at the time?"

"This," she said, pointing to her soiled outfit. Wynter presented an empty metal tray.

"Remove your clothes. Place them in the bin to your left."

Quinne complied, tenderly easing out from her outfit. Black and blue welts were staggered across her back.

"Now," said Wynter, "I will perform the collection of forensic evidence. Please attempt to relax and stay still."

Cee Cee remained outside, while Wynter darkened the room and swept a black light over the naked body. Quinne closed her eyes and moved as asked, standing still for the physical sequence. In a way, she appreciated the corporately-sponsored android program, which largely automated the hospital. The last thing she wanted was the touch of a man's hand. The scientists who designed the medical droids programmed them to emote, act, and even sound human. But at the end of the day, the machines stayed true to their nature; pretending to be something they were not.

Minutes later, Wynter indicated that the pair could go, and

she departed herself. Cee Cee reentered the room, blindly passing Quinne a fresh pair of clothes and undergarments. The crime scene clothes would be kept for evidence.

*It's "right" to him, what he did. He had the power. But I'll have the power someday.*

"They'll catch him, Q."

"No," said Quinne, putting them on. "They won't. And I'll spend the rest of my life clean on the outside but filthy on the inside."

"You don't know that. Forensics has come so far and now. . ."

"Don't lecture me!" she warned. "You don't know what it's like, do you? Especially when you ain't want it. You think about it. You think, am I pregnant? Do I gotta disease I can't get rid of? I remember it all. How do you get rid of that? And don't give me any of that Jesus crap, either."

"It's what I believe," Cee Cee shouted. "Get angry at the world, your situation, God, whatever. But who took off two days to be there? Whose shoulder did you cry on? Mine. Show me some respect, Quinne, or you're going to lose the only real friend you've got."

The two stared one another down in silence for a moment. Wynter reappeared just as Quinne pulled down her midnight green football jersey over her black sweatpants.

"Miss Ruiz, one of the hospital's benefactors, The Genesis Institute, provides counseling services for trauma and crime victims." The android offered her a thumb segment-sized, blood red disk. "One of its best psychoanalytic doctors, Dr. Adharma, is on staff here at the hospital, and. . ."

"No!" She recoiled. "Not one more person tellin' me what to do, or what to take or not take. I got it, had enough. I'm done."

"Thank you." Cee Cee accepted the disk on her behalf. "She'll give him a call."

"No, I will not! You call them. You need counselin', if you think I'm going. If I ain't go to the other place, this wouldn't have happened in the first place."

"You'd be in jail, if you didn't go to group," Cee Cee argued. "And if you hadn't gotten hooked on sniff, you wouldn't have had to go to group and we wouldn't be having this conversation."

"Or if you had taken me home, like a true best friend, and not left me on the street, I never would've gotten picked up. And, for the last time, I'm not hooked on sniff. You, Mason – when are ya'll gonna start listenin' to me?"

"So, that's it then? It's *my fault*? I guess I put the drinks in your hand, too? Sooner or later, it would've caught up to you. You and I both know that. "

As the examination drew to its conclusion, the room lost its soundproofing. Noticing this, Quinne stood up and exited with as much of her dignity intact as possible. Cee Cee followed. They waited at the front for Cee Cee's black Tarpan to pull up.

"So, you think after blaming me for everything that's happened to you that I'm just gonna drive you home like everything's okay?"

Remembering what happened the last time she traveled by herself, Quinne humbled herself. "Please?"

Cee Cee melted beneath the sudden show of sincere emotion. Regardless of fault, Quinne had experienced a lot in the past three days. "Look, Heifer, I called in again. Let's go to breakfast later – my treat. I'll catch Sunday service on the Internet."

Quinne nodded and sent a text message on her holophone. "Go to early service and we'll do lunch instead. I need some good sleep. And, can we go to that place on north 24th?"

"You want to go *downtown?* I know the food's good, but. . . alright."

After Quinne spent the morning in bed, showered and changed, Cee Cee picked her up in front of their apartment building and motored to their destination; a family-owned diner in a slightly better neighborhood than Quinne's alley. A drugstore, a liquor store, and a few abandoned brownstones surrounded it. Still, Cee Cee locked her doors and set the Tarpan's anti-theft mechanism.

"Let's go."

"Wait." Quinne rounded the vehicle and confidentially spoke to her friend. "Let me hold some units. I need pads."

"What do you need pads for? The hospital gave you enough for a week."

"Yeah, but it's like wearing a diaper."

"Then let me go buy them for you, and you can get us a table. Heavy, right?"

Quinne scrunched her eyebrows. "You seriously won't let me buy my own pads, Cee?"

"Then let's both go."

"I get it. I ain't exactly been trustworthy, but I don't need that much. Just transfer me about 70 units. Let me do this one thing for myself."

Her friend reluctantly authorized the transfer via holophone. "If you're not back in ten, I'm coming after you, Ordnance blazing."

Quinne slipped into the drugstore. While strolling down the appropriate aisle, just in case Cee Cee followed her, she sent another text message to her dealer. Sunday mornings followed his busiest night and she hoped he'd be able to quickly get to her. Her holophone chimed Cee Cee's ringtone.

Cee Cee's face popped up. "What's taking so long? The coffee's getting cold."

"Go ahead and order, I'll be right there. You know you eat slow anyway. I'll order, eat, and be done before you even pick up your fork."

"Whatever, Heifer. Hurry up." Cee Cee's face vanished. Quinne picked up a box of pads and dropped it when a familiar pair of hands surrounded her waist.

"I'm guessing if you're getting those, you'll be paying me in units this time."

"How'd you get here so quick?" She pretended to adore his grasp to avoid alerting the desk clerk. "I just messaged you a minute ago."

"Was close by. Said all you got is 30? That'll barely get you a taste."

"What you talkin' 'bout? Thirty's good."

He produced a vial of aqua blue liquid. "Not for this."

The color mystified Quinne. "What's that?"

"Sniff base chemical." He closed his palm. "Pharmaceutical. Better high without the side effects. I'm out of the regular 'til Friday."

"It's traceable? They pee test me every day."

The dealer sucked his teeth. "Went and got yourself caught. Heard about that." He noticed the hospital band on her wrist. "You look awful. What's up?"

"Nothin'." She dug her hand into her pocket. "Look, traceable or not, you gotta give me somethin'. I'm itchin'."

"I like you, Q. So, I'll tell you what. Float me your 30 units and you owe me."

Quinne made the transfer but allotted herself enough to buy a sample size of sanitary napkins. To her surprise, the dealer put the vial inside a miniature syringe and slipped it in her handbag. "What? I ain't doin' no needles."

The dealer silently dipped behind a New Year's Day ornamental display. Quinne hurriedly bought the pads, pocketed the box inside her handbag, and joined Cee Cee at their table next door. She poured herself a cup of coffee and ordered a combo breakfast platter. Several police officers sat at the counter.

"Got what you need?" Cee Cee's voice contained a small twinge of suspicion. "Where's the box?"

"In my bag." She remembered the needle and her probation sentence. "Which reminds me. I'll be right back."

Quinne darted for the bathroom and entered a stall. The syringe did not intimidate her, but she wondered; *if the drug's got side effects, what are they?* Without much other thought, she tied off her veins below the bicep with the string of her pants, stuck herself in the left arm and pushed the liquid into her veins. She discarded the syringe in the sanitary napkin container and waited. Her eyes tingled a bit, but the sensation reminded her of tickling. Her body no longer stung. And the smell of her attacker's drunken breath evaporated from her mind.

Quinne opened her eyes to her old room in her mother's house. *How'd I get here? Is this a dream?* Already, she felt suffocated from the lack of space. She could walk in a straight line and stretch out her arms, but if she leaned in any direction, her arms would touch something. Her broken audiodome lay in the room's right hand corner. It cost about 100 units to repair – an amount Anibel Ruiz was loath to pay.

"You can get that thing fixed," she'd remembered her mother saying, "or eat for a week. Your choice."

When it had broken down, Quinne felt that sacrificing entertainment for eating was no decision for a seventeen-year-old high school junior to make. Her poor term grades encouraged Anibel to ground Quinne from having a job or dating boys. Those rules and regulations made her rebel. Anibel had also formulated rules for Guillermo and paid the price. He left her to start a real life and his jilted, knocked-up girlfriend got stuck in a job as a public transport driver. When she wasn't drinking her cares away over it, Anibel cussed out Quinne for existing. The girl remembered having peace in her life when her mother passed out.

Quinne brushed her bare feet across the texture of her bedroom's carpeting. She did not remember it being this soft and plush. The vibrant, violet walls were almost mystical in sheen. The resonant snoring coming from the living room let her know that her mother had called it a night. Quinne relaxed. If this was the drug's lone effect – dreaming of her miserable upbringing – going cold turkey should be no problem.

"Q," said a familiar male voice. *Troy?* "You decent?"

Quinne pulled him inside the room and kissed him with voracity. "When's that stopped you?" Confused by the realistic sensations, she continued kissing him, her hands wandering to his belt buckle. "Don't stop."

"Hey," Troy said, backing up. "What's the rush? We got a lifetime for all that. Besides, your mom's in the next room."

"Anibel'll never hear us." Quinne removed her blouse. "And we ain't got a lifetime, we got *now*. Trust me. Why you actin' like we ain't done this before?"

He pushed her away. "Because you're not here for that."

Quinne crossed her arms and cursed over and over again. "Then why am I here?"

"You know why."

"You gonna get set." She choked up. "I'm gonna lose our

baby. And my life ain't gonna be right side up again."

"You can't go back, Q."

"Why not?" she cried. "Why I gotta continue in this messed up life, where don't nobody care about me?" Her left cheek went numb and then her right followed. "Troy?"

"Come back to me, Q!" No longer masculine, the voice sounded like a woman's calling after her underwater. "C'mon Q, don't go out, not like this."

Quinne's eyes fluttered open. Cee Cee hovered over her in the bathroom and stopped slapping her cheeks. A female policeman read Quinne her rights.

# CHAPTER SIX

*January 4, 2050*

The tightly-wound bandages around his head and arm startled Damario, as did the throbbing. Stinging, dull metal barbs in his right eye socket shot waves of lightning through his brain. Frantic, he thrashed everything he could move until a medical droid named "Ellis Murtaugh" anesthetized him.

Madison sat to his left. He wished she hadn't. While the details of how he got into this particular predicament were fuzzy, the reason why remained clear. In the quiet moments, he pictured Justin Rochester, Yvette's ex-husband and a police medical examiner. He and Justin played basketball at the gym. They had conversations about women – with lurid details. Justin spent time at the house and ate from Damario's table. Justin slept with Damario's wife. He wondered if Justin bothered to use protection with her, given his proclaimed "allergy" to it.

He did not know the attendant at the hotel, except by his bulky physique. Damario caught his wife looking at the boy on more than one occasion. Summer, 2049 was the hottest recorded season in a century and the four-star hotel relaxed its dress standards. As such, the young man handling their luggage had rolled up his sleeves. She spotted the tattoo on his forearm and nearly swooned. He thought nothing of it, until he mistook her holophone for his and received a graphic picture message. Shell-shocked, he marked it as unread. When Madison confronted him about the mix-up, he claimed that he had been signal-free most of the day and did not notice.

The private investigator he hired found another, but suspected one or two more before Damario called him off the case. It certainly explained why Madison had been cool to intimate touch for half a year. He'd wept over his broken marriage. Thinking about it made him tear up again. He fought it. Madison did not need to see him more vulnerable and damaged.

The tube in his throat itched so badly that he had to be restrained from bothering it. He'd tried to scratch it once, before anyone could stop him, and paid a steep price. Now, with his wrist limited to a range of motion not exceeding more than a few inches, he had to swipe his fingers on a glass pad to be understood. This frustrated him, as he was not ambidextrous. Also, the machine did not have a volume control function.

"Hey there." A cheery Madison approached his bedside.

His fingers pecked *Hi* into the keyboard. The male voice he'd selected sounded like that of an old-time game show host.

"Can I get you something?"

"Date."

"It's the fourth, 3:05 p.m."

Three days had passed. When not in surgery or semi-conscious, Damario requested for the time followed by the date. Though he intended to ask a question, without punctuation, his requests sounded like commands. Madison compressed her frustration and irritation at it, but extra sweetness bothered them both. Keeping this part of her vows – to love him for better or worse – challenged her will infinitely more than the others.

Immediately after the accident, she notified Justin and her other lovers not to contact her; that she must devote herself to the recovery and wellness of her husband. At first, it felt like a morally-binding duty to her. From the litany of injuries – the collapsed lungs, the broken nose, right knee contusion, and the right eye and arm they had to replace – she owed him loyalty. Betrayal helped put him in there, and love and devotion would bring him back. Perhaps he would not forgive her, but she must try. She did love him, and hoped that merited forgiveness.

Damario's eyes tightly squinted. The first occurrence of phantom pain happened following the amputations. Damario moaned in terrible agony then, though machines routinely pumped his body with medication. The sensation of missing appendages would not totally subside until the robotic prosthesis process took place. That could take days, or months, depending on his body's reaction to the new drug his psychiatrist had introduced to the daily regimen. But not even that comforted him.

Nothing gave him relief, save for the presence of Dr. Nandor Adharma – the sole human cog among Ellis and the androids tending to her husband. He reminded Madison of a man she hated, though she could not remember why she disliked him. Obviously intelligent, Adharma spoke with a calm, superior intellect – especially when it came to Damario's treatment.

Perhaps what bothered her was the way Damario's face lit when Adharma arrived, for relief would soon come in the form of a psychotropic drug. The substance, which Madison stumbled in pronouncing, contained the addictive base chemical that produced sniff. In controlled amounts, it did wonders, but uncontrolled on the street, it killed.

The doctor inserted a tube of aqua-blue liquid into Damario's bloodstream feed. As it drained, Damario's left iris matched the color of the drug. Madison tapped her foot.

"Questions, Missus Coley?"

The sterility of his tone bothered her. "N. . .no," she stuttered. "Why do you ask?"

"Each time I administer this particular drug, you appear nervous."

"I don't like it," she spurted out. "Isn't there another you can use?"

"He's experiencing a great deal of inflammation that will keep the prosthetic eye and forearm from bonding with his nerves and muscle tissue."

"What about anti-inflammatories? They work."

"Not with simultaneous neurotransmitter application." Adharma docked his eyeglasses on the bridge of his nose. "Your husband's full recovery will take weeks; a fraction of the time that it would have under normal circumstances. You're doing the right thing."

Madison rubbed her eyes. Adharma convinced her to do it in the first place, and again to up the dosage despite her misgivings. "And the side effects?"

Ellis flashed a lightscope across Damario's intact eyelid, which fluttered.

"The dreams?" Adharma asked. "We've been over this. Maybe if you see the ADA's report on the research being conducted on the psychoana. . ."

"Just explain it to me again," she interrupted. "In layman's terms."

Adharma sighed. "Your husband's dosage is the maximum allowable and without the customary side effects of high usage; hives, dehydration."

For once, through Adharma's condescending tone, she understood exactly what he said.

"The enhanced brain activity comes from an additive, an

artificial protein, if you will, that simultaneously suppresses those symptoms but also reactivates the dorsal lateral prefrontal cortex and neurotransmitters to a degree. In other words, Missus Coley, his brain has the ability to control what he sees and remembers in his dreams. It's temporary and harmless."

Damario's bare feet sunk a bit into the moist, dark brown loam. It had been turned and contained no rocks, insects, worms or foreign bodies. He knelt and squeezed some between his fingers. The soil squished and turned to patties of earthen clay. He returned them to their native home, rose, and inhaled. The farm-like aroma reminded him of summers at his grandmother's country house in Georgia. That place lacked every modern convention of the mid-21st century, and she refused to conform to them. He hated visiting there for any extended length of time because of its remoteness.

"Hello there. Offer you some lemonade?" An elderly black woman approached him with a sweating mason jar of pale yellow liquid. Damario's grandmother looked just the way he remembered her the last time he saw her alive. He grasped the jar and almost choked on the frigid drink as he gulped it. It quenched a thirst he did not even know that he had.

*Nothing in my dreams has ever felt this real.*

"You ain't gotta admit it. I know it's good. Ain't nothin' like it on a day hot as this. Weatherman say it's s'posed to be 90 degrees. Swear it's more; ain't no wind movin'."

He gazed into the clear sky. She led him through the parlor into the kitchen. Sure enough, an antique high definition television covered in dust and a digital telephone sat near the front door. Despite that, the parlor showed an attention to cleanliness. His grandmother kept the maroon shag impeccably vacuumed, and the wooden panel walls retained their original color. Damario ran his hand over the ivory cloth furniture and detected the scent of dinner cooking in the air. Three places were set with napkins and silverware.

"Who's joining us, Ma'Dear?"

"Who you think? Have a seat. She'll be here soon."

Damario did not have to dig through the compartments of his memory. Soon, the screen door opened. In came a female vision of a woman in a purple flowing silk evening gown and flowing thin dreadlocks. Suddenly, he felt underdressed and conscious of it. Robinne Glasse greeted his grandmother by name and assumed the chair next to Damario, which urged him to slide away from her.

"Be civil," his grandmother warned him. "Ain't Christian to be mean and nasty like that."

"Please stay out of it, Ma'Dear." At that, she vanished like a wisp of steam. He looked around for her. Had he wished his grandmother away? He wanted Robinne to do the same.

"It doesn't work that way," the beauty said. "I think you know that."

Damario huffed. "I don't know much of anything here, wherever I am."

"You know." Robinne moistened her lips. "Love the dreads, Copycat."

"Why are you here?"

"You know the answer to that, too, D."

Frustrated, he pounded his right fist against the table. When it struck, he realized that his fist had regained function. So did his eye. He wiggled his fingers and touched his eyelid. He shook salt and pepper into his hand and tasted it. Real. The linoleum floor and the cheap plastic dining room furniture were authentic, as well. With much hesitation, he touched Robinne's arm and stroked its skin.

"That tickles," she giggled. "What more do you need to understand?"

"Senior year. Why?"

She smiled. "You don't waste time. Why do you think?"

"I never bought that crap about someone else. I know you better than that." The atmosphere behind them shifted, from that of a southern home's kitchen to a nighttime garden in the midst of a college campus quad. "You thought it couldn't work long distance. I told you it would, but to not answer my calls for 13 years? C'mon, we're at least friends, aren't we?"

Tears formed in her eyes.

"I heard you'd asked about me, and I got married, but that doesn't mean there's nothing left for me to say. I went to business school, not the end of the earth."

"We were friends, but we were lovers, too. No wife wants that kind of friend for her husband."

Damario's heart pumped a little harder. "And if I hadn't gone?

"I know what you want me to say," Robinne sniffed.

He took her hand in his and held it tightly. His pulse quickened as they came closer. Their surroundings and clothes had changed again. "Let me say it for you."

The couple leaned into a passionate kiss that continued – longer, deeper, and more passionate than any he had ever remembered experiencing. Breathless, they parted enough for him to directly speak into her ear.

"You're still in my heart," he said. He felt the skin of Robinne's cheek shift backwards from smiling. He also smiled. "Would you have me again?"

There needed to be no answer. He sniffed the perfume

emanating from behind her ear – a mixture of sweet flower nectar and a summer breeze. She giggled with delight. Robinne. For the first time since his early 20's, he said her name, over and over again.

A paralyzing pain dropped him to the ground. Damario unintelligibly moaned.

"Relax, Mister Coley." No longer feminine, her voice resembled that of Ellis. "Settle down and try to relax."

His arm beneath the elbow ached. Then, stabbing flared at the right knee. Damario struggled to catch his breath and lost vision in his right eye before passing out.

When Damario awoke, Ellis monitored his racing heartbeat. A red-eyed Madison crossed to the right side of the room. How much of it did she hear? He typed into the keypad. "Date."

"Ask Robinne," Madison sniffled before storming out.

# CHAPTER SEVEN

*January 5, 2050*

Since the mid-1960's, the James family mandated that its dead be in the ground after no more than three days. The ceremony rooted in superstition would be the manner in which Harper buried Micah. Pronounced dead late last Saturday, he would be interred Wednesday.

Next to Micah's mother, Laverne James, Harper held court in the funeral home's parlor and popped a few saltines into her mouth. Her pregnancy limited her to the amount and type of medications she could take. The nurse said to avoid stress, which might be possible, after today.

Both the James and Lowe families flew into town. The former did not wear black or navy blue, yet another decades-old tradition. Micah's great-grandmother, Joséphine Coutiér-James, had insisted on the wardrobe for funerals ages ago. The family observed it for her and each of her four children – Darrion, Jr., the oldest and Micah's grandfather, Betty Joséphine, Kelley, and Leroy – before making it an unspoken expectation.

The picture of composure for a grieving mother, Laverne donned a royal purple suit jacket and matching dress to celebrate her son's life, and possibly more. After all, who knew if Micah would be resurrected on earth instead, warranting celebration? God had intervened like that before in her family, though most of them now debunked it as a hoax once all of the eyewitnesses died.

"Welcome." Harper greeted those who passed the front row of chairs, occasionally substituting salutations with a hug. The fatigue and guilt of the past few days caught up to her. In those brief moments of respite, the baby in her belly reminded her of it. She did not do what she and her boyfriend agreed to do and because of it, he died. If she had aborted their child, all three of them would be gone. His daughter and their son would be orphans. That thought alone tethered her in the weak moments.

Christian sat on Harper's lap and Gabrielle fidgeted next to Laverne on Harper's left, with Charlotte Lowe, Harper's mother, at her right. Gabrielle's mother, who refused to attend the wake or the viewing, did not care whether Micah lived or died, as long as her child support payments kept coming.

The music slowly dragged during the closed casket ceremony and the building's heater sputtered out bursts of temperate air. Micah desired to be buried here – not in Zyonne, North Carolina where his people originated. Harper's insistence on following his wishes to the letter caused a rift with Laverne so large that Charlotte stepped in and paid for everything. While this resulted in a lecture about how Harper should have conducted herself differently when it came to finances, it lifted a weight off of her shoulders. Harper would use most of Micah's life insurance policy to help their family maintain a slightly better quality of life. *It's what he would have wanted*, she thought.

Laverne asked the pastor of the local assembly to say a few words, before speaking herself – after which she expected Harper to represent Micah, as the mother of his son.

Just yesterday, she regained the power to talk and retain composure. *And they want me to eulogize him? He wasn't saved. Laverne should ask someone else to do it, but she won't.*

"Talk from your heart," Laverne told Harper. "You don't have to be long."

"You know, Harper." Charlotte moistened her thin pink lips. "You don't have to say anything, no matter what these people think of you."

"These people?" Laverne reared back. "What do you mean, 'these people', Charlotte?"

"She loved him in her way," retorted Charlotte. "She should say goodbye to him the same."

"I know, Mother." Harper set Christian in her place. "This is how Mike wanted it. And don't say 'these people'. It's offensive."

Charlotte tugged the ends of her suit's coat. "You know, that's not what I meant, Laverne."

"No, Charlotte, I don't. But now's not the time."

Harper walked to the front. "I wanted to do things *his way* today, and not the way we thought it should've gone. I know that's hard for some of you to understand because of your rich spiritual tradition. I would never want to disrespect that about you. But Mike wanted things done his way."

Her soft voice cracked with sadness. "The last thing he wanted me to do, I couldn't do. There are a million reasons why I should've. But there's one reason I didn't and, because of that, he's no longer here with us. I chose. I chose our unborn child and it cost him his life."

Charlotte rose and tried to escort her daughter back to her seat. They struggled for a second until Charlotte accidentally said, "It's not your fault he's dead!" out loud for all to hear.

"A group of hateful people killed my husband." Tears rolled down Harper's face. "But we gave them the opportunity. All I could see was the money. How could we afford another baby?

"We've borrowed money from some of you down the line and couldn't repay it. Soon, I will. But the love of my life is gone. My children have no father. And if you have a sense of loss, but there's money in your pocket, maybe you know what it's like to be me a little. Does it ease your pain?" Harper rushed out down the center aisle. Charlotte, Gabrielle, and Christian followed.

Members of both families muttered among themselves until Laverne quieted them. "Please, everyone, let's show reverence." Once it became clear to her that Harper, Charlotte, and the children did not intend to return to the main room, she instructed the undertaker to call the pallbearers forth.

After the families bid their goodbyes, the men loaded the casket into the rear of a stretch black Marque. From there, a caravan led by Charlotte's canary yellow Spirit proceeded to the cemetery. Micah's final resting place would be a compartment inside of a climate-controlled building. There, a bronze placard emblazoned with his name, birth, and death dates would mark it.

Following the interment, Charlotte invited both families to her home for a repast. The socialite's prim but stately opulence left no doubt to the type of culinary spread she planned; ham, turkey, and all the trimmings. Most of the Jameses, including Laverne, did not care for the pretentious woman, but they would not give up a free meal – especially after traveling so far and so long. But, while Micah's mother recounted old stories en route to her transport, Charlotte, Harper and her children did not move from the mausoleum's foyer.

"Miss Lowe." The undertaker placed a gloved hand on Harper's shoulder. "The rest of the family is readying to leave. We are waiting on you."

Harper did nothing that indicated an awareness of anything around her, including the man at her right.

"Ma'am, with all due respect, I have another funeral I must prepare for."

Charlotte approached. "Leave us."

"It's part of my duties. I must insist that. . ."

". . .and we must decline. Thank you for your service. Now go."

The kindly man donned a hat and walked back to the main transport. While Gabrielle minded after her brother, Harper and Charlotte stood next to one another in front of Micah's blank marker. Harper rolled a small object inside her closed hand.

"The droids and service staff will take good care of them," Charlotte said. She checked her appearance in a compact mirror. "Formalities are the last thing you need to worry about right now, but your family will be everything you'll need later. It was that way for me when Harper had his accident. Afterward, I needed you and you were there. Micah and I had our differences, but I loved him." She squeezed Harper's fist. "Let me be here for you now."

Until now, Harper's ability to keep it together had strained under the day's emotional weight. Her mascara did not run. Tears had been in limited supply. "This morning," she forced out. "I scrambled eggs."

"Yeah?"

"Mike liked them with a bit of pancake mix. . .makes them fluff up more. I used the stove, you know, old fashioned. He said it retains more heat that way. But he stirs them with a fork. It makes them look like crumbs."

"I didn't know that."

"The kids eat them whatever way. So, I forgot this morning and used a spoon. He didn't correct me, like he usually does. I forgot he's gone, Mom. His got cold, so I ate them."

"Keep up your strength."

"Dad said all the time, 'You can always make more money'."

"I suppose that's true."

"Because, if so. . ." Harper trailed off with sudden vigor. She opened her closed fist. In it rolled a fire-damaged, thumb segment-sized, blood red disk. "Why didn't we have it?"

Charlotte knew the correct answer to the question, because she had asked a similar one of herself years ago. In time, her daughter would discover it, as well. To their left, another funeral gathered and would soon intrude upon them.

"In weeks, I'll have more money in my account than I could want."

Aware of the approaching company, her mother stood up and encouraged her daughter to do the same. "Harper. . ."

"Three times as much as we've ever earned as a household, at least."

"It's time to go. Say your peace."

"There is no peace!" Harper's bellowing frightened the children present. The grieving elderly ignored the outburst and filled in around them. Composing herself, Harper approached Micah's placard, touched her lips and gently fingered the placard. The next service was for a woman who peacefully died at the nadir of life and not its zenith.

Harper would not say goodbye. "So long."

The ride to Charlotte's home went speechless. When the mother-daughter duo entered the room, the conversations continued. Glasses were filled and eating commenced without a pause. Silence and stares would worsen the already present discomfort. Robbed of many of their traditions, the James contingent expressed displeasure through mumbling. Their beloved would stay dead this day, but little had been said of his spiritual condition. He came from a rich lineage of faith and preachers, but those raised close to the faith often shunned it under pressure.

Harper did believe, and she took the children to church with her. But if Micah did not personally confess Jesus Christ, it explained the dark pall over the proceedings and her discomfort.

Some of the more radical believers there thought his violent end balanced the scales for his attempt at aborting his child. None would voice it. But Harper knew that they thought it and talked behind her back – even if they would not say so. Mentally, she strangled Micah's trio of busybody, opinionated female cousins.

Someone finally came to check on her: Jackie, from the Genesis Institute. Harper never introduced her to Micah because of his affinity for exotic-looking women. She never remembered the woman's ethnic name, so she named her "Jackie."

The woman sidled up to Harper and passed her a plate of food. "How are you holding up?"

Harper stuffed a finger sandwich into her mouth. "This baby's been kicking my butt. Half the day, I'm nauseous, the other half, I'm ravenous. Don't worry, I still have your money."

"Don't worry about it. Try the cous cous. It's *amazing.*"

She scooped the salmon-colored concoction onto a cracker and wolfed it down. "Seldom wrong and right again," she said with a full mouth. "It's fantastic."

"The managing partners and I talked. Take as much time as you need. Don't worry about your sick days. A bunch of the others kicked in, so you've got time. I reallocated your patients."

"Thank you for everything."

"Listen." "Jackie" reached out and patted Harper's thigh. "There's no right time to say this, but you should consider talking to someone. Go see Dr. Nandor Adharma. He's a psychiatrist and fantastic at what he does. He might be able to help the kids cope. Understanding death poses a difficult challenge for people at any age."

Harper considered the offer a good omen. "I know the psychiatry spiel, thanks." She gave a slight smile to her superior. "I think I'll take a week or two."

"Take three. You'll need it. Arranging your life after something like this takes longer than you think and you never know how long until you're knee deep in it."

Her superior's kindness overwhelmed Harper. For reasons unknown to Harper, all of her coworkers referred to their superior as a conniving, silver-tongued serpent. "I don't know what to say. I think I'll call him."

"Good. Call him any time. Tell him Kareza Noor sent you."

# CHAPTER EIGHT

*January 13, 2050*

"My name is Andre. I'm an alcoholic, but I'm beginning again."

Piano music swelled and broke into a dramatic, sweeping decrescendo. Quick choral chords built as each different person introduced themselves.

"My name is Kelly. I'm a sniff addict, but I'm beginning again."

"My name is Tamara. . ."

"My name is Jennifer. . ."

"Terran. . ."

"Sophie. . ."

"John. . ."

"Devon. . ."

". . .I'm a thief. . ."

". . .white collar criminal. . ."

". . .gang member. . ."

". . .quadriplegic. . ."

". . .wife beater. . ."

". . .I'm terminally ill. . ."

". . .and we're beginning again."

The commercial ended with the Genesis Institute logo and a phone number, 1-888-BEGINAGAIN. Madison redialed every few seconds she spent alone, while Damario rehabbed his new synthetic arm and eye. Adharma's advice proved true. The miracle drug stimulated healthy growth of the severed nerves to bond with the artificial ones wired to his new appendages.

When he slept, she assumed the dreams were vivid, as her husband's moaning indicated pleasure. He'd awaken and stayed mum on what he had seen. The object of his enjoyment was his college sweetheart, Robinne Glasse. They broke up prior to Damario accepting his internship at G.R. Cooper and attending business school at Stern. Robinne lived in Philadelphia.

With the busy signal operator in view from Madison's holophone, Damario entered the room. He employed the use of a crutch and wore sunglasses to hide his eye, which looked like an antique LED. Soon, it would be fitted with synthetic skin to make it appear normal. "Still busy?"

She snapped the display shut. "How's therapy?"

"If I didn't know any better," he said, limping towards the bed, "I'd think you were hiding something."

"Have me investigated then." She snapped her fingers. "Sorry. You already did that."

"Ouch," he winced with sarcasm. "Those lines are going to be jammed up forever. Everybody in America wants to know what 'beginning again' really means. The advertising is a little deceptive, but brilliant."

"I think you wouldn't be half as high on life, if they stopped giving you that drug."

"I'm healing." Damario sat at the edge of the bed and swung his good leg into it for leverage, then his sore and bruised one. "I have sensations other than pain."

"Good for you," she said, while loading a virtual magazine.

"Look, you don't have to be here, Maddie. The bedside vigil's really not necessary."

"I guess not, since you have Robinne."

He sighed. "Will you stop it with the Robinne stuff? Seriously!"

"Stop dreaming about her, D. Stop whispering her name in your sleep. If you want to reconcile, I did my part. I apologized, I severed the relationships. You do your part."

Damario wondered if he could control the dreaming. Thus far, he had not tried, thoroughly enjoying each rendezvous with Robinne – the picnics in the quad, the college dances, and impromptu dates. Each journey lasted longer the previous one, and all ended before the physicality got extremely involved. Madison did have a point. Internally, he wanted a free pass to do what she had done. "Alright."

"Don't sound so enthused. It's just our marriage."

"I'll do it," he joyfully resigned. The change in tone satisfied her. "Do you have my holophone?"

She passed the silver object to Damario. "Here. Why?"

He dialed 1-800-BEGINAGAIN. "Let me give it a shot." To his surprise, the phone connected right away.

"Hello, and welcome to the Genesis Institute and the Begin Again Initiative." A brunette female greeted him. "Please wait while we verify your identity with an iris scan."

Damario removed his glasses and hoped that the prosthetic had been coded with his genetic information.

"Good morning." The holographic image arrested Harper's attention. Other than a few blips in its presentation, the administrative professional looked authentic. A few of her curls even wobbled as her head moved. "Welcome to the Genesis Institute. May I have your full name?"

"Harper Charlotte Lowe. I have. . .had a 9:30 meeting with Doctor Adharma, but the crowd outside. . ."

"You're fine," she reassured. "We allow an extra 45 minutes for his appointments. The excitement surrounding our "Begin Again" initiative is spectacular, isn't it?"

"Yes, but what is it exactly? And why do people want it so badly?"

"Everything in time, Miss Lowe," said the annoyingly pleasant program. "Follow me, please." She rose from the projection machine seated in a high-backed office chair. As she did, the hologram replicated itself at the desk. Harper wondered how the hologram's stiletto heels clicked against the black marble floors, as if the secretary actually existed.

"The Genesis Institute exists for the betterment of humanity," she explained. "Accordingly, we focus our talent and resources on revolutionary advances in the physical, mental, relational, and financial well-being of the international populace."

What does all of that mean?

"In other words," said the assistant, as if reading Harper's thoughts, "if there's a way to push mankind to the unlimited depths of its potential, we will be involved."

"Does that include the 'Begin Again' initiative?"

The smiling assistant waved her hand in a welcoming flourish, which opened the sliding door in front of them. "Doctor Adharma will see you now."

Harper entered the door and watched the assistant vanish into a miniscule light diode embedded in the baseboard of the hallway.

"Miss Lowe." A thick Indian accent beckoned her. "Please join me."

Harper complied and shook hands with the doctor. "Pleasure to meet you. My boss just raves about you and the work that you do."

"Ahh. . .Kareza." He relished saying the woman's name. "I would not be able to accomplish much without her helping hands. Please have a seat."

"Thank you."

The two sat a few feet apart, separated by a thick fiberglass desk. It housed an enlarged computer projection console. To operate it, Adharma wore specialized gloves with memory chips implanted in the finger pads. Harper coveted the technology for her office.

"I heard your boyfriend had been killed." The doctor's words exuded sympathy. "My condolences and apologies."

"Thank you."

"What's your mental state right now?"

Harper tasted the inside of her mouth and paused. "When I close my eyes, I still see the accident. I smell the burning, and. . . it. . ." She stopped to collect her thoughts and to keep from weeping.

The doctor pushed his fingers a few times in the air on a display that Harper could not see with her naked eyes. "Have you slept?"

"Barely," she admitted. "The kids sleep on his side of the bed. That helps me to forget."

"Taken anything for the insomnia?"

"I'd rather readjust naturally. I don't believe in medicating problems away. Not everything can be cured by a pill or solution."

"A peculiar ideology for a psychiatrist." He swept his hands across the desk and typed on a virtual keypad. "Look at it as a means to an end. Your body needs rest to heal – even mentally. Open wounds get infected and fester. Then, what's healthy becomes unhealthy."

"I understand, but I disagree. What did insomniacs do before drugs were developed? How about different methodologies instead of pharmacology?"

"They drank themselves to sleep," he chuckled. "Depressants have existed since the beginning of time, you know. I'm talking about a pill, not a hangover-inducing binge."

"And the side effects are a small chance of heart attack, stroke, and blood clots, right? Aren't there medical cases of insomniacs who die because of sleep aid side effects?"

"There are more documented instances of insomniacs falling asleep while piloting a transport and killing themselves and their children. Don't you agree?"

Harper did not protest further, as she had fallen asleep at a red light a few days ago. When she awoke, the automatic pilot had already taken over. The thought of losing Christian, Gabrielle, or her fetus overwhelmed her.

"How pregnant are you now?"

"Eleven weeks."

"I can prescribe something safe for you and the baby, with limited side effects. Prevalent among them are vivid, memorable dreams. But you will sleep."

Harper suppressed her personal opinions about the subject and consented.

After administering a battery of questions and mental health tests, Adharma authorized a prescription to the pharmacy of Harper's choice. "Before you go to sleep, take one pill," he instructed. "Your dreams will be vivid, palatable. You will remember them, but you will sleep soundly."

"Anything else?" She braced herself.

"Other than a slight aftertaste, no."

She accepted the news and walked out. The holographic assistant emerged from the floor and escorted Harper to the lobby. Outside, a throng of people shielded their eyes from the sun to peer into the building. From this vantage point, they viewed the building's architectural and glorious design. Micah would have loved the chance to design such a magnificent work of metal, wood, glass and polished marble.

If only Miles Chu had not laid him off.

Despondent, Teanna rolled her head towards the sunlight. A few geometrical yellow shapes warmed her forehead, nose, and across her cheeks. She whispered dim and the tint on the hospital window darkened to a higher grade. The ceiling lights barely illuminated the room beyond an auburn glow. It remained that way until the doctor or Stan Witmore, her attending medical droid, entered. Then, the lighting matched that of a sports stadium.

". . .wife beater. . ."

". . .I'm terminally ill. . ."

". . .and we're beginning again."

The holovision played the Genesis Institute commercial ad infinitum. It ran before and after every major show, as well as during the news. Teanna let it run. Today, she would return to an empty home cleared for habitation a day ago, when a policeman notified her that they had cleaned up the crime scene. They buried Meleasa over a week ago, and Stan sedated her after delivering the news. But he could do nothing about the construct of her mind; something Adharma told her, as well. Erasing the past took time. Teiji did not wish for her to contact him. She imagined word had reached his father overseas and that he would finally come to see what a mess his former lover had made of their son's life.

"Good morning, Miss Kirkwood." Stan greeted her warmly. "You will be discharged today at noon; approximately one hour and 15 minutes from now. Please prepare yourself and your things. I will come at a quarter until noon to sign you out."

Teanna rubbed sleep from her eyes and entered the shower. As the hot water dribbled across her body's full contours, she thought about her next move. She could not stay in the house alone, where Tiny and Meleasa had died. In a matter of days, the state would pull its aid due to her discovered drug use. Then what?

For one reason or another, she had alienated her friends. No one came to visit her – not even to settle a score or to curse her out. The satisfaction of her failure could be discovered from a distance. She had chosen a boyfriend over her children before – only to later discover that they had told the truth. *If I'd believed Tay, or done somethin', he'd be goin' to his internship and Meleasa would be alive!*

She had barely gotten dressed when Stan returned. "Good morning, Miss Kirkwood. Please affirm your signature on the following release documents by pressing your thumb against the plate located on the front of my arm." Teanna did so without reading them. "Thank you. Please follow me to the exit."

"I thought I got a final check up with Doctor Adharma?" she inquired to Stan's back. He continued to move forward but swiveled his head around to address her.

"Please feel free to visit him. He has offices at the Genesis Institute."

"I ain't gotta make an appointment?" she asked, still following.

"No. He marked you as a priority case."

*Priority case? What's wrong with me?* Teanna waited for a public transport at the corner. Two transfers later, she would be dropped off on the same street as the Genesis Institute. She hoped that whatever the doctor told her, it included more of that blue drug that gave her sweet dreams and a pleasant taste in her mouth.

Cee Cee had been to the women's detention facility a few times to visit her best friend, but Quinne would not have her. This time, she noticed the inmate from afar, dawdling about the yard. When Cee Cee drew close enough to call her name, Quinne glowered back and said nothing. Her stare quieted everything conciliatory her friend could have thought. The bigger woman cornered Quinne and projected enough hostility to impose her will. "Sit or stand."

Quinne did not speak, but cursed Cee Cee with an evil grimace. *You turned me in.*

"I commissioned a lawyer to speak with Kareza Noor and the judge regarding your release. Good behavior alone will get you reduced to 45 days."

*Wasting my time.* Quinne crossed her arms and sulked.

"I identified your dealer and they caught him."

*You snitched?* Her eyes widened.

She held a hand up. "It's anonymous. But he turned on his supplier, who they've been trying to catch for a while." Cee Cee's voice bubbled. "Noor made a big deal out of it, so my lawyer negotiated an earlier release for you."

*When?*

Cee Cee noticed the wonderment in her friend's eyes. "Counting time already served. . .next Wednesday."

Quinne contained her excitement with pursed lips. "Can I still enlist?"

"She talks!" Cee Cee snapped her fingers. "Expunged record! Yep. Forgot about that."

"You didn't have to do all that for me."

"Yes I did. And you're right. I haven't been a good friend."

Quinne swiped the corners of her eyes with the backs of her hands. "What do I owe you?"

"Well, you still have to behave for another week. Can you do that?"

"In this place? What else is there?"

"Been going to your meetings?" By "meetings," Cee Cee meant the addiction support group.

She nodded. *Sat through every gut-wrenchin' question and discussion. Talked about Troy, our baby, my actions and the consequences.* "Yes, Mom."

"Noor did insist on one small sticking point and wouldn't budge from it."

Quinne rolled her eyes. "I knew it. What, community service?"

"Sort of. Without it, the deal goes away. You get the full 120 and it stays on your record."

"Shoot, sign me up. What I gotta do?"

Cee Cee dug into her purse and produced a thumb segment-sized, blood red disk. "You get phone time in here?"

"Once a night. I ain't got no one to call but you, though."

"You do now." She handed the disk to Quinne. "Since you wouldn't see me earlier, you have to respond by midnight tonight. I'll see you on Wednesday."

"Wait! What if I don't get through?"

Cee Cee smiled and kissed her friend on the cheek. "You'll get through."

That night, phone privileges could not come fast enough. To the amazement of her fellow prisoners, who ribbed her, Quinne jumped in line for the first time, One joked that her man must have visited. Another one had seen Cee Cee kiss her and assumed that she and Quinne were lovers. Quinne endured the jokes without response, which egged on her provocateurs. When her turn came, she dialed the number five times and received a busy signal every time.

"Try another number, Ruiz," warned the supervising officer, "or get out of line."

She tried one last time, crossed her fingers and held her breath.

A hologram of a Hispanic male appeared. "Hello, and welcome to the Genesis Institute and the Begin Again Initiative. Please wait while we verify your identity with an iris scan."

# CHAPTER NINE

*January 18, 2050*

Absolution. Teanna had never heard of it until her psychiatrist used the term to describe her recent emotions. He refused to define it. Instead, he persisted in making Teanna clear up the matter for herself. During their Friday morning session four days ago, she excused herself to the bathroom and looked up the word on her holophone. Satisfied, she returned to the office with bravado.

"Forgiveness? Could've just told me that, Nandor."

"Yes." Adharma manipulated an invisible display. "But what would that accomplish?"

"Umm. . .not trying to confuse me?"

"Your confusion lies deeper than you think. I said you needed absolution. However you define it, that's your problem and your solution."

It started and ended with Teiji, who had refused to see her. At her last attempt, she asked the man in charge of visitation to show her Teiji's list of visitors. Only one person successfully saw him – his girlfriend, Kelly Roshenburger. Though multiracial herself, Teanna did not approve of her son's choice of a white Jewish girlfriend. Yet, Teanna herself did not practice a religion. But something about the girl put her ill at ease. She appeared to be well-mannered and behaved. At the end of that same day around three o' clock, she approached the girl. "Kelly!" She waved as discreetly as possible. "Kelly Roshenburger!"

Kelly turned. When she noticed the disheveled black woman walking towards her, she cursed and sped up. Teanna also stepped up her pace too but not enough to aggravate her scabbed-over knees. They arrived at Kelly's transport at the same time. Teanna laid a hand over the door's thumbprint panel and locked eyes with Kelly.

"You're harassing me. Give me one reason why I shouldn't get a school policeman. One."

Desperate, Teanna pled her case. "Hear me out, just this once. I'm Tay's mom."

Kelly crossed her arms. "I know. You want a chance, Miss Kirkwood? One more chance than you ever gave me? You don't even know me, and the first thing you do is ask me for something. You're everything Tay said you were."

"I need to see him, and he ain't seeing me."

"He doesn't want to see you!" she snapped. "Why do you need to see him anyway? Isn't it enough that he's in prison because of you?"

Teanna swallowed the criticism. "I need your help. That's why I'm here. You the last shot I got."

Kelly smiled with contempt. "It's burning you up that he'll see me anytime I want."

"I got it. . .you're angry. Sorry, I was wrong about you and Tay. Ain't fix nothing, but it's the truth. Believe me, I done run up a lot of mistakes in my time and paid the bill for every last one of 'em myself. . .all but this one. I want to try, can't do nothing else but that. And you right – I don't know you, but I can't get to know you unless you let me."

Kelly moved Teanna's hand and opened the driver's side door. "What difference do you think it'll make, if you're with me?

Then, he won't want to see either of us."

"I don't know you, but I know my son. All he wanted me to do was accept you. And I ain't do it because I didn't think you was right for him."

"Because I'm white? Jewish? Who cares? We're good for each other." Kelly blustered. "You'd know that, if you'd try to see it. Say he does see you. What good will it do?"

"Won't bring his sister back," she admitted. "I lost her, too. I ain't always do the right thing, but try to see it through my eyes. What would you do?"

Kelly thought about telling her to back off, but she knew better. If Teiji told Kelly to stay away, she would continue trying until the day of his release. She slumped into the driver's seat and shut the door. Teanna's shoulders dropped with defeat until she heard the transport's automatic door click open. Kelly was going to take her after all.

With the prison 20 miles outside of town and the rush hour traffic approaching, it would take up to 60 minutes to reach him. Teanna braced herself for a long, silent ride, but Kelly would have none of that. She often switched satellite radio stations to skip commercial interruptions and incessantly talked on her holophone device. About 15 minutes from the prison, she veered off an exit and pulled into the parking lot of a fast food restaurant.

"Oh, I forgot to tell you, Miss Kirkwood. I leave straight from school to come here, but he eats at five o' clock. The traffic usually pushes me close to then and there's no visitation when they're eating. So, I usually stop here and get a quick bite."

"Sure," she absentmindedly replied. "Whatever you need."

Kelly unlatched her security harness and parked. "It's a little too chilly to sit out here. Why don't you come inside? At least have something hot to drink."

Teanna snapped back from her thoughts. "Yes! Okay, sure. Let's go."

At the counter, Kelly ordered more food than Teanna thought an 18-year-old girl weighing no more than 100 pounds could consume. She paid for a cup of coffee and a pastry.

The pair sat down and ate. Before Teanna had enough time to get a third of the way down her cup, Kelly had already consumed most of her double cheeseburger and a half container of shoestring French fries.

"Can I ask you somethin', Kelly? It's kinda personal."

A dot of ketchup stubbornly lingered at the corner of her mouth. "I guess."

"You always eat like that? You makin' me nervous."

Kelly giggled with a full mouth. "Tay says the same thing."

She never noticed Teiji had been dating anyone until months into the relationship.

"Our first date, we went to the movies to see an old romantic drama, The Experiment. Tay picked me up with a single violet rose, which is my favorite. He thought the female lead, I forgot her name. . .she's gorgeous. And the guy who played her love interest – he's yummy.

"So afterward, we came here and sat in this same booth. Tay thought I'd order something cute. When my order cost as much as his and I ate through it twice as fast as he did, he said I made him nervous. I think it's the first time a boy didn't think I had an eating disorder."

Every once in a while, Teanna posed a question. But for the most part, the teenager went on and on about Teiji without provocation. The girl knew more about Teiji than Teanna did. They discussed his favorite music, activities and interests. Kelly credited the visible changes in Teiji's attitude and behaviors to her erstwhile boyfriend's presence, while Teanna had dismissed them as teenage insolence.

When Kelly finished stuffing her face, Teanna checked the time on her holophone device. 5:25. "How long's their dinnertime? You know?"

"An hour." Kelly crumbled her food packages and slid them toward the table edge, but kept her soda cup. "We can go now. By the time we get there, he'll be waiting."

"Waitin' for you, not for me."

"He doesn't know you're coming." They slipped through the exit door. "No matter how much he says he hates you, he still loves you."

"No. Not after this."

"In spite of this," she insisted. "It's not really love, if it can't stand testing."

Kelly's wisdom caught Teanna off-guard. "What you know 'bout that?"

"I don't yet," she admitted. "Teiji told me that when he considered the internship."

The internship! Heaviness formed in Teanna's stomach. She had cost her son the chance of his short lifetime. Even with time off for good behavior, he would be in his late 20's, with no college education, and a felony on his permanent record upon his release. Who'll hire him? Not Senator Mateo. What'll Tay become?

The path to the meeting room wound around various prisoner facilities. Men in bright jumpsuits lifted weights, read books, played indoor basketball, or loitered by leaning against building supports and chewing the fat with one another. Many did not appear hardened by their confines, but a few looked downright scary. Neither Teanna nor Kelly made eye contact with the more nefarious looking. Those men stared, as the women passed by. Just a couple whistles and profane comments passed before the security guard warned them of impending discipline.

When Teiji came into the room, his pleasure at seeing Kelly got tempered by his mother's presence. He greeted his girlfriend with a hearty hug and kiss on the lips. Teanna stood and opened her arms, but Teiji shunned her. Kelly smacked his chest for doing so, but his position did not change. The three sat down. Only then, did Teanna notice Teiji's face bore an assortment of cuts and bruises at various stages of healing.

Filled with emotion, she reached out for her son's hands, which he withdrew from the table.

"Only a matter of time," he deadpanned. "Using Kelly to get me to see you? You hate her. You don't even know her last name!"

"It was my idea, Tay," Kelly explained. "She doesn't hate me. And it's Roshenburger."

"Watch. . .wait until she's done using you. See how much she likes you then."

"Talk to me," Teanna implored. "What they doin' to you up in here?"

"I'm locked up with real criminals. I'm just the kid protecting his family when no one else would. What do I get for that? Fifteen years and I missed my sister's funeral."

"I missed it, too. I'd trade places with you, if I could."

Teiji rolled his eyes. "Sure. You had your chance with Tiny. You didn't take it. I did."

Kelly had never seen this degree of hatred in him. "Calm down, Tay."

Teanna composed herself. "I lost the house 'cause of the sniff. Got me in a halfway house now, drug rehab program."

"Just tell me one thing. It's the only thing I think about, and I gotta know." Venom rose in his voice. "Why did you even have us, if you were going to be high half the time? You ruined my life and took Mel's!"

With sudden life, Teanna sprung to her feet and pushed the chair back from the table. Teiji did the same, which alerted the security guard. He carefully approached to assess whether there was a threat. Kelly backed away.

"Since you 'big man' now, I'm gonna look you in the eye and tell you straight."

Unlike a few weeks ago, he did not cower from confrontation. "Good."

"Only difference between what you goin' through and what I been through? Can't see my scars. Ain't been the best mother, but I sure ain't the worst. Tried to do my best for you and your sister, and I ain't succeed all the time. But you ate, every day, even if you ain't like it. We moved from time to time, but you had a roof over your head. And yeah, I messed up, got high and fell in with the wrong guys, but Tay, this ain't what I had in mind for you or her!"

Teiji's tough façade shattered. "Then why. . ." he trembled. "Why didn't you protect us from him? Why didn't you do anything? How did you not know?"

"I swear. . .I ain't know. If I knowed, I'd have done somethin'."

For several minutes, mother and son bathed each other in tears as an emotional Kelly stood nearby. Whenever Teanna pulled away, Teiji scrambled back into her arms – like he did as a toddler. Injuries, insomnia, and sickness drove him to clutch onto Teanna for dear life, as he did now, and his mother never refused him. Kelly wanted to include herself in the moment, but recognized it as a two-person healing.

Absolution. Teanna scooted her mouth toward his ear and whispered. "I know, I know. I love you, no matter what you done, no matter what you do. I'm so sorry for everythin' I done to you.

Can't blame you, if you never forgive me."

"But I. . ." Sniffles muffled his words. Teanna wanted to erase the guilt he felt over accidentally killing Meleasa and the eventual remorse he may experience for shooting Tiny. He would carry it until he died. A prison sentence and a long parole would not change that.

"Three minutes remain in this visitation period," the security guard announced. The other prisoners bade goodbye to their loved ones. Teanna and Teiji released one another and settled back into their chairs. Kelly smiled. This was not the end, but the beginning of a better ending.

"I'm gonna be going away for a special treatment on Thursday, so I ain't gonna be seeing you anytime soon." Teanna used a balled-up tissue in her pocket to finish the assault on her running mascara. "Gotta kick this thing for good. But I'll see you again. I'll let your dad know. Maybe he'll come. Until then, Kelly'll take good care of you."

"Yes." Kelly blew her red nose. "Yes, I will."

"Counting on that." Teanna squeezed Kelly's free hand. Teiji issued a smile towards his girlfriend, who returned one just as bright and wide.

"What kind of treatment?" His mother had never entered Alcoholics Anonymous or anything like it. She always insisted that she could go cold turkey.

"Honestly, I'm not sure. The hospital arranged it. Wish me luck."

# CHAPTER TEN

*January 19, 2050*

Quinne dipped her stiff hands inside of her woolen coat pockets, a smile creeping across her lips. She had served her sentence victoriously, and with *humility*. The atmosphere had not stained her soul. It had with others. Her cellmate – a middle-aged white woman awaiting trial for a domestic crime – blanched a degree or two each day. Quinne thought the woman would rather drop unconscious from pain than to use the commode in front of her. On their second day together, she gave in and dropped her pants. Quinne stifled a laugh. "It's no big deal," she assured her.

"It is," she had uttered, deeply exhaling. "To me, it is."

"Okay, I gotta know. What you in here for?"

"Stabbing my husband, actually." She cursed him. "We have plenty of money, but he won't bail me out. He's actually pressing charges!"

Quinne asked nothing else, but her cellmate gushed forth a confession. "He hit me, once, at first. I thought it was a fluke. He did it again. The third time, he broke my nose. This last time, he threatened to kill me, so I figure I'll do him one better. I never reported him, so it looked totally one-sided. And here I am."

That final morning, the stench in the hold startled Quinne awake. Her new friend squatted on the toilet in plain sight. She chuckled and turned over in bed, shielding her nose. It took almost two weeks, but the woman had grown to be an acquaintance. They agreed not to forget one another on the outside.

The group sessions, on the other hand, would not be missed. By a remarkable coincidence, the same doctor she resolved to never visit moderated the group once per week. Dr. Adharma was part of the Genesis Institute's outreach program to prevent recidivism. The man's bedside manner was brusque and to the point. While Quinne appreciated candor in her personal life, she preferred a softer touch in psychoanalysis.

She checked her watch, which she appreciated having the ability to do. Cee Cee's transport pulled up, just as she dropped her hand back into the shielding of her coat. She lifted the Tarpan's butterfly door and entered the passenger's side. Her friend offered her a mint coffee from Caribou- her favorite holiday hot drink. Quinne giggled and sipped from the insulated steel mug. "You just might be the best friend ever."

"I'm glad you think so." The engine revved into gear. "Welcome back."

They rode in silence for a minute, absorbing the moment. Quinne drank the cappuccino to its last. "Sorry you missed Wednesday mornin' Bible study to come out here."

"I didn't." Cee Cee turned on the dashboard's screen console, which showcased her pastor concluding his morning message. "Do you mind?"

"No," she said convincingly enough to placate Cee Cee. "Enjoy."

Quinne zoned out on the sermon until the call for discipleship, but she picked up enough religious buzz talk to know the message had something to do with "tricks of the enemy" and "resisting the devil." *Her* devil no longer had a foothold in her life. Generally, after she remained clean for at least two weeks, she could deal for a while without an illegal stimulant in her system.

"Hungry?" Cee Cee asked after the service faded out. "Split a pizza?"

Quinne thought of the cost. "We could eat in. E'erythin' they give you in jail's kinda starchy. Keeps you full longer for less."

"Got it." Cee Cee noticed a twinge of anxiety in her roommate's voice. "Your supervisor called and he said. . ."

". . .that I'm no longer needed? You ain't gotta sugarcoat it, Cee. I ain't the first girl to get hemmed up and fired. Seen it happen a couple times."

"Well, there's unemployment in the meantime. You can do it online."

"Thanks," she deadpanned. "Now, all I gotta do is commit check fraud, claim some kids that ain't mine and collect some disability, too."

"No, Q, you are not Anibel."

She stared at the passing buildings. "Ain't I, though?"

"No. You're different."

"Look," she redirected. "I owe you big time. Say the word and I'm out."

"And what would I do with an extra bedroom?" she mused. "Who's going to call me on my crap and drink all the coffee? Besides, I hate interviewing roommates. Avoiding that is worth half the rent and utilities for at least a couple more months."

Quinne shook her head violently. "No, I gotta put in equal share."

"Right now, you can't. You can take it, or leave it and live on the street."

"Fine. But I'm payin' you back."

"First, we eat. I want pizza, so you can get something else, if you want. And we can talk."

"Troy's dead, baby's dead. I get it. Let's move on and talk about something else."

Cee Cee stopped in front of a pizza parlor and they slid into a booth, where she ordered for the both of them. Despite Quinne's expressed preference to the contrary, her friend knew her heart's desire. Quinne heartily ate four slices. The food in jail had been doughy, but unpleasantly so. This collection of cheese, sausage and pepperoni slathered in delectable grease was a different story. She even devoured the crust. At the conclusion of the meal, Quinne sat back and relaxed a little.

"So, I guess they weren't feeding you in there after all, huh?"

Quinne muffled a belch. "Yep, but it just ain't good food."

"I've been in the prison ministry before, but not inside. What's it like?"

"Prison?" She wiped her mouth with a napkin. "An extended time-out with bars."

"Stop it."

"Think about it. . .what lil' kids do in 'time-out'? Stand in the corner and think about what they did, right? Jail's the same thing. You got this small concrete box with a toilet, sink and bunk beds. It's way too noisy to sleep 'til lights out and since you can't read the noise out you try to think it out.

"What do you think about? What you did. You talk in group about what you did and why you did it – sometimes promise yourself you ain't gonna do the same thing the same way again.

"I mean, really – if you take Troy, put him on that same corner and he still dies. . .do I miscarry? Maybe. Do I start drinkin'? Probably. Does that lead to sniff? It did before. Lil' kids do the same thing. They just gotta bump they heads enough so that they stop."

Cee Cee sipped soda from a white straw. "Have you bumped your head enough, or do you need to stand in the corner again?"

Quinne waited to answer until some other patrons passed. "I know this gonna sound like some wild junkie talk," she whispered, leaning over her plate, "but when I took that last hit, I *saw* somethin'."

"Save it Q." She pressed her thumb against the plate on the table's edge and added gratuity with a few finger grazes. "Ready?"

"Dead serious." She grabbed Cee Cee's hand. "I gotta tell someone."

The seriousness in Quinne's grasp startled her friend. "Tell me about it on the way home."

En route to the apartment in Cee Cee's Tarpan, Quinne unraveled the tale. "I went back to Anibel's, and she's sleep after doing whatever. Anyway, Troy opens the door. We start kissin' and what not, and then, he stops me. . .says he ain't there for that. I ask him what he there for and he tells me I already know. So I flip out and he say I can't go back. Next thing I know, I'm in the bathroom. . ."

". . .for the record, I didn't call the cops. The droid cashier did. . ."

Quinne waved her off. "Whatever. So then, I woke up."

"And since then?"

"Nada," she lamented. "No more dreams. But I ain't havin' nightmares, neither."

Cee Cee turned into the apartment's parking deck. "That's a good thing. It's a miracle nothing else happened to you. What if you OD'ed on it?"

Quinne exhaled. "I know, Cee. I thought about it."

"And?" She cut the engine off, waiting for exposition.

Quinne looked blankly ahead. "What if I did die. . .in that

alley, or on that bathroom floor? Straight up? Who wanna die in an alley or a bathroom floor, or a prison cell? If I gotta choice. . . I'd wanna go in battle, fightin', doin' somethin' for somebody who can't do it themselves. Not over somethin' stupid."

"Of all the things I believe God allows us to do, Q, controlling how we die isn't one of them. People do stupid things every day and die for it. They do heroic things, and die too. And sometimes, they just die. Whatever you do, just make the best out of what you do, right here, right now. That's all I really want for you."

"I know." The friends held hands. "But I have to want it for myself. And right now, I want to lay down in complete silence without some chick fartin' in my face."

"What?"

"You don't want to know."

Quinne napped well. In fact, she had slept clear through until early evening, waking only to use the restroom. She lazily returned to bed and set the HTV to two dimension images instead of three. A virtual flat screen appeared and displayed a syndicated rerun of her favorite sci-fi drama.

When the second act broke for commercial, a representative from the Genesis Institute appeared in front of the corporation's building. "Hi, I'm Kareza Noor and I'm here to announce our four participants for the Begin Again initiative. Before we do that, I would like to thank the nearly 300 million people who applied."

*Hey, that's the chick who handled my case!* As part of Quinne's release, she had called the Genesis Institute. The automated message informed her that she should attend a briefing tomorrow at 9:30 in the morning.

"Out of the hundreds of millions to respond to our recent advertising campaign, we have chosen only four for our initial intake cycle."

Quinne sat up in bed. *This is what I signed up for?*

"In addition to having a month's worth of their life expenses paid for donating their time, those lucky individuals will have the unique opportunity to right a wrong, fix a regret, be freed from a habit, reunite with a long lost love. . .'begin again', so to speak.

Pangs of excitement fluttered in her chest.

"These four people will join us tomorrow at our main building located at 216 Xavier Street downtown in the business district. There, they will be briefed, handed their promised stipend, and fully immersed in the program. They will be our first volunteers to begin again.

"Let's get to those lucky four people."

Quinne watched the commercial in its entirety, then rewound it and watched it three times before vaulting from her room to find Cee Cee in the kitchen.

"Cee!" Quinne prodded her in front of the HTV. "Watch this."

"Hi, I'm Kareza Noor and I'm here to announce our four participants for the Begin Again initiative. Before we do that, I would like to thank the nearly 300 million people who applied."

"Wow," Cee Cee said with astonishment. "She's gorgeous. Why am I watching this?"

"Shh!" Listen."

Cee Cee watched the commercial in its entirety, pausing with shock as the names were announced. Hands on hips, she looked Cee Cee in the eye. "Ain't that what I signed up for: the 'Begin Again' thing? Focus group? Four people? Sure sounds like it."

"I don't know, girl! You signed up for something. Who knows until tomorrow?"

"Ain't you say I have to have faith? That's what I'ma do. And half a trillion people trying to get into this thing. . .it can't be bad, right? You'll get your rent. . .maybe even some back utilities. . .and all I have to do. . ."

". . .you have no earthly clue." Cee Cee smiled. "C'mon, dinner's almost ready. I fried some chicken for you! Eat up, then get some more rest." She patted Quinne on the shoulder. "Tomorrow's a big day for you."

Yeah, thought Quinne. The first time in a while.

Harper wanted to ignore the announcement.

Adharma said the recent widow had eligibility for it; the "Begin Again" initiative. To be a candidate, one simply had to call the toll-free number and get through, which, like millions of others, she could not successfully do.

At their most recent session yesterday morning, Harper burst into fits a few times in reaction to Adharma's antagonistic therapy techniques and her increased hormone levels. Harper's boss, Kareza, coldly dismissed the painful process as "weakness leaving your mind." Besides, "even head shrinks need to be shrunken sometimes."

Harper checked her degrees and certifications at the door and submitted. But if Kareza had not suggested him in the first place and insist that he sign off on her return to work, she would have quit long ago.

"That's it for today. Our time together has expired."

Still rattled, Harper's alto dropped off parts of words, as she spoke. "I tried for the 'Begin Again' thing, like you said, and I couldn't get through."

"You and the rest of the free world."

"I've never gotten anything with great odds attached to it." She tossed the wet balled-up tissue into a silver trash can. "But, I need this."

He laughed, as if she had cracked a self-deprecating joke. "You need it? You don't even know what it is. Nobody does!"

"Then, why am I so drawn to it?"

"Because it has money attached to it."

"That's not why I want it." Her voice steadied. "I've been numb for weeks. . .living in a world where everything I need exists but nothing's real, or I can't get to it. It's an out-of-body experience I can't escape or control, and I just need to change something. This might be it. Help me. . .please?"

"It may be." His glasses hung onto his nose's edge. "I'll see what I can do."

From that point on until later the next night, all that remained was the confirmation of her exclusion. Harper cooked generic macaroni and cheese and chicken nuggets for her children and braised a chicken quarter and steamed vegetables for herself. Her food would be done in a few minutes, which gave Christian and Gabrielle's food enough time to cool off and be edible.

"Mommy Harper! Mommy Harper!" Gabrielle scooted across the hallway floor in her socks. "The six! Look!"

Harper stationed Micah's four-year-old in front of the living room clock and asked her to say when the clock display showed a six. After 5:56, the next time she said something would be 6:00 p.m.

"HTV on, volume level 15." Harper sat on the couch. Christian climbed into her lap and Gabrielle sat beside them. The Genesis Institute's logo preempted the regularly-scheduled cartoon program they were watching.

". . .here to announce our four participants for the Begin Again initiative. Before we do that, I would like to thank the nearly 300 million people who applied."

Harper's eyes bulged. Three hundred million people?

"Someone must've fudged those numbers."

"We have fudge? Mommy Harper, I want fudge please?"

"I want fudge." Christian perked up.

"Let's get to those lucky four people." Kareza opened a digital display.

Harper frantically waved her hand. "Shh. . .not now." Her heart skipped. The insurance money would not transfer for another week and bills were way overdue. A stipend would do the trick.

"Quinne Ruiz."

Harper did not know anyone named "Quinne," but she liked the name for a guy or girl. It was unique, but not overly so, unlike the names of some of her client's children.

"Teanna Kirkwood."

"Mommy Harper, can I have fudge? Mommy Harper, please? Mommy Harper! Mommy Harper!"

Harper clenched her fists and shouted. "Gabrielle! Be quiet!"

"Damario Coley, and our last participant. . ."

*I have one shot left. One out of 299 million-plus.* "We don't have fudge, baby," she grumbled. "Wait for your dinner. You know what, let's. . ."

". . .Harper Lowe."

Harper's mouth dropped. "I won!" She jumped to her feet and leapt up and down. Her children screamed with joy.

Ten seconds later, the home line rang. "Incoming call from Charlotte Lowe," it proclaimed.

"Answer," she giggled. "Block all other incoming calls." The HTV turned itself off and a projection of Harper's mother beamed down from the ceiling. "Hello Mother! Guess what?"

"I heard." Charlotte crossed her arms, the bluish veins in her temples nearly visible. "You're not seriously thinking about doing this."

"No, I'm not thinking about doing it, I'm doing it."

"I know you're excited. Calm down and think about this. I suspect, since I'm retired and have nothing better to do, that you want me to watch them tomorrow night?"

Even Charlotte's disapproval did not dampen her spirit. "Would you? If not, someone will take them in, maybe Laverne. I have to do this."

"Harper Charlotte. . ."

"Mother, look." She sent the children in the other room to watch holovision and set the area to *soundproof.* "You're not here when I dream of Mike at night, and all that's on his side of the bed is a pillow that barely smells like his cologne anymore, except for when I spray it."

"Harper, I know, but. . ."

"We have conversations, Mother, in my dreams. We talk about our kid and our baby that'll never know him. I go back. I look back in my mind and think about all of the times we argued about money, and bills, and his career. We're not rich, like you, but we could've made it. Soon, I'll have money and I couldn't care."

"That'll change!" Charlotte interjected. "In time, that'll change."

"How much have things changed since Daddy died? How happy have you been, all these years? You've seen the world, done things I've only read about. I'm a shell of a human being right now and I need to be more – for all of our kids. Help me do this."

Worry materialized on Charlotte's brow as well as at the corners of her mouth. "I miss your father every day. Nothing I do can bring him back, though I'd give everything I ever owned to try. You can't live like that, Harper. Thinking like that will kill you."

She shook her head. "No, Mother, I can't live like this. It's like I'm already dead."

Charlotte huffed. "You were like this once before. Look at where it's left you."

Her mother never let her forget that solitary time of defiance, when Harper supported Micah's decision to follow God's call to start his own business instead of applying for other architectural positions. Inside, she questioned whether things would have worsened had he found another job. If she ever saw his former boss, Miles Chu, she would have words for him.

"Maybe I can get back some of my deposit from the trip."

Harper smiled at Charlotte's admission. "Sorry about that."

"No, you're not. At least I get my grandbabies all to myself. Don't you dare ask Laverne."

"Soundproof, blocked calls off." The transparent orb surrounding them vanished. "I won't."

"Get going. I'll see you tomorrow morning."

"Seen you then. And thank you."

Once the call disconnected, Harper rushed into the kitchen to rescue her dinner from overheating. Though it violated every parental instinct she had been born with, she allowed her children to eat in the playroom unsupervised. At the dinner table, she ate and listened to the 13 messages that had been left on her voicemail. Most were from family members who wanted to know the nature of what she had been selected to do. She also wondered.

An automated representative of the Genesis Institute left the one message of note. She should report to the main building tomorrow morning at 9:30 a.m. sharp and wear comfortable clothes. She did not, however, have to pack a change.

*Why don't I need clothes? Will I be naked?* Harper wished that she had not muted the line to incoming calls, as she surely would have answered that one. *Will I be able to come home?* Charlotte would want to know, and Harper would give the answer as soon as she received it for herself.

# CHAPTER ELEVEN

*January 20, 2050*

Damario placed a canary yellow golf shirt atop the other clothes he had packed and zipped the luggage shut with his human hand. Though the Genesis Institute instructed him that he would not need a change of clothes, he assembled the outfits. Madison had not been in on the call and, therefore, did not know his wardrobe assembly was unnecessary. She naturally assumed he'd be leaving their high rise apartment for no more than a few days.

He wavered on whether or not he intended to stay, but he had stored the papers that Yvette Sloan had sent over to Madison. Playing his final decision close to the vest meant going to great lengths to clip his responses. When his wife prodded him for information on the Begin Again program, he shrugged his shoulders. He really did not know much. She had wondered about the date of his return, and he responded "soon." That satisfied her. But when she inquired about his intents concerning their marriage, he kept mum. "We'll see," or he said the occasional "I don't know."

Madison compulsively tapped her fingers on the bedpost, as he finished. "Tell me what they told you on the call again? Where are they sending you? Out-of-state maybe?"

The well-discussed topic exhausted Damario. "Don't know what you want me to say. There something you think I'm not telling you?"

It wouldn't be the first time. "End us or continue this. I can't stand the in between."

Damario flexed his artificial right hand, which intermittently transmitted sensations. "I got in a major accident, underwent surgery, PT. . .I'm still getting accustomed to it all. You can't make a major life decision on a whim."

"Yes," she admitted. "Yes, you can."

He understood the reference to their past. "I need a break."

"From me?"

"From everything." He dropped the suitcase onto the floor. "The currency deal was stressing me out before the accident and, when I get back, I'll need to concentrate on that. . .which I can't do if I'm worrying about my arm, my eye and us all at the same time."

"And if you weren't going, what then? What would we have done?"

"There is no if." He rolled the suitcase toward the door. "I'm going."

A wave of nausea crashed in Madison's stomach. Not now, she thought. "What about Robinne? I checked the home holophone records. Nobody you know lives in Philly but her."

Damario stopped without turning. She's checking up on me? "You think I'm going to see her. It's 12 hours, round trip. I'd barely be able to say hi and be back tonight."

Madison anticipated his building anger and backed away from her comment. "I just want to know why you're dreaming about her, calling her."

His college ex entered his thoughts more than he cared to admit, which increased with the administration of that drug. "I don't know. She didn't return the call."

Madison's smile shined with disgust. "I thought you were

holding something back from me, all this time. It wasn't me or my career ambitions; it's Robinne. Why rush to propose and marry me, if you felt this way? You thought I'd leave you, too?"

At the mention of their impromptu marriage, Damario wheeled his suitcase to the door. "I don't have time to do this now, Shenk."

"You're still in love with her," she shouted at his back. "Tell me!"

Damario's attempt to press down his rage failed. Quickly, he turned, swiveled his hips and punched a hole in the drywall. He knew the electrical sparks jumping into his brain's pain receptors were manufactured attempts to imitate pain and they did not hurt as much as he anticipated. Damario brushed off the dust and fragments from his metal fist. Breathing heavily, he pointed at Madison, whose body trembled. "They're thoughts. And I told you that I need time. Leave it at that. Give me that."

Madison nodded, and then violently threw up onto the Berber carpet. At first, Damario credited the sickness to taut nerves, but he knew better.

Disgusted, he stormed out of the apartment and entered the elevator chute at the end of the hall. Later, on the bottom floor, he used his holophone to access his personal computer server. Then, he opened a set of Sloan's documents, authorized his signature, and sent them back over to Madison. *Our marriage is over.*

He hailed a public serve Crown Alice, got in, and gave the address of his storage locker. There, he stored the bag he packed along with some belongings he had stashed away. When he returned tonight, he needed a new place. Whatever she had not ruined, given away, or shredded, he would retrieve later.

From there, they drove to the Genesis Institute. At the entrance, a holographic assistant greeted Damario. "Hello,

Damario Eugene Coley and welcome to the Genesis Institute."

"Whoa, easy on the Eugene."

"My apologies. Please remove your glasses and verify your identity by allowing us to scan your retinas."

He did so, but before he disclosed information about his artificial eye, the scan completed. "Not to worry, Mister Coley. We have the latest in retina scan technology."

"Nice to know." The hologram led him to the left and into an elevator chute.

"Please hold your feet together, as tightly as possible. I will meet you on the fifth floor." The hologram dissipated, as soon as Damario entered the tubing. The sensation of pressurized air beneath his feet instead of something tangibly solid always put him ill at ease. As he ascended, he closed his eyes and refused to look down. The sensation of flying thrilled him as a child, but not so much now. Soon, he exited the tube, and the receptionist greeted him again.

"Hello, Mister Coley, and welcome to the Begin Again initiative." The whitewashed room reminded him of a hospital emergency ward, or what he imagined the seventh floor of the city hospital – the level where they kept the crazies – must look like. To the right were bagels, a bowl of fresh fruit and carafes of imported coffee. He fixed himself a cup, smeared a bagel with strawberry cream cheese, and sat in a padded chair.

Next to him, a young woman – of about 17 or 18-years-old – listened to alternative music from her personal audiodome. She would not be interested in conversation. If not that, the camouflage hat pulled low over her hair sent the message. Two seats down, a heavy, light-skinned woman in pedal pushers used the "audio only" setting on her holophone. She'd wiped her running eye makeup all along her cheeks and kept making reference to someone named "Tay." In the last seat, a finely-dressed woman read something on a holographic computer screen with great intensity.

Damario checked his watch. 9:15. He hoped that someone would clue him in soon. When that did not happen, he moved his chair next to the reading woman, who repositioned herself. Both of them wore wedding rings, so she would not think he was flirting. But rings do not stop everyone, as he recently learned.

"Excuse me, miss?" Damario forgot about his coffee, and accidentally spilled a little on her and the computer projector. She frantically searched for a napkin, as did he. When one could not be found, he voluntarily fetched a few and gave them over. "Sorry."

"It's fine," she said, smiling. "Clumsiness is an incurable disease."

"Terrible way to introduce myself. Damario Coley."

She quickly cleaned up and shook his hand. "Harper Lowe."

"Nice to meet you." He nodded his head to the left. "Do you know them?"

"The woman to my left: her name's Teanna," she said under her breath. "I don't know the girl's name at the end, but I think I heard the assistant call her 'Quinne' or something like that. Matter of fact, I think it's Quinne. Pretty girl."

"Do you know why we're here? I'm assuming you got the message?"

"Yep. Genesis Institute, 9:30 a.m. Wear something comfortable. I know what you know." Harper and Teanna had exchanged brief notes; Adharma had counseled them both. Just then, a watch alarm beeped. "I'm sure we're about to find out."

"Good morning."

Damario recognized the voice of the beauty in front of him. He first remembered her from the commercials and from the brief time they spent together on New Year's Eve. Buttoned up in a burgundy business suit and Zara Hristoff high heels, Kareza was still attractive. Damario noticed the light of recognition in Harper's eyes. "You know her? Kareza Noor?"

"I knew her as my boss," she admitted, "not the CEO of this place."

Kareza started with the young girl on the end. "You all don't know each other, but, in one way or another, I am familiar with every one of you. Everyone, meet Quinne Ruiz."

"I know you," Quinne insisted. "But I thought you was a shrink?"

"That's how I started off my career; psychiatric counseling for troubled people." She moved down to the next woman. "Teanna Kirkwood, welcome."

"Thanks." Teanna dropped her holophone into the pocket of her cargo pants. Teiji's cursing mad father wanted nothing to do with her.

"And Harper Lowe, who also knows me from my counseling background."

"CEO?" Harper's brow furrowed. "That explains a lot."

Kareza laughed. "Missing staff meetings and the pot lucks? I've been personally evaluating each department, one by one, since last year. December was psychiatrics' turn. My internal promotion to CEO had to be kept under wraps until I finished my assessments." She reached Damario and their handshake heated his neck and face. "And Damario Coley. Mister Coley and I have seen a lot of each other, haven't we?"

He smiled nervously at the double entendre. "We have."

"I gather that you all want to know why you're here. Follow me, please."

Teanna, Harper, Damario and Quinne – in that order –

walked behind Kareza. Damario focused on the back of her head and not the body he had seen half-naked. None of them had any clue of what type of business the Genesis Institute conducted.

From what he read and heard from financial sections, it did billions in 2049 alone. Much of that came from the holographic technology and software it had patented. Now, one could not make a call, watch a sitcom, or drive a transport without it. In fact, Damario's savvy investment in its stock at the ground level afforded him and Madison the luxurious lifestyle they enjoyed.

"Ever have someone you thought that you could not live without?" Kareza asked, while ushering them through a black marble corridor. The area starkly contrasted the completely white environment they had just left. "I did, a long time ago."

"A long time ago?" Teanna said, perplexed. "You ain't no older than 35."

"I've aged gracefully," she said matter-of-factly. "I'm older than I look."

Quinne approached Kareza's left side. "How old? What's your secret?"

Kareza wagged a finger. "A lady never tells her beauty secrets."

*People still say that?* Teanna stepped up her pace to stay in front, though her knees ached. Thankfully, they reached the elevator tubes.

"Please, step in." The quartet joined the CEO in one large tube. "Top floor." Since the building was almost 60 stories higher than their present floor, the trip took longer than the one from the ground. The elevators emptied into a room resembling that of the waiting area, but the floors and walls were black marble with white trails running through it. As the girlfriend of a structural engineer, Harper knew these materials were top notch.

"I made a decision one day and five of my friends joined me. Because of that one decision, I never saw them again."

Harper touched her pregnant belly. "My God."

"I swore to myself that if I ever got the opportunity to make things right, I would do it . . .wouldn't even think twice about it. I never got that chance and still regret it."

The theme of loss connected with each one of them for different reasons. Quinne broke the silence. "No disrespect, but what's that gotta do with us?"

"You're about to get the second chance that I never had, Quinne." Kareza stepped forward into the range of the retina scanning device, which verified her identity. She placed her hand on an access panel, and said her name.

Harper, Teanna, Quinne and Damario looked at each other. The door slid open and they all stared in wonder.

"This looks like an old-school dentist's office on sniff." Damario's eyes bulged at the technology-draped ergonomic blue chairs.

"You know what an old-school dentist's office actually looks like?" Quinne wisecracked. "Never actually seen one outside the History Channel."

Damario sighed. "I am so freaking old."

The machinery did intimidate the quartet of volunteers. At first blush, holographic images and scenarios randomly emerged, focused, and vanished – a chorale of monotone, automated voices echoed behind them. Damario recognized some of the equipment, as it belonged next to a hospital bed.

"Welcome to our Begin Again initiative!" Kareza announced with fanfare. "I have a ten o'clock, so I'll be handing you over to the project's chief medical counsel, Doctor Nandor Adharma, who's capable of answering all of your questions and concerns."

Kareza's departure disappointed Damario, but Harper appreciated it. Suddenly, like her cohorts, she did not trust Kareza.

"Miss Noor." Adharma nodded. "You are all here under your own volition?"

The group looked at one another, then at the doctor.

"Your attending medical droid will assess you, after which you will be briefed regarding the next step you will take in 'beginning again'."

The four splintered off into solitary soundproof stations. Harper stretched out her legs into a comfortable position.

"I am Wynter Dawn, of the pilot medical android program. Please start by stating your full legal name."

"Harper Charlotte Lowe," she said. "And I'm 13 weeks pregnant."

Wynter's robotic female feigned glee. "Congratulations! What is your date of birth, Miss Lowe?"

"July 18th, 2015. I'm sorry, but can't you just scan me for this information?"

"It is vital to the process of the project to do it manually. Height and weight?"

"Five-foot-six and I weighed 145 pounds at my last checkup."

"Place of birth?" The questions came quicker now.

"Cleveland, Ohio."

"Current address?"

"3815 Whisper Lane."

"Marital Status."

"Single," she replied with more remorse than she ever had.

"Single." Teanna had always been unattached, rarely in a relationship, and never within breathing distance of a marriage, but she preferred it that way since her first "date" 30 years ago.

Her mother thought it unusual for a 13-year-old girl to have such an early interest in so many boys.

Thirteen years later, Teanna became a mother for the first time to a son conceived with a foreigner Teanna's mother would never meet.

"Annual income?"

"Ain't got one. Zero."

"Do you have any prevailing medical conditions we should be aware of?"

Teanna unraveled a mental list. "High blood pressure, diabetes, cholesterol. tendonitis in both knees, arthritis in my joints. Depression, fibroids, and got asthma on top of all that." She imagined that if Stan Witmore was human, he would have shaken his head at the physical condition of the 42-year-old. Instead, it instructed her to rise and follow it to another part of the room. She appreciated that the Institute had transferred a droid familiar to her. It made her comfortable – as comfortable as one could become with a machine.

"We will need to stabilize you before we proceed."

Teanna hobbled over to a sequestered cot. Soon, an opaque barrier erected itself between her and the others. Stan attached a pack to Teanna's flabby arm, which distributed medication to control her blood pressure and insulin levels. While she leisurely turned her head, two needles stuck her in the sore spots of her knees and dispensed medicine. She cursed and yelled in temporary pain but, when it subsided, the joints felt better than ever before.

"What'd you just stick me with?" She eyed the three-inch long needle.

"A proprietary solution; anti-inflammatory, pain, and analgesic compound," said Stan.

"That's all?" she joked, surprised. Teanna flexed the now-healthy knees. "How long it'll last? And can I get a case of it?"

Though programmed to act human, Stan failed to see Teanna's humor. "A case of the medication would provide short-term benefits with long-term implications. Continued injections would result in muscle freeze or paralysis."

"It's cool. Never mind, just a joke."

"I see." He observed the flexibility in her joints and the improvement in Teanna's vital signs. "We shall be ready to proceed with your participation in another few minutes."

Teanna exhaled, dangling her pain-free legs over the side of the cot.

"Do you have any prevailing medical conditions we should be aware of?"

Damario flexed his new hand, and he felt warmth where it connected to his natural tissues and skin. "Two prosthetics. . .right arm and the right eye."

Ellis perceptibly shifted modes, from one of an inquisitive nature to that of an assessor. "Please stand by for evaluation." Without warning, the machine scanned Damario's entire body from top to bottom, with particular attention to the improved areas. Ellis had done the exact same thing in the hospital. What made him uncomfortable, though, were the permanence of the attachments and the idea of being something other than blood and bones.

"Your prosthetics continue to bond and adapt well, and should no longer be compensatory, but complimentary, almost human."

"Great," he deadpanned.

"This does not please you, Mister Coley?"

"I'd rather be myself, or at least have the choice not to wear these things." He knocked his right knuckles against the frame of his metal chair, and the sound of metal against metal repulsed him. "Electricity isn't pain. It's a current; like licking an alkaline battery. This looks like my skin, but it's painted to look that way." He stood up and swatted a hologram with his artificial hand. "It's not real!"

His outburst drew Adharma into the fray. "Settle down, Mister Coley." His voice, sounding ruffled, heightened in pitch as he talked. He laid a hand on Damario's left shoulder. "You're making a scene and frightening the others."

He clasped the wrist of the doctor with his right hand, releasing only upon realizing that the intensity he intended was not the grip with which the hand responded. Damario released him. Adharma rotated his own wrist until the circulation returned.

The first to finish the questioning, Quinne sat in an empty chair. *I ain't gotta STD!*

Overjoyed, she observed the others. The eldest of them all, or so she assumed, would finish next – her face downcast and worn. Damario – she remembered his name because of his cuteness and she liked his dreadlocks – concluded his study by throwing a tantrum and nearly breaking the doctor's wrist. And the fat woman with the loud voice did not finish at all, but a droid remitted her to further medical treatment. When the loudmouth cursed about a needle, Quinne stifled a laugh. Whenever she thought about it, even minutes later, it caused her to chuckle.

"What's so funny?" Harper asked. She occupied the chair to Quinne's left.

"Nothin'," she said, still laughing between syllables. "One of them things, where you just remember it later and laugh? Ain't funny to nobody else but you."

"Ah, got it." Harper folded her hands onto her lap and tapped her foot. "You wouldn't happen to see a bathroom around here?"

"Nope. You may want to ask. Looks like we might be here a minute."

Harper did so and Ellis escorted her to an unmarked door at the corner of the room. She did what she needed to do. Quinne did the same. Satisfied, the two sat down again without a word passing. Soon, Damario joined them, sitting to Quinne's right. He shook his hair and secured it in a ponytail.

"I love your dreads," said Quinne, with much enthusiasm. "You don't see them much anymore."

Damario brushed off the compliment with aplomb. "Thanks."

"What made you grow 'em? Just curious."

Still irritated, he clipped his answers. "A girl."

"Nice. She your wife now?"

"No," he bitterly said. "I'm not married anymore."

"O-kay." Quinne rolled her eyes. "Forget I asked." She turned to her left. "What's your name again?"

"Harper Lowe."

"Harper, why you think we here? They keep saying, 'Begin Again' like it's one of them catchphrases and such. . .like that dude's gonna lead us into the desert somewhere to worship him and then kill us all before we can prove him wrong." She eyed Damario when he laughed. "Somethin' funny?"

"No, no, not really," he smirked. "Just reminded me of something."

"Actually," Harper interjected. "I'm a counselor and there's this breakthrough psychotherapeutic research developed in Europe that I've read about in medical journals. It's extremely experimental, though. The government has to sign off before we even think about using it here in the US."

Eavesdropping on the conversation, Damario's interest increased. "I've been doing some currency work with banks in Europe to replace the Euro. Do you think it'll pass – this research?"

"It already has." Adharma smiled and revealed a set of coffee-stained teeth, which were otherwise perfectly groomed and straight. "Please, join me."

The Indian man indicated that they should flow to his right. Quinne touched one of the chairs and the suppleness of the material amazed her. Damario and Harper tried it for themselves. The material sank around their fingertips. After a few seconds, Harper snatched back her hand.

"Electronic muscle stimulation, Miss Lowe. As you lie here, every muscle in your body will be electronically massaged."

Harper's face screwed with worry. "What are you planning to do to us?"

"Not do to you, but do for you. Each of you endured a major life change in the past month." Adharma was insistent but not condescending. "That life change resulted in an unhealthy response; a habit, a behavior, injury, or death." His voice hung on the last word death, as he briefly paused. "That, plus a number of other factors and a bit of mathematical luck made you eligible for the Begin Again initiative."

Before any of them could ask, he answered. "The Begin Again initiative is a practical study," he said, while producing a blue vial. "In one form or another, it's a drug you have all had exposure to. It has anti-inflammatory and dopamine-boosting properties and it possesses a neurotransmitter stimulation protein. We believe that protein will allow us to guide and stimulate unconscious thought and behavior. We affectionately call it, 'The Solution'."

Most of the language escaped Quinne, except for the "guiding unconscious thought" part. "Mind control?" she asked.

"Not controlling the mind, Miss Ruiz. Stimulating it. Say you like to smoke cigarettes but it negatively affects your health. We'd use The Solution to guide you through your subconscious memories to the first time you had a cigarette. There, you will exercise your choice to decline it. By severing that mental and behavioral tie, when you return to your conscious state, the appetite for nicotine has left. You have never had it, as far as your mind is concerned. When you return, your world will be different."

Teanna's ears perked. No more addictions? It sounded too good to be true.

Skeptical, Damario raised his hand. "But, what if you don't have an addiction?"

"You were selected for a reason native to your particular circumstance; maybe not an addiction, per se. Tell me, Mister Coley, there's not one thing about the way you live your life today that you would elect to go back and change; that, if you had the opportunity to alter your emotional, psychological connection to it, that you would?"

He thought of Madison and what a quick emotional slicing might do for him.

Harper, however, remained unconvinced. "I'm sure that you'll agree, doctor, that health professionals strike an uneasy balance between healing and playing God. Using a drug to alter connections to old memories? Sounds like science fiction, if you ask me."

"Hypnotherapy techniques are really not that different. You disagree?"

She thought about it for a brief moment. Not really. "Then, why not use the drug in widespread fashion, if the government approved it for use?"

"The Solution has been approved for our purposes here first," he asserted. Damario's eyes brightened. Cornering the market with a drug holding so many benefits would be lucrative. He thought to investigate and invest into the Genesis Institute after the study's conclusion.

"I did not sign on to be an experimental lab rat for a drug and a clinical trial."

"You did not sign on for anything, Miss Lowe. None of you have. Yet."

Quinne raised her hand and quickly lowered it. "Okay, so then how does this work? I mean, we get The Solution, and then what?"

"First, we'll conduct a psychiatric evaluation to identify the source of the problem. We'll explore from all angles why you picked this addiction or event in the first place. This could take anywhere from 20 minutes to hours, depending on your willingness to be transparent. That point in time will become your focal point. Then, we administer The Solution."

"What's it gonna be like?" Teanna asked, with sincerity.

"Like living in yesterday. But you will retain the knowledge of today. You will touch, taste, smell, hear and see."

"Will it hurt?" Quinne's voice piqued with interest.

"As much as a thought or a memory can harm you." The answer held a different weight for each of them. "When you make your decision, your journey will not necessarily end there. Once you are ready, you will return to consciousness."

The concept of "readiness" concerned Harper. Shouldn't it be quicker? "Putting me in a coma for hours isn't doing something for me," Harper argued. "And if we are not 'ready' in those hours? How do we return?"

Adharma looked at her directly. "You will be weaned from The Solution and fall into a normal sleep. Think of it as a medical procedure for which you need anesthesia. When you awake, all will be well."

# CHAPTER TWELVE

Harper's hesitation in signing the consent form, which indemnified the Genesis Institute from litigation, gave Damario enough time to erase Madison's profane messages. In the first one, she angrily rattled off expletives. By the beginning of the second, she broke down into hysterics. For years, their marriage had been the lone flagship of hope in her family. She loved him and pledged to be committed this time, if he granted her a second chance. Damario erased them all. The death of his marriage depressed him, but "beginning again" would change it all.

After investing his stipend, he called his supervisor. Nothing else crucial had come across his desk – none more than usual. He would swing by the office after treatment.

Paramount to everything was the research for the international currency deal. Haggling between liberals in Congress – who were led by Senator Ramsey Mateo, the House of Representatives, members of the Federal Reserve and the United Nations threw the deal into a holding pattern. Started by a rookie Italian prime minister, the drive to unite the world's top ten economic heavyweights under an intangible currency called "the mark" had gained tremendous groundswells of support.

The World Bank and most members of the International Monetary Fund fell in line, but the eyes of several countries stayed on the US. America held out the longest – due, in part, thanks to Damario's small contributions to research. He took pride in it. Worldwide, economists slammed G.R. Cooper,

Mateo, and "short-sighted" legislative liberals as "digging a deep, water-filled grave" for the national economy. The conversion predictions boasted numerous advantages to the unit: a digital form of currency adopted decades ago. Having the same, biologically-exchanged form of currency as nine other countries frightened Damario. After all, no one could accurately prophesy the effects of such a momentous decision. They could only hypothesize and hope.

Damario glanced over at Harper, who still discussed matters with Adharma. Since he had a little extra time, he checked his video mail server. There, he found one from an Internet provider address that he did not recognize, with *Robbie* written in the subject title. After turning down the volume, he pulled it up.

"Hey. . ." Robinne appeared haggard, as if she had woken up from a three-day-long nightmare. Her bloodshot eyes darted to and fro, and her dreadlocks were knotted atop her head. She appeared a shell of the college-educated, free spirit he remembered. "Don't know how you found me, but I'm good." She sniffed. "How you been? Saw from your message that you done well for yourself."

The muscles in his cheeks sagged. *What happened to you?* In the background of her bedroom, he noticed an uncovered hairy leg sticking out from under the bed sheet. The private investigator – the same one who found Madison's lovers – had a hard time tracking her down. Nothing of record existed in Robinne Glasse's name; no apartment, bank account, possessions, or utilities.

Police records showed that she had been arrested five times last year for public drunkenness or being under the influence. The address on the last citation, on New Year's Eve, by coincidence, is where he found her. The holophone number was registered to a man's name, so he left her a message as "Cousin Damario," hoping to get in touch.

"So, if you wanna get together," she said, pausing to wipe her nose with her hand. "I stay at this place downtown, off Broad. . .on the corner. Apartment four. Call before you come. Maybe we can do lunch. Bye, cuz."

Teanna knew that the types of holographic computers they had been afforded used the same technology as a holophone. After paying some overdue bills with her stipend, she called the prison. According to Tay's girlfriend, they could receive visits during recreational time. That time included calls. She used a subdued voice when the prison administrator answered.

"Teiji Kirkwood, please."

A few minutes passed before a prison medical staffer showed up. She thought nothing of it, except that Teiji might have gotten sick.

"Miss Kirkwood, that prisoner is unavailable at this time."

"He sick?"

"He's unavailable at this time," he repeated. "You're welcome to call again, later today. Visitation hours are seven days a week, at. . ."

"You're not telling me anything!" Teeth gritted, she barely maintained composure.

". . .recreational times, which occur after breakfast. . ."

"I know when visiting hours be at! What's wrong with my son?"

"Anything else I can help you with, Miss Kirkwood?"

"What's-wrong-with-my-son?" She cursed the man and shook the computer.

"Your call will now disconnect. Goodbye."

Frustrated, she connected again and received a busy signal.

Hoping she remembered the correct number, she hung up and dialed Kelly, who might be accessible. "Hello?"

Bedridden and her voice unsteady, Kelly looked up. "Miss Kirkwood?"

She pressed to the point. "What's going on with Tay? Stupid man ain't connecting me."

"The same thing happened to me yesterday." Beads of sweat dotted her forehead. "Channel Zero news reported a riot up there yesterday."

"What?"

"I got food poisoning, Miss Kirkwood. Can you get a ride up there?"

"Not now," she admitted. "I wish I'd known ten minutes ago. I might be able to go later."

Kelly's voice trembled. "Call me, if you do. Bye." The hologram disappeared. Teanna had no choice but to trust that she could get to him after her treatment. She bowed her head and said a quick prayer, asking for her son's protection and healing, if he needed it.

Hardly sentimental, Quinne compiled a playlist for Troy that brought it out every time. She used her tablet to access her home network, and then quietly played it, but not loud enough to distract. The first, a driving rock sample, set an atmosphere that no one outside of her deemed romantic. The words to the chorus said it for her: *All I need/everything that's dear to me/someday you'll see/the end of you and me.* The liner notes said the band's lead singer dedicated it to his on-again-off-again girlfriend, who promised him that they would die together one day. She rewound the song's bridge to drown out Teanna's belligerence.

The next track, an R&B ballad by a collection of female crooners, mellowed her out more than the previous song. She closed her eyes and remembered her lover – his chocolate skin, the thickness of his shaped eyebrows and his muscular build. In the summer, he walked around in boxer shorts without regard for whoever saw him. She would lay with him, hypnotized by the rotations of the ceiling fan. Soon, the chair had massaged her muscles into complete relaxation and she closed her eyes with a smile on her face.

Harper snapped back to attention after a few minutes of Adharma's explanation. Yes, there were minimal risks involved. No, her baby would not be in immediate danger. Yes, they would monitor the child. And yes, they would pull her from the project, if the situation necessitated it.

"One must have an element of trust in their physician," he had said. But this operation toed a line between science and experimentation – too much, she believed, for her to be a part of it. She would pray for the others to get what they needed.

"Thank you for your time." She closed the holographic release forms. "I won't be a part of your experiment."

The doctor became alarmed and waved to one of the droids. "Nothing will make you reconsider?"

"I'm afraid not."

"But the stipend, your life expenses. . ."

"I spent years of my life worrying about what I'd do if I didn't have enough money for this or for that. I'll get that soon, and you know what? There's nothing on this planet worth that much worry." She pointed to the door where she first entered. "I should exit this way?"

"Y-yes, but you need authorization from Miss Noor to do so. She'll be along soon."

"Doctor," said Ellis Murtaugh. "Quinne Marybeth Ruiz is ready."

"Really?" The lilt in his voice rose. "Connect her to an intravenous drip pack and run the preliminary anesthesia protocols. Do the same for Mister Coley and Miss Kirkwood."

"Yes, Doctor." Stan Witmore trailed Ellis.

"Do you have a problem, Miss Lowe?" Kareza appeared almost out of nowhere.

Harper jumped at the sound of Kareza's voice and the touch of her supervisor's silky smooth hand against her exposed shoulder. "No problem. I've just decided against doing it, that's all."

A sly smirk crossed Kareza's face. "Oh, you have?"

"I'm not comfortable with the project. It's not what I thought it would be."

She looked at Harper's small baby bump. "Can I be honest, Harper?"

Questions from the woman had always been mandates. "Can I sit down? I'm a little dizzy."

"Of course." Kareza maintained a close distance and held Harper's hand in hers. "Harper, you and your boyfriend, Micah, were handpicked for the Begin Again initiative."

*We were?* The disorientation continued. "Why?" The scent of Kareza's lilac and vanilla perfume tickled Harper's nose.

Kareza accessed the release forms once again. "When I came to Micah's funeral, I saw a longing in you, and I thought you and this initiative would be a perfect fit."

She wanted to know more, though her decision stood firm.

"The life you were living wasn't meant to be yours."

Harper bit her lip. "I think I'm going to be sick."

"No, you won't. You'll be fine." Kareza squeezed Harper's fingers. "At one point or another, everyone believes they should have a better life. You have the chance at a better life, but you're not taking advantage of it. It's not wrong."

Immediately, Harper's mind keyed in on a choice she'd made years ago.

"Don't walk away, Harper." Adharma handed Kareza the computer with the release forms. "Sign. Get started on the life you could have had; the life you deserve to have."

Still uneasy, Harper lazily applied her thumbprint to the appropriate spot, indicating her consent. Kareza had Ellis escort a lethargic Harper to the last chair, where Stan attended to her. Afterwards, Kareza carefully peeled a thin latex layer from her hand.

After the four had been thoroughly evaluated and anesthetized, Adharma joined Kareza at a curve in the circular shaped room. "It's expensive and troublesome. . .this experiment on four nobodies. I fail to see the logic."

"There's much logic in it, my friend." Kareza patted him on the cheek, which drew immediate worry until she displayed a clean hand free of the drug she had used on Harper. "You simply lack the vision to see it all."

"Enlighten me."

"It's almost noon. We must begin."

"You drugged the Lowe woman and had her sign legally-binding documents. That alone could shut us down, cost us billions, trillions! Why risk everything for her?"

"I risked nothing."

Frustrated by her clipped answers, Adharma shouted with passion. "I have served you without question. And you would deny me a simple explanation of your 'grand design'?"

Kareza carefully formed her response. "Once, I worked in the shadow of an overbearing man. He rarely explained and expected me to fall in line. I swore never to do the same. Ask."

"This 'Begin Again' initiative is a charade, isn't it?"

Once Damario, Quinne, Teanna, and Harper fell into stasis, Kareza positioned herself near their heads. She spread her fingers at Harper's temples. Crimson threads of electricity jumped from her impeccable fingernails into Harper, whose body vanished with a pop of pink smoke. Seconds later, Kareza aged a number of years. "Indeed."

Adharma drew back, speechless at Kareza's actions, which appeared to dim her physical beauty.

"In 2035, Harper will retake Applied Physics instead of switching majors and it will make her wealthy." Kareza slid over to Teanna. "Teanna will stop pining over the father of her son and spare the boy and his sister her dented brand of parenting."

*Not possible*, Adharma thought.

Now with graying hair and a curving posture, Kareza vaporized Quinne. "Quinne would have become a military sharpshooter and had a decorated career. With her boyfriend alive, she won't care anymore."

Adharma's awe was rivaled only by this vivid delusion. "What's happening?"

"I am a god!" she bellowed, "living a worthless existence on a miserable rock beneath my birthright. I was created to rule."

"By whom?" he wondered aloud. "What are you?"

"Without his interference, I will rule nations." Kareza finished off Damario and erupted into a coughing fit. "I dispatched them back into the fabric of time. These four played roles, small or large, in my defeat. No longer. But I need five."

Adharma patted his chest. Only two of them remained, and he doubted his aging benefactor intended for him to know these things and survive.

"The Solution dangled the temptation, but I needed their permission." She slapped Adharma's back. "My power, teamed with their choices, opens the gateway."

"What part do I play in this?"

Kareza grunted with disdain. "You are not half-Indian, as you claim, but a Jew by birth."

Adharma did not refute the statement. His father's ancestors migrated from Portugal 700 years ago and settled in what would become New Delhi. His mother, a native born Italian, converted to Judaism before they exchanged vows. The foreboding in his belly would not go away. "So what of it? I do not practice any religion."

Kareza stretched her wrinkled hands toward Adharma's temple. "You always desired power for yourself, Nandor Adharma. Now, you shall have it."

With that, he vanished like the others.

# CHAPTER THIRTEEN

*January 20, 2050*

A caravan of stretch Bentley transports halted at the entrance to an upscale eatery with a considerable dining hall. The procession drew the attention of the parking attendants, who found themselves captivated by the apple, white and green-striped flags. The contingent emerging from the opening doors were European men with distinctive taste pallets. It made sense that they would dine there. The management prided itself on the authenticity of its Italian cuisine.

The last of them to enter was Nandor Adharma: a fine looking, dark-skinned man a few inches above six feet. His woolen black coat hung from his shoulders with distinction, and the starched shirt and blood red necktie were crisp. Adharma exhaled, with a sense of disappointment and high-mindedness, as if the ground praised him by submitting beneath his weight. His arm cocked out into a hook, and a feeble Kareza Noor joined him. In her prime, she would have been mesmerizing, but now, she labored to keep the façade of beauty. A trail of graying hair cascaded down her back and lapped over the back of her fur coat.

The two brought up the rear behind the potentates preceding them, entering the main avenue of the restaurant to applause. They proceeded through a who's who receiving line of firm handshakes and political heavyweights. Of course, President Ramsey Mateo did not attend. Due in part to Kareza, he had just taken his oath on the west front of the US capitol building hours ago. She also positioned Adharma to become the Prime Minister of Italy and to receive the credit for rescuing the US economy.

Over the past year, Adharma had led the charge to unite the nation's ten largest financial markets under one, biologically-transferred currency, dubbed "the mark." In the process, he built a friendship with Mateo, whose endorsement of the mark and popularity among Hispanics pushed him to a crushing electoral victory. Unlike his friend, Adharma held more esteem and sway as Prime Minister.

"So, this is the infamous maker of kings?" A member of the Italian parliament winked at the woman and kissed her right hand. "A pleasure."

Kareza hid her discontent beneath a glimmering smile and tender knees slightly bent in a curtsy. "A misnomer, I'm afraid. A few congressmen and representatives here, a Prime Minister there – I do it for the cause."

"Lovely and modest." He reluctantly dropped her hand and faced Adharma. "Mister Prime Minister, you exerted diplomacy in getting the Americans to validate the mark. President Mateo will soon sign it into law. I have heard that the mark's popularity will lead to others adopting it, as well. You must be proud."

"When a man desires, truly desires, peace and prosperity, he will do anything he can to secure it." Adharma delivered his words with perfect diction. "The United States has been financially enslaved to the world for over half a century. Ramsey's a progressive thinker who's not tied down to the dictates of the religious right or the leftist liberals. The mark will secure this country's financial future."

"Regardless, you have to admit," responded the diplomat, "that it's a risky gambit. If it fails, more than a few economies will fall into ruin."

"But they will not – not with a new, united currency." Kareza concluded her retort just before falling into a coughing fit. A potentate signaled for a waiter to give the older woman a drink. The water helped cease the hacking, but it did not remedy the metallic taste of blood.

Adharma patted her on the back. "Are you alright, dear one?"

"Yes." She cleared her throat a final time. "A little cold, that's all. I don't suppose you have another body I can inhabit, do you?"

The response drew a nervous chuckle from Adharma. "I believe the scientists have discovered a way. Right after that, they solve the mystery of time travel!" His nonpareil charm commanded attention and respect wherever he went.

The throng of foreigners proceeded to the reserved banquet room inside the restaurant. There, laid a buffet outfitted with a selection of rich meats and Italian delicacies.

"Excuse me, my friends." Adharma drifted to an almost vacant corner of the room. There, Micah James fidgeted in a fine designer tuxedo – nondescript, except for being one of the select few African-Americans at the dinner. Adharma plucked two lamb kabobs from a silver platter and approached him. "Mister James, you have the look of a man who does not believe he belongs here."

Micah dug his hands into his pockets. "I don't, Mister Prime Minister. Why did you invite me anyway? You leveraged your foreign influence to revoke the Exodus Foundation's federal funding. You eliminated 40,000 jobs, including mine."

Adharma removed the skewered lamb with his teeth. "Where's your boss? Off somewhere licking his wounds?"

Micah's eyes rolled back. "Let me see. . .he said 'the authors of the Exodus Foundation's destruction don't deserve my presence'."

"Pretentious," he mused. "That's Chu for you."

"Well, you did strip away the substance of his life's work."

"I did no such thing. Miles Chu's life's work consisted of extremist experiments and needless social work. Your founding fathers supported separation of church and state."

"The state out of the church, not the church out of the state," he corrected.

"Regardless, the two entities should be separate and exclusive, and Chu used federal funds in the name of God. Your government that took action and your people elected the representatives that voted for its downfall."

"Weren't a majority of them strong-armed by your mentor?"

Adharma chuckled, while patting Micah's shoulder. "Enjoy the dinner."

Micah watched Adharma peel off to glad hand a couple of politicians before rejoining the main group.

Soon, the dinner hour began. Following a half-hour of eating and idle chatter, champagne made the rounds for Kareza to give a toast. Dubbed "Princess of the Airwaves" for her captivating rhetoric and uncanny ability to tap into the pulse of her audience, she would give a speech enticing enough to keep the populace silent. At the point the spotlight shined on her to perform, the room went silent.

"Good evening." Kareza muttered, stifling a cough. "People often ask about the mystery behind what I do. In other words: how do I breed success in the men and women whose campaigns I run? Politicos around the nation have interviewed me on this subject. But have I reserved the true answer for only you."

The audience took a collective gasp. Micah speculated her direction. *What's she doing?*

"Politicians, the good ones, increase their odds for success by going out and meeting the people. They make promises that

special interests groups will never allow them to fully realize."
Kareza took a little water. "So, what then is the solution? Simple:
fix the odds."

Kareza's words stunned, until one of the oldest dignitaries
heartily laughed. Merriment whisked around the room from
corner to corner: a humorous political roast!

"How else do you think an inexperienced, private sector
businessman like Nandor Adharma captured President Giovanni's
attention? Motivation."

There was more laughter. Various statesmen pointed fingers
and shot at one another, still laughing. Adharma did not play
along. Nothing about Kareza's demeanor suggested jest, which
made it funnier. The circumstances surrounding his rapid ascent
did gnaw at him from time-to-time; especially when he spent
time in President Giovanni's presence.

"If I discover a weight that tips the scales in my favor, I apply
it. If there's a weakness, I expose and exploit it. The Palestinian
president's opponent was a whoremonger, no? Israel's acting
prime minister – the first woman in history to assume power
there – did so because her predecessor, a chain-smoking glutton,
snuck pork to his table. And the U.N. Secretary-General. . . well,
I bribed someone to poison his challenger."

*My God, why are they laughing?* Micah excused himself
without garnering attention.

Adharma knew the truth of the situation. No one in the
audience knew Kareza like he did. In 2017, he became CEO of
his father's corporate finance firm at the age of 25. Twenty-six
years later, she politically seduced him. From the start, he found
nothing attractive about what the old political magnate had to
say. But she convinced him; first to have a sumptuous dinner with
her, and then a nightcap. He remembered little else about the
encounter, but the next day, Kareza told him that he had a great

future in international politics. And he believed her.

Critics gave him less than a 20 percent chance of victory, but his unprecedented rise as a Prime Minister candidate in the '46 appointments culminated with an overwhelming win.

"But, in all seriousness, my career in shaping the future of the world comes to an end. I hereby resign as Prime Minister Adharma's campaign manager, effective immediately, but I will continue to advise him. It has been a fantastic run, fashioning his ascension. His selection sits among the highlights of my career. After uniting the ten most powerful nations in the world beneath the mark, I look forward with great anticipation to what Nandor Adharma does next."

Though he applauded like the others, Adharma assumed Kareza's icy stare was meant for him. She flourished an accepting hand upon her return to the round dinner table. He took her free palm and squeezed it, signaling their exit.

In a hallway, replete with hand-carved, marble Roman pillars, Adharma cornered her once he ensured they were alone. Following them from a distance, Micah ducked behind a pillar and extended the recording range of his handheld to pick up the conversation yards away.

"What sort of business do you mean in there, quitting?"

"Cagey until the end," she uttered through a cough. "Widen your scope. Thus far, I have advised you. From now on, I will lead you."

No, she meant she would advise me and not lead me, he thought. "And what's that nonsense about fixing the elections?"

"Can't take a joke, Prime Minister?"

"That was hardly jest. Have you perpetrated a crime?"

"Have a little faith. Mister Prime Minister. Haven't we come a long way, you and I? Do you not have luxury transports at your disposal? What about all of the women you've slept with and the palatial mansion? Why doubt me now? Has the world suffered for it? Where's the crime?"

"But. . ."

"Largely due to your overtures, the ten most affluent nations in the world have adopted a united currency. You selected a majority of Italy's parliament, and have gained worldwide notoriety and influence. Most men would be pleased with this and not question my infallible methods."

"If your 'methods' include extortion, murder, and blackmail, you're a criminal," he said impetuously. "And I am not most men."

"Precisely why I selected you. Surely, you don't think my success comes from lumps of clay too difficult to mold? The potential to rule an empire bigger than that of the Romans lies within you, and I will personally see to it that it comes out."

Adharma's shoulders slumped. "I thought you to be driven – relentless even – but you have lost your grip on reality."

"Not so," Kareza said, as Adharma turned his back to her. She laid a strong hand on his shoulder and exerted enough force to cause him pain. "I used 80 years of my life force creating this reality, but my time has run out. I am soon going to die."

Adharma attempted to move. "What have you done to me?"

"Given you a life you never would have otherwise known; plucked you from obscurity and fashioned the spotlight for you on the earth's largest stage." Kareza licked her lips, not unlike an animal. "I have prepared you for this – a grand moment! The world's population will kneel before the man who brought it peace and prosperity. He will be a god in their eyes, and they will tremble beneath his feet, as he commands them to do his bidding."

Adharma found that he could not speak without struggling. She has subdued me, but once I am freed, I will go to the authorities, he thought.

"I have much to accomplish and a short period of time in which to do it, Mister Prime Minister." Kareza concealed her free hand behind her back. "Breathe. At this point, I cannot be stopped. But my form must change, one last time."

"What. . ." he blurted, "do you need. . .me for?"

"Frankly. . ." She stopped short of finishing her sentence before violently plunging a blade into Adharma's back and watching him die. Once his breathed no more, Kareza knelt at the prostrate corpse, which landed face down on the hand-woven carpet.

As she reached for the wound, Micah straightened up, and then peeked at the scene. Kareza removed bloodstained fingers from Adharma's back. He did not wish to know whether she wiped off the blood or sucked it like a vampire.

"You served me well," she said with distinction. "You were the key to my ascension in the former world, and you will do so once more, here in the latter."

Speechless, Micah continued to stare without betraying his position. What he saw next defied logic; visible crimson waves emanating from Kareza's fingertips dissolving into Adharma's back. Naturally, as an expert mathematician, Micah searched for scientific answers as to how it could have occurred. Simple physics dictate that matter cannot be created or destroyed, but changed. But the change happening – the inspiration of life transferred from one body to the next – was not possible.

Adharma now stood over the fallen Kareza's body – apparently victim to his former demise. His shoulder blades, including the navy blue silk suit jacket, showed no sign of being punctured. No blood soaked the tapestry beneath his feet. This

new version of Adharma checked them all with the intensity of a
forensic scientist searching for telling clues – except in this case,
he did so to prevent discovery of his own mischief. Why he did
so, Micah did not know. Surely, a being able to transcend death
could not be concerned with mortal laws?

Prior to that moment, Micah separated faith from his
profession. When his relatives spoke of his great-grandfather,
Micah responded with spiritual reverence – never science. The
two were mutually exclusive in his mind; unrelated, one
undetermined by the other. Spiritually, one could explain what
happened to Darrion James; he had risen from the dead and gone
on to live almost 40 more years. But, without a physical
explanation, Micah never considered one with respect to the
other. What now occurred bridged the two.

"Help!" Adharma's yell, unmistakably female, readjusted to
male. "Help!"

Micah vanished into the ensuing ruckus and snuck out. How
could he remain inconspicuous and be sure that no one followed
him? He stowed his Casper several blocks away and proceeded by
foot, as public transportation could also be traced. He said a
mental goodbye to his favorite vehicle. If its loss meant avoiding
suspicion of tonight's events, he would sacrifice it to the criminal
element. *Wait, my holophone!* He dropped it onto the street,
intending to crush it with the heel of his shoe when Doctor Chu
called. He bent over, answering it on its voice-only setting.

"How was the dinner?" Chu's inflections conveyed an air of
expectancy.

"Nothing I can talk about right now." Micah increased his
walking pace.

"Then when can you? Where are you going now? And why do
you whisper?"

He looked around. "It's not safe."

"Come to the laboratory, the west door."

Micah removed the holophone's memory before disposing of it. The foundation building was at least two miles away, and his feet were freezing. Still, he soldiered on through the residual puddles of rain, mentally dissecting what he had just seen.

In the Bible, Jesus cast out evil spirits from people many times. Was it illogical to assume a malevolent spirit could move from one human body to the next? He had never actually seen it done before. The event even fit the profile of matter – the spirit – moving from Kareza to Adharma, and Kareza needing to free Adharma's spirit before replacing it.

But why?

Chu had asked him to attend the celebratory dinner to plea for the restoration of the foundation's funding. The legal team had worn out its welcome, and so Chu sent Micah instead. It posed a risk, as his presence could result in a harassment charge. Though stealthy in his approach, one of them had slain the other before he could talk to them.

Indeed, Chu had left the west door to the Exodus Foundation unsecured. But the area was dark and, without his holophone, he had no way of lighting the way. Micah ran his fingers along the walls until he reached the elevator tubes, stumbled inside, and ascended to the top floor. Power still flowed there, he assumed, from a backup source. He accessed the handprint security panel.

"Voice recognition required," said the automated voice. "Please state your full name."

"Micah Darrion James."

"Micah Darrion James. Access granted."

Micah entered the top-level laboratory, where Chu – a kind dark-haired Asian – piddled about with the technical equipment remaining inside the round room. Their research concentrated on neuroscience, the brain's behavioral tendencies, and holistic procedures. Close to discovering a method to power their research, they lost funding. The angel and capital investors had dried up, as well. In a few days, the building would be destroyed and the work would have been for naught.

"So, what did the Prime Minister say? Did Kareza still pull his strings?"

With a fair degree of shellshock, Micah handed over the holophone's memory and he narrated as the audio file played.

Chu, of slight stature, tinkered without pause, even at the point where Kareza assumed the Prime Minister's place. "Hand me that vial over there, the one with the red liquid in it." Micah did so. "It'll have to do."

"Nothing I just said surprises you? Or you don't believe it?"

"Oh no, I believe it." The man set his tool on a black recliner. "But do you?"

"It violates every scientific principle that I've ever studied."

"And those scientific principles are immutable?" asked Chu with false gravitas.

"Aren't they?"

"Hmph." The recliner automatically leaned back. "What about the metaphysical? How much more do you need to see to be sure? You saw a woman stab a man to death and reanimate his body."

"It makes even less sense now that you said it out loud. I don't know. Metaphysics were always more philosophy than mathematics to me."

"Separation between belief systems and finite systems." He patted the chair's padding. "Why don't you have a seat and relax?"

"I just witnessed a murder, sir. Relaxing isn't the foremost thing on my mind."

"Five people besides me can open or close the door to this room and none of them would try to kill you."

Micah complied and felt immediate relief. His legs and feet needed respite from the two-mile walk. "Why am I here?"

"Why are any of us here?" Chu quipped.

"No, sir, I meant in a smaller sense. Why did you want me to come here?"

"We have a project to finish."

"The hexagonal probability theory? How can we finish with no funding or method?"

"Will you help me?" Chu asked in a calm alto.

Micah nodded. "Should I cue up the Sixth Equation files?"

A cool hand touched Micah's forehead. "No. Just try to relax."

He closed his eyes and, before he could react, a needle pricked his arm and blackness covered his face. Immediately, a blitz of mixed images played across his mind's eye. Before he knew it, they stopped and he saw Chu again. The taste in his mouth reminded him of sponge cake.

"You injected me?" Flustered and woozy, Micah stared at him. "Are you insane?"

"What did you see? Answer my question."

"Answer my questions first!"

"It's an analgesic and anesthetic. Without them, the process could cause unconsciousness, pain, and might drive you insane."

"Why did you do that to me?"

"Metaphysics; an alteration in your perceptions of time and space. Most scholars believe those concepts to be progressive and linear, like the path of an arrow." He pantomimed the action of aiming and shooting an arrow. "Is it truly unreasonable to assume that time and space are malleable, even reversible, just because no human being has found a way to successfully do it?

"Have you ever had a dream familiar to your emotional

intellect but foreign to your ability to reason? It's long been a belief of mine that our dreams are escaped manifestations of primal codes embedded in our subconscious."

The lightning-fast linguistics confused him. "I don't understand."

"A baby comes from the womb, innately knowing that he must suckle at a breast to live. He must inhale and exhale to survive and sleep to function. Codes to regulate these behaviors exist in our lower brains, along with clues to our destinies. God engineers them into our bodies so that we cannot forget them. We, who embrace these clues best, are those considered to be successful. Those who do not have 'dreams' about what could be; live life as ordinarily as they see fit."

"What I just saw was really a clue to my destiny?"

"Something like that, yes."

"I can't accept that."

"Then it's a dream. But suppose the inventor of the AIDS cure never pursued his purpose? Billions would have died. No wonder the world has so many problems. Nobody risks believing in themselves. The future will find you, Micah. Here's the true question – will you recognize it when you see it?"

Micah never considered it from that perspective. The doctor defended the position with belligerent conviction, as if he really believed his probability theory to be the truth. "We've literally been over this a million times and there's just no answer to the Sixth Equation."

Chu handed Micah a pair of black-rimmed visors. They had the weight of eyeglasses, but held a greater importance. Micah held them as such. *Has Chu solved the mystery?*

"Half an hour ago, you had a peek," Chu said, extending the visor's arms. "Now, take a look."

# CHAPTER FOURTEEN

Suddenly aware of himself, Damario slid over on the bed and massaged his lower back, which ached from the dip in the old mattress. Vintage scotch whiskey mixed with a sugar-like sweetness lingered on his tongue. Even through a mild hangover, he had dreamed again.

"No more Sweet Georgia Brown." Robinne Coley stirred from her husband's movement. "It's late and I'm sleepy."

Damario retrieved his navy blue flannel pajama bottoms from the floor. "I'm good. Go back to sleep, babe."

He padded to the in-suite bathroom and set the lights to dim. After swallowing some aspirin, he scratched his bald head and looked in the mirror. His face bore three vacation days worth of beard, which he intended to shave off later that morning. He'd been too busy with domestic duties to do it during his day off. Meanwhile, Robinne home-schooled their daughter Christian, and Gabriel, their toddler.

Damario's clean-up efforts led to an unexpected lovemaking session that his wife initiated. During his off-duty periods, Robinne sprung up with life, but inactivity drove him nuts. If he dreamed and insomnia struck – like it did now – only one thing granted him true peace. He scooted down the hall to the study and silently secured the door.

There, he used the computer to pull up the bank account where he stashed his investment earnings. Now that the figures transitioned from units to marks, the digital totals were even more robust than before. He cracked his knuckles and glanced at the clock. At a quarter after 1:00 Thursday morning, the American exchange would open in five hours, but the European trading hours had barely begun.

As the operating system loaded, he wistfully thought about how much he'd earned last week. He studied economics in his undergraduate college days, but eight months ago, he whimsically played the market by guessing which stocks he would buy – if he had "mad money" to use. Robinne would never approve of anything so financially risky. If they stayed their austere course, their house mortgage would be paid off by 2065, and then, the middle-lifers would live a relatively comfortable life.

Comfortable was not an option in his mind, and only Madison Shenk, his longtime partner on the force and "work wife," understood that. Last April, she loaned Damario a week's worth of lunch money to play his risky hunch. When it hit, he rewarded Madison with fondue and drinks at her favorite restaurant. To cover for his winnings, he worked more overtime and inflated its monetary worth to Robinne. He also purchased her a pair of heels she'd window-shopped for months to smooth over the tension. His wife suspiciously eyed them before placing the box into the closet.

Bit by bit, Damario accelerated the percentage of his monthly pay into the stock market. By July of last year, he flipped his entire check twice over by the time the next one arrived. Since Robinne did not ask about the overdue bills that suddenly disappeared, she did not need full disclosure. It brought him unmatched joy – almost as much as solving a lengthy and puzzling crime.

Another hour later, Damario transitioned the excess money

into an independent account, powered down the machine, and eased back into bed.

The doorbell frantically rang at a quarter past 7:00. Maddie's date must've gone south, Damario thought. He scooted to the bathroom to make himself presentable before joining the adults in the kitchen. There, wearing spandex black running tights, worn grey sneakers, and a powder blue Spelman College sweatshirt, Madison nodded with fresh eyes at her partner and tipped her coffee mug to him.

"Morning, D." She playfully sniffed. "You smell Irish this morning. Don't go over there before you shower. Robinne, I'm warning you – you might get a contact buzz."

Damario popped his A-shirt at the collar and sniffed. A faint whiff of alcohol assailed his nostrils. He slid over to his wife, who scrambled eggs and fried turkey bacon at the stove. "Morning, doll. Do I smell that bad?"

*Probably*, she thought, but she would not say so. She rustled her naturally kinky hair with her fingers and shed her blue terrycloth bathrobe to the elbows. Her pink tank top revealed a ton of cleavage. Robinne bent close and slowly inhaled, her lips brushing his beard. "No," she said with confidence. "I don't smell the Oban at all. Don't worry, I'm immune to scotch, Madison."

Pleased, Damario gave his wife a quick peck, though she yearned for more. "See," he replied, directing his attention to the coffee pot. "It's you, not me."

Robinne uncomfortably smiled and slipped back into her housecoat. Regardless of Madison's presence, she had hoped for a smack on the rear at the least.

Damario noticed copious amounts of red lipstick on Madison's ivory cup. "So?"

". . .it-did-not-go-well," said the trio in singsong unison. A few sips into his coffee, Damario refreshed Madison's cup.

"So, it was a blind date. We've established that?" She watched Damario pour and halted her hand when the coffee reached a half inch from the lid.

"Yeah." He returned the pot to the brewer.

"Mommy!" cried Gabriel from the living room. "I want juice!"

Robinne rolled her eyes. "How do we ask?" she yelled back.

"Please!" Gabriel responded.

"Want a plate, Madison?" Robinne poured apple juice into a spill-proof cup. Her politely curt tone contained a hint of the expectation she'd say *no*. But the single moocher never turned down free food. "We've got plenty. You're welcome to it."

"Sure." Her morning jog had made her ravenous, and Missus Coley effortlessly made restaurant-quality food. "So, Yvonne, you remember Yvonne Rochester. . .real deep southern accent? She introduced us. I forgot his name, it was that bad. Every time I let her fix me up, they have some big flaw or obvious mental defect. I don't know. Give me a woman's opinion, Robbie. Am I being too picky?"

*Yes, definitely. Who cares? Get a boyfriend already. It's been too long.* "No."

"Listen." She slapped Damario's forearm. "This one kept asking me dumb questions all-night-long, like. . ."

He anticipated the end of her sentence. "He didn't ask to. . ."

". . .hold my Ordnance? Yes, he did." She mocked her date's deep voice. "'Can you handle mine? What's it like on a stakeout?

Do you guys really drink a lot of coffee and eat doughnuts? What is it with guys, anyway?"

"Don't go in blind next time," Robinne said. "Soup's on." Robinne left to feed the children, and Madison and Damario served themselves.

"I'll be right back." Madison excused herself to the bathroom to wash her hands.

Robinne returned and jabbed her finger into Damario's chest just below the neck. "Why do we keep having the same conversation? I don't like having people over this early in the morning! We're half-dressed; I've barely washed my face. Look at my hair! She poked fun at my sobriety, too? And I don't care what happens, you-aren't-going-to-work-today. You're hung over, anyway. So don't think about it."

He rolled his eyes. "What's the big deal, Robbie? It's just Madison. She's like family. You said we've got enough food. I just bought a couple dozen eggs the other night."

"That's not the point – she's a single woman and she's not like family." Robinne angrily portioned her own food. "You work together. She's your partner. Put a real shirt on, for God's sake, and learn some professional boundaries."

Madison returned and noticed the marital tension. Undaunted, she sat next to the two of them at the breakfast table and bowed her head during Damario's prayer, though she did not say grace herself as a regular practice.

"So, he paid the check, about 500 marks." Madison said between bites. "He got gassed about it, too. He talked the whole time about how he loves to work out and the kind of property acquisition work he does."

Robinne's eyes brightened. She cared little about Madison's life, but the woman scoured real estate listings as if she meant to move every week. "Look at the bright side, Madison. . . you two have something in common, then."

"You'd think so, wouldn't you? Well, somehow he thought he'd get some. Since I drove to meet him, he walked me to my transport and. . ."

"Left or right cheek?" Damario figured the poor slob did something else to offend Madison; slapping was her go-to move.

The sparkle in Madison's eyes affirmed it. "Left. I almost used a closed fist."

"Wow." Robinne marveled at the ridiculous tale. "You didn't have to hit him."

"He grabbed a handful of my butt, Robbie. He needed to be slapped. Not everyone's a gentleman like your husband. It's a shame Brian and Carla couldn't pop out one more like him."

To Robinne, Madison's easy camaraderie with her husband felt worse than a torrid physical affair. *I love my in-laws.* "Glad he's mine then."

"You should be. D is the only guy I know with half the sense God gave him."

"I've got at least 75 percent." Damario changed the subject. "Any more word on the James' case?"

Robinne's eyes narrowed. "You're not working, I said. You look half in the bag."

Madison agreed. "She's right. You're off-duty and you've been drinking. Stop obsessing and enjoy your long weekend."

But he couldn't. No one had seen the renowned mathematician and scientist since the inauguration of President Mateo and the death of Kareza Noor last Thursday. The other detectives wanted James for questioning on the "convenient" disappearance of his boss. With the absence of more than circumstantial evidence, only Damario and Madison shared the suspicion of foul play – though he had to convince her, too, at first.

"Fine." He bumped fists with Madison. "I'm gonna catch a shower." He parted their company, bathed, and dressed in a black sweater and grey jeans. Even if he wanted to wear his street blues and work off the clock, Robinne had washed all of his uniforms and not dried them. He did have a spare at the station, but it did not fit well.

Robinne entered the bedroom, followed by Gabriel. "Almost ready, babe? Christian's watching her cartoons, but after I do her hair, we're out – 15 minutes, tops. Dad's barbecuing this afternoon. Make sure you drink some extra water, so you don't get dehydrated."

Damario picked up Gabriel and braced himself for a fight. "I'm not going."

"I told you to stop drinking so late at night. Fine, I'll drive there. But you're driving back. I need a big virgin margarita and I'm going to have one."

"No, it's not that. I'm fine," he said, as his son pawed at his face.

Robinne examined her husband's demeanor. "Christian!"

In a few seconds, her daughter rumbled into the room. "Yes, Mommy?"

Robinne pulled a kicking Gabriel from Damario's grasp. "Take your brother in the living room to watch HTV. I'll be there in a few minutes."

Christian obeyed and dragged her brother out of the room by the hand. "C'mon, buddy, let's go." When the children cleared, Robinne secured the door and set a soundproof barrier.

"Where are you going?"

"Work. There's something I have to do."

She hissed through her teeth. "You can do it Monday, when

you're sober and scheduled to work. Madison can handle it until then."

"She can't — not by herself. Look, the sooner I get to the bottom of this, the better. It'll all be over soon. And for the last time, I'm okay."

"I'm not having this conversation again, Damario." She crossed her arms. "Excuse yourself from the case and come with us."

"I can't do that, baby. Not this time. It's mine to solve."

"It doesn't have to be." She gestured at the space between them. "I hate this. All you do is work! Your son misses you. . .we all do. When's it our time, Damario? When do we get to be your number one priority, instead of some violent crime or random kidnapping victim? When's it our turn?"

*This kidnapping isn't random.* Damario wrung his hands. "I don't know what else to say. But, trust me, when I can talk about it, I will."

She kicked off her shoes — the same Zara Hristoff heels he'd bought for her months ago. "If you're not going to be watching me wear these, I might as well wear flats."

He sidled up to her. "You were wearing those for me? Can I have the Sweet Georgia Brown tonight, when you get back?"

She gave him a sideways glance and eased away. "I'll be too tired from driving for the Sweet Georgia Brown. Maybe on the next vacation day you don't skip."

Robinne pulled the room's barrier down, opened the door, and quickly kissed her husband goodbye. She loathed the routine; being a detective's spouse meant the last time she saw her husband may be the last time she saw her husband.

Damario grabbed his badge and Ordnance, hugged and kissed his children, and then joined Madison on the brownstone's front steps.

"I have to stop being so daggone predictable," he grumbled.

"First her, now you. . ."

"It's not like you're a kaleidoscope of variety, Coley. You're constant like the tide, but that's a good thing. Unpredictability means you might get me killed."

He huffed. "I guess."

"You had another dream, didn't you?" she asked, concentrating on the remains of her fourth coffee. *I hope Robbie didn't spit in it again.*

"Yup."

"Still haven't told your wife about the dreams, have you?"

He exhaled. "Nope."

Madison rested her cup beside her left thigh. "You're going to fail your next psych eval if you don't start sleeping."

"Relax," he scoffed. "It's only been a week." *That's when the dreams started.* "I slept fine before that, all the time."

"What happened? The round room again?"

"It's like I'd been operated on, or something. I pull this breathing tube out of my mouth. There's one empty chair, like an old dentist's chair, to my left. A Hispanic girl's in that one, and there's three others to my right. A mixed-looking woman is in one of them and someone else's there too. I get up, and go to this high rise apartment building. When I handprint the door, I wake up."

"What if a new opportunity will open for you? Something like that? And the operation means you have to go through something painful first? I don't know. I still don't see how two people you don't know and have never met have to do with it."

She assumed two because he kept Harper James' presence to himself. "I don't either," he admitted. "Maybe I do need to see someone."

Madison put a hand on his shoulder. "Don't be ridiculous. You're as sane as they come. It's just another case you have to crack, Detective. I know you haven't contacted them."

He self-consciously looked down. "You expect anything less?"

"Hardly. I bet Robinne's *pissed.*"

*In a word, yes.* "I hope she'll get over it faster this time."

"Robinne's a good woman and you blow it every time you ditch her. Tell her what you've been going through. It's not like she'll leave you because you're making money and having crazy dreams."

"Thanks Maddie," he deadpanned. "I really appreciate the love."

"No problem. If you're checking in to the station, you better sober up first."

"I'm good." He planned to check his blood-alcohol levels anyway. "I'm going to question Harper James again. I'm missing something."

Madison stood up. "Let me know how it goes. Good luck."

Hesitant to open the door at 8:30 a.m., Harper did so, thinking it might concern Micah. She peeked through the one-way panel inside the door. He had an Ordnance but did not wear a policeman's uniform. She feared the worst. But dressing down might have been a psychological ruse to keep her calm. Trembling from an overdose of caffeine and sugar, she asked for identification. The officer pressed his badge against the access panel. *Damario Coley, badge number 086114.*

"Just have a few more questions for you, Missus James," he said with a tint of hope. *Perhaps she can shed some light on why she haunts my dreams.*

She waved off her hired bodyguards and released the compound security locks on the door. "There's a sizable reward for my husband's safe return," she said as the door slid up. "I must screen my visitors. You understand."

Bare-faced with her hair barely combed, Harper wore plain navy blue sweatpants and a sweatshirt. Her bloodshot eyes alerted Damario to the fact that she had not sufficiently slept in a couple of days – standard for a relative of a missing person. He entered the palatial foyer. Its gold inlaid, crystal chandelier in the vaulted ceiling provided light, while the space's complimentary maroon and chocolate brown highlights muted the bordering-on-garish appearance of it all.

Harper escorted him to a smaller, modestly decorated receiving room. There, a service droid poured them coffee and served a series of delicate, fruit-filled pastries. The lone peculiar one, a cone-shaped golden sponge cake, looked particularly appealing to Damario, but he did not eat one. "I'd like to ask you some questions about your husband, Missus James, if you're up to it."

"Please, have a seat. There's not much more I can tell you that I haven't already, and you'll be better at piecing it all together." She tapped her fingertips together like she connected a round-shaped thought with her hands.

"Let's go over it, all of it, one more time." He sank his long frame into the comfortable burgundy leather loveseat. "Start with everything you remember leading up to that day, please. Don't leave out any details."

Harper's eyes purposefully eased to a high resolution rotating photo album displaying an image from their wedding. "We've been married ten years. Neither of us has ever cheated. We barely fight at all."

"Are you sure? That he never cheated?"

"As sure as a wife can be. We're happy, Detective. He has a regular Sunday afternoon tee time. We vacation abroad once or twice during peak season." She added the next comment for effect rather than fact. "Our love life is satisfying."

"When you say 'satisfying'. . ."

"Good. Great even." She stopped from further description. "Satisfying."

"What do you do for work, again?"

"I head up the applied sciences and weapons division for the west coast branch of the federal government." She eased the recitation, so that it sounded more genial.

"And your husband?" He sipped deeply from the coffee cup.

Harper waved her hand, as if his occupation did not matter. In truth, she did not understand an apt way to describe it. "He worked at the Exodus Foundation."

Damario choked on the contents of his mouth, almost spitting it out. He coughed heartily, to the point where Harper became concerned. "Are you alright?"

Finally, he could swallow normally. "What does he do there?"

"Mathematical physics. He reports directly to Miles Chu, the Chief Executive Officer. He's far more hands-on, from what I've heard. He's missing too. Do you think the two are connected?"

*Maybe.* The detective found the lack of explanation curious. "Were they working on a project? Something where Micah and Chu could have made enemies, maybe ticked off a rival?"

Harper sipped some tea. "I'm sorry. . .again?"

"Your husband: did he have corporate enemies?"

"The economy, you mean?" She faked disgust. "It's a non-profit. The foundation lost its solvency a few months ago – rather abruptly, in fact. Congress passed that bill removing its public funding and it didn't take long after that."

He would stop skirting the issue soon. "Again, how did your husband react to being let go?"

"He isolated himself," she said, mentioning e-mail messages they had exchanged where he claimed being "lost" and "without purpose." "As you can see, he loved his job and there's not much work out there – much less for a mathematical physicist – outside of the educational sector. Mass-produced droids occupy many of those positions at a fraction of the long-range cost."

"What did he do, then?"

"I took a short sabbatical and we traveled."

The police had surveyed the James' credit records. The couple had spent hundreds of thousands traipsing the Caribbean in the past year. "When we got back, he spent a lot of time in his study during the day, and some nights." She paused. "I started to worry, so I started recording his movement down there, in his study."

"What did you see?" he asked with intrigue. "Did you turn over the recordings?"

"No, but they don't show anything I didn't already tell you. He left around seven o' clock last Wednesday night. You know how they found it," she said about her husband's favorite transport; a gold Casper. "I don't know where he went."

"Mind taking a ride with me there?"

Harper agreed and notified her head bodyguard that they need not be followed. Damario opened the passenger door of his Jupiter station wagon for her. Though a passenger riding in the front seat with a policeman violated official protocol, she entered without a second thought.

Their animated rapport ceased during the drive. This suited Harper, as she did not wish to talk. *But why aren't we slowing down?* They neared the crime scene location where her husband's stripped vehicle had turned up, but Damario passed it without stopping.

"We should have turned back there," she said, also noticing the navigation service locked on to the Exodus Foundation site.

"Why are we going to an abandoned building? I'm not sure that it's even safe for us to go in there."

"It's safe," he reassured her. "I'd like to see his office."

"The security might not let us in there. But you can override that, can't you?"

*I hope so.* "Yes."

# CHAPTER FIFTEEN

The duo ducked past the warning signs and postings, and entered the high-rise through an open door on the west side. During the daytime, the structure looked far less imposing than the beam-and-girder tombstone it resembled at night. Small wildlife scampered across the wooden floors, littered with dead leaves and branches. Harper led the charge to the elevator tubes. In front of them, a glowing marquee directory indicated Micah's division, *Mathematical Physics, 77th floor.*

She fingered the display. "That's odd. The electric is off, but this thing isn't?"

"Elevator tubes work on a battery-like power source."

"These things make me squeamish. If it wasn't on the top floor, I'd walk."

Damario offered his hand. "Here. Take my hand."

They entered the center tube large enough to transport them both. A solid platform of forced air formed beneath their feet and they instinctively clenched fingers. Within two minutes, they were transported to the building's top floor. Unlike the bottom floor, which had been left to the dogs, the level looked to be completely intact, including an active security system.

Damario applied his right hand to the handprint security panel. After scanning him, it turned red. He attempted twice more. The handprints of emergency personnel were supposed to open all manufactured doors. *Is my blood alcohol level too high?*

Curious, Harper laid her hand onto the plate and the panel

turned green. *It worked!* "Voice recognition required. Please state your full name."

"Harper Charlotte James."

"Harper Charlotte James, access granted." She held up her hands in wonderment as the door opened to them.

"Have you been here before?" Damario asked as they walked inside.

"Never." Her voice wavered. *Not that I remember.*

The massive backlog of information Damario possessed on the James couple faded away. All that mattered now was the connection he felt to Harper and the information she did not share.

He repeated the question, while activating the room's backup electricity source. "Have you been here before?"

Harper looked around. Damario followed her into the round room of his dreams, and the door automatically closed. He lingered around the dark impressions on the metal floor, where machinery must have been.

She counted the chairs facing one of the curved walls. Patting the dust free from one in particular, she sat down. According to her fractured dreams, in a room much like this one, a Hispanic girl named "Quinne" had been to her right with the detective just two chairs down. She clasped her hands together and tapped her foot, which attracted Damario's attention. He stared at her feet. "Do you have to do that?"

"Sorry. Can you come here for a minute?"

Damario approached the row of chairs and chose one. The mystery grew more complex. He placed a private call to medical examiner, Justin Rochester, the lone human among the forensic droids.

"Rochester." Justin looked up from his desk. "Coley? Shenk

warned me you'd be calling. I shouldn't be surprised. What can I do for you?"

"Missing technology from the Exodus Foundation. Do you have it?"

"Had it. We seized it on one twenty-one. They took it on one twenty-two."

Damario turned his back to Harper, who attentively eavesdropped. "They?" he whispered. "How? Who?"

Justin smiled. "Both answers higher than our pay grade, Coley. They swiped it so fast that I can't even tell you what it was."

"Thanks." Damario ended the call. *Who took the machines?*

Madison placed a hand on his shoulder. "What are you thinking, Detective?"

"Whatever he and Chu were working on, it was serious."

Urged by her unsettled stomach, Harper cleared her throat and confessed. "I have not been totally honest with your superiors. What I'm about to say sounds insane, even to me, and they're my thoughts."

He suspected some duplicity, but braced himself. "What do you know?"

"I've been to a place like this before. So have you."

The revelation rocked him, as he closed the distance between the two of them. "I don't understand. . .you and me?"

"We were here, or in a room exactly like it, together. Once before. . .you and I."

He experienced a degree of recognition regarding her name and face, but not much else. "You're confused."

"I'm sure of it," she protested. "You and I were here; us, and at least three other people. One of them sat here between you and me; a cute Hispanic girl, named Quinne."

The name stopped both of them in their tracks. He had no idea as to his connection to Quinne.

"Maybe you should tell me what you know."

Damario weighed the benefits of doing so. She could not do much with what he could tell her because it would necessitate her telling others what else she knew. "I have this recurring dream, where I wake up here, or somewhere like here, in the dark." He pointed out the particular one. "I had these tubes in me, and I don't know how I got here or what I was doing."

His story would have sounded crazy to anyone but Harper.

"The other people you mentioned. . .could one of them have been Micah?"

She ventured to the most familiar ergonomic chair and laid down on it. "Definitely not. You think Micah's disappearance is connected to this."

"I don't know. Why can't we remember?"

Harper stared at the ceiling. Everything in her life felt disjointed and dislocated. The master bed in her house, her designer clothes – both were almost too perfect. The huge bed and 1,000 square foot walk-in closet full of designer outfits and shoes may as well have been rented. The antiseptic house made her itch inside her own skin. The only things granting her comfort were snippets of blurred dreams. Verbalizing this discomfort fell short of her vocabulary, so she did not try. She had told no one and was fairly positive the detective had not either.

Her emotions surrounding her husband's disappearance were even more disturbing to her. She refused to give voice to them, as they were unnatural and would suggest to the policeman that she may have had something to do with it. And she did love Micah. But the absence of her husband felt natural, like it should have happened. Harper believed in God granting peace in the midst of emotional storms, but she never personally experienced it. Still lying in the chair, she blinked her eyes to keep herself from falling asleep.

Damario touched the reclining chair he dreamed of lying in, hoping something might trigger a memory, a clue, or something. His surroundings were quiet enough to notice Harper's breathing patterns shift from that of someone awake and vibrant to sound slumber. He let her sleep. *She must need it.* Harper looked peaceful, like a child. Her bottom lip drooped slightly, enough to reveal the crown of a bottom tooth.

The puzzle irritated him; an equation with five factors. It had three unknowns; Quinne, Micah James, and another person. The laboratory they discovered had been stripped and would only exist a while longer.

Without a forensic droid or backup collection material, he started snapping pictures with his police issue holophone. Its high resolution and settings provided enough variance for him to capture it from different perspectives. The infrared did not reveal anything he already did not suspect. The pictures would have to stay off-the-record. If his superiors found out he had gone behind them without prior authorization, they would suspend him first, and then have him psychologically evaluated. While not fragile, his psyche certainly would not pass strenuous testing at this point. At a point of stress, he might blurt out information – like he had been dreaming about his partner, too.

"Missus James," he called out. "Harper, wake up."

"Hmm? I fell asleep?" She propped herself up and rubbed her eyes. Damario lent her his arm for support and she used it to slide safely to the ground. "Did you find something? Anything?"

Damario's face fell downcast. "No. I'll take you home."

At the room's entrance, Harper approached the access plate. When the door opened, she and Damario barely had time to react to the young girl in front of them before she dropped to the ground. Damario carried her to a chair and laid her down; Harper followed them. When she came around, she would speak and verify what Harper had already suspected.

Damario studied the quiet face. "Is this who I think it is?"

"Quinne," Harper responded without hesitation.

They would not understand the significance of her presence until she awakened, but Damario started postulating outcomes. If the pattern held, she would have had some memory or link to this same room and the people within it – Harper did and so had he. This laboratory allegedly belonged to Harper's husband. Its ventures included equipment for a secret project that might have been off the official books. Micah could have instituted an experiment on all three of them.

The venture could have been of a criminal nature – the likes of which he did not want to even imagine. Experimentation on human beings dated back through the annals of time; the most recent recorded instances to increase adaptability of robotic prostheses. It did not explain why someone, or Micah, would have chosen five random people and why he would have done so in the laboratory of a not-for-profit foundation.

Gradually, after minutes of Harper fanning Quinne's face with her hands, the girl roused. She opened her eyes and stared at the exact location of the ceiling that she dreamed. Quinne shot up into a sitting position, screaming and thrashing. Damario tried to calm her. Harper did the same.

"Take it easy." He gently touched her arm. "You fainted."

"What?" The scenario had all the markings of a dream to Quinne, who only recently stopped breathing heavily. "Who 're you?"

"I'm Detective Damario Coley," he said, "and this is Harper James. You're in the laboratory of her husband, Micah James, in the Exodus Foundation building."

Quinne massaged her cramping right quad; the reason why she'd stopped halfway into her four-mile run. While supporting herself on a nearby tree, she noticed Damario and Harper entering the abandoned building. Quinne's only other recourse was a liquor store a block away. By that time, someone could have attacked her.

"They do not-for-profit work to improve the human condition," Harper explained, reciting the company's tagline. "Or, at least they did until a few months ago."

Quinne stared at the familiar masculine face. "Ain't you have dreads before?"

"What?" Damario's brow furrowed. "Haven't had dreadlocks since college, about 13 or 14 years ago."

"You that old?" she asked unconvinced. "Guess you got one of them kinda faces."

Harper moved closer. "How'd you get in here?"

Quinne held up her palm and jumped to the ground. "Like you did, I guess? I ain't never been up here, though."

"You might have," Harper assured. "How else could you get in here?"

That question remained. "I ain't do it on purpose." Quinne cleared the hoarse rasp from her voice. "I called out, at first. You must not've heard me. My leg's hurtin' real bad, so it took me a minute to get to the tubes. Found out you was up on this floor, so I followed and banged on the door."

"But how did you get in?" Damario tried to extract the details. The door's metal alloy would not have readily responded to the strength of a 125-pound teenager.

Quinne's eyes rolled. "You ain't hear me, so I banged on the door. That ain't work, either, so I smacked the panel."

"Why would it read her prints?" Harper turned to Damario. "Any idea?"

He signaled no. "Did you hack it?"

"I look like a hacker to you, man? No, I ain't hack it! It asked for my name, I said it, and it opened." When it did, two apparitions from her dreams appeared and dropped her to the ground. "Pain must've knocked me out."

Damario knew different; she likely fainted because she had dreamed of them. "Since you said you've never been here before, let's go back to the events leading up to you getting here. Start with when you woke up and be as specific as you can."

Like the past six days, Quinne had awoken completely covered in sweat. Sleeping in just a pair of black mesh shorts and a tank top did nothing to cool her off, and Troy, her cool-by-nature boyfriend, insisted on full covers. They lessened the effects of the cooling mechanism at her bedside. She told him her night sweats were from hormones or the apartment's overactive heating system, but she secretly feared Post-Traumatic Stress Disorder.

"I woke up 'bout 7:30. Turned the window tint down to get some light in the bedroom. Washed my face, threw on tights and a hoodie, grabbed my tunes and went for a run. Helps clear out my head." *Or make sense of what's in it.*

"Whereabouts?"

"East side – Lowery homes."

When Quinne mentioned the low-income neighborhood, Harper visibly recoiled. She hated that run-down side of town.

"You always run that early?"

"Not always." She twiddled her fingers. "Why? Does it matter? I get up early. I run early. Ain't got no job. Might as well."

"Rough neighborhood to be running in the dark," muttered Harper.

"I ain't scared. You sound like Troy. He thinks I should be scared, too. For what? You gonna stay in the house, scared all the time? Not me. I gotta Ordnance for all that. And yeah, gotta license for it, too."

Damario mentally dissected the answers. "Right. Continue, please."

"Ain't much else to it but that. 'Bout a half block from here, got a cramp. Thought you and her was better than anyone in the liquor store."

"Have you been having dreams, Quinne?"

*Gunshots fire. Troy lyin' in black blood. His eyes stickin' open like a deer crushed in traffic. Blackout. I scream in a hospital bed, pregnant – 'bout five months or so. Blood. Lots of blood.* "No."

"Nothing?" Incredulous, Harper pressed. "Seriously? Both of us have."

"I said, no!" she yelled back.

Damario knew different, but he would not push. "This Troy. . ."

"My boyfriend? Moved outta my momma's house couple years ago and we moved in together."

Anibel Ruiz, a Bible-thumping Catholic, did not approve of her teenager's active sex life, so Quinne moved out. The concept of an afterlife, or a prior life, as it were, was a waste of thought to Quinne. The present – where she lived, breathed, achieved, and failed, held more importance.

"And you've never been in a room like this before? Officer Coley and I have, and we both possess these dream-like memories of all three of us being here. . .in a round room.

"You were sitting here," Harper said, pointing out a specific chair, "between us. Another woman beside you, and, we think, someone else on the end. It could've been my husband, Micah. He's been missing for about a week."

Damario stepped forward. "My dreams are much less conclusive, but I am in one of these chairs, strapped down, with a tube in my mouth. Had the same dream over and over. Keeps me awake at night. You don't remember anyone? A name, or anything?"

Quinne put a hand to her lips. Her memories were reminiscent of Damario's and Harper's, and while she did not remember encountering them before, she did not completely doubt it. With folded arms, she divulged her dream – from murdered boyfriend to pregnancy gone wrong.

"If what we're describing are dreams," Damario said aloud, "it makes sense why we only remember bits and pieces, doesn't it?"

The women agreed. "But it doesn't make sense that you were here, totally conscious, or why we all see different versions of the same things. All this started happening for us over the past couple days. What about you Quinne?"

She shook her head. "Four days."

"Detective?"

"Same."

"Why ain't your boys handlin' all this and figurin' it out?"

"They've been here, Quinne," he corrected. "The machines are all gone."

"Great." Harper sighed. *That technology might have provided a clue to Micah's whereabouts.* "So, what do we do now?"

"We leave," he said with certainty.

"Wait, to go where?" She limped in Damario's direction. "The two of you ain't gonna just show up, throw my life around, and go about your business. I ain't goin' nowhere 'til I get some more answers."

"Nobody's saying we step out into the hallway and forget." Damario's temperature rose. "But sitting around in an empty room, trying to remember isn't going to help, either. You don't solve a puzzle by looking at the shapes of the pieces you don't have. You look what you do have and how the missing pieces fit the spaces." He pointed at the room's front. "*Five* chairs: you, me, plus Harper then Micah, I'm guessing, that's four."

Harper thought the policeman had a valid point. "And the fifth person?"

"Teanna Kirkwood," Quinne blurted without thinking. "Her name is Teanna Kirkwood."

# CHAPTER SIXTEEN

*January 28, 2050*

Harried by the delayed red-eye flight, Teanna ordered alcohol, starting off with a Fuzzy Navel on the rocks. The event called for a celebration. After a month away from the west coast, the trip demanded she let loose. Teanna wore her best business suit, designer heels, and a Zara Hristoff clutch with no practical use.

A tumbler ascended from her first-class armrest. Shaking the ice cubes back and forth until her palm cooled down, Teanna sipped, her lips filtering the liquid from the ice. *Exactly what I needed.* Soon, her stilettos found their way to the storage area beneath her seat. The passenger sitting next to her – an impeccably-groomed Asian in his mid-30's, smiled at her. She hoped his warmth originated from mutual attraction and not an alcohol-fueled illusion.

"Hi," she laughed with a tipsy lilt.

"Hello," he responded, with a slight Korean drawl. He had been too busy manipulating his computer display to speak. The man rested his chin on his left hand, which bore an expensive-looking band on his ring finger. That did not deter Teanna, who had fooled around with a married man before. The risk of getting caught jumpstarted her heartbeat. She had a thing for Asian men.

"Teanna Kirkwood." She extended a hand, which he tenderly accepted.

"I know who you are, Teanna." His throaty baritone plucked her strings. "I saw you at the police precinct, by the tree."

"Oh yeah?" She volleyed more flirtation his way. "We've met? I don't think so 'cause I would've remembered you."

He flashed a winsome smile. "You don't remember me?"

"Really don't." She swallowed the last hint of her drink. "You a cop?"

"No, I'm not. Why do you ask?"

"Met this guy, right? Boxes like Pacquiao, but he ain't a good boyfriend. Go out of town for the real estate conference I just came from, he follows me, makes a scene." She stifled a belch. "That's when they got him. They prolly want me to press charges."

"You're a chatty one, aren't you?"

Teanna adored the way his lips formed words underneath a trimmed mustache and chin goatee. "Yup. Guess I am, mister. . .?"

"Chu," he answered. "Miles Chu."

"Miles Chu. You were at the police precinct? What for?"

"Mistaken identity. You can imagine the amount of problems that can cause."

"Wow!" Her response rang with fake amazement. "What do you do. . .Mister Chu?"

"I'm a scientist." He reached into his jacket pocket and produced a vintage red die – the kind used in Vegas gambling – and placed it on her tray table. "I've been studying a complex mathematical theory, but I'll give you the short version, if you like. Pick a number, from one to six."

Teanna blinked her eyes. "Hol' up. I need a drink 'fore all that." She disposed of her empty glass inside the automated tray table and summoned another Fuzzy Navel. After sipping it, she waved her hand for Chu to start. "Why six?"

"It's complicated. Pick a number, from one to six."

"You pick one."

"Alright, I'll pick the number five. No matter how many times you roll this six-sided die, it has a one-in-six chance of falling on the number five."

Teanna made sense of what he said, even while weary, with impaired faculties and an empty stomach. "Okay, I'm with you."

"If I fix the die on one side, the odds increase that you will get that five."

"I'm not a bettin' girl, but I'd take a fixed bet."

"Of course." Again, he grinned. "Who wouldn't?"

"Wait. You an odds maker? That sounds borin'."

"Let me finish. Apply that concept to a person's life. Everyone has regrets; things they want to change about the past. Given the opportunity to go back and fix a bad decision, would you do it?"

Besides her ex-boyfriend, the heavyweight, no regrets immediately popped into her head. "No doubt."

"Not if your second chance had an 83 percent chance of going wrong."

The explanation caught on. "Fix the odds 'fore you choose?"

He nodded. "Essentially."

She realized he was not finished. "So, what's the problem?"

"The impossibility of time travel and, as with all gambles, your win is another's loss. The house would not exist, if it lost more than it won. What would the betting world be without it?"

Now, the man did not make sense. "Not followin'."

"Ecology, economics, politics, sociological studies – the change or unsettling of one unchecked factor could throw the entire system into anarchy."

Like that, the stranger had drained all of the joviality and flirtation from their conversation and reduced it to a diatribe on consequences. It killed Teanna's percolating libido which, prior to this conversation, had been humming along like an engine needing spot tuning.

"Somethin' changes and destroys whatever – so what?" She snatched the die into her palm. The alcohol plus hunger made her flippant. "However the odds change, no one will ever know they caused it, will they?"

"If you can figure that part out, use this." He handed her a thumb segment-sized gold disk with *Exodus Foundation* printed on it and returned to his reading.

She did not continue the discussion. His theory interested her in the silence of her thoughts. Teanna examined the die. He fired her up over the potential of a wild hypothesis and now it bothered her without further explanation. Chu left his seat for the bathroom.

Teanna crossed her arms and flicked on the in-seat HTV to a documentary about President Ramsey Mateo's rise to power and recent inauguration. Mateo's parents were native Mexicans, who fled to the US in 2009 as illegal immigrants. But, Mateo's birth occurred on US soil and, by all rights, it enabled him to run for president. During the feature on his brief background as a grassroots representative in the House, Teanna dozed off.

She dreamt of a dark-skinned man, who said little but irritated her with his presence. Next to him stood an exotic beauty whose face blurred and phased into different forms. The ingénue asked for Teanna's hand. Suddenly, the woman morphed into a drooling beast with jagged white teeth that repeatedly stabbed Teanna in the limbs with knives. Body rigid with fear, her eyes shot open with Chu's disk and die still in her hand. She would look him up when she settled in at home. The disk felt rough on an edge. *Is it broken?*

Over breakfast and for the remainder of the flight, she thought about her foreign companion, his rather wild musings on probability, and where he could have gone. They were in first class. *Could he have relocated to bother someone else?* She wondered, though, about the theory of six and pondered it all the way to the stop on the landing strip.

Still searching for Chu, she waited until most of the passengers exited the plane. Then, a stocky, chocolate man emerged from the rear of the plane with a container of garbage. Catering to commercial flight passengers was one job that still relied on human beings.

"Ready to go?" One of the plane's stewards, Theodore Mitchell was pleasantly handsome to boot.

"Sure, Ted." The redheaded stewardess attending the flight loitered at the front row of first class next to Teanna. She made eyes toward Ted, who indicated with a gesture that he was talking to Teanna.

"Think so." Teanna giggled at the woman's lack of tact. Finally on her feet, she could manage her drunkenness. "Excuse me. . ." she looked at the stewardess' nametag. *Rhianne.* Teanna produced the gold disk. "A nice man, Miles Chu, was on this flight next to me. Did he move to coach? I ain't see him when I woke up."

"Sorry, ma'am," Rhianne said. "We don't give out customer information to people who aren't employees of the airline or next of kin. It's a violation of privacy and protocol."

"C'mon," Ted argued. "It's a 'yes' or 'no' question. I'll do it for you."

Rhianne stepped up. "Database check passenger first class or coach, last name Charlie-Hotel-Uniform, first name Mike-India-Lima-Echo-Sierra."

"No passenger with that name traveled on this flight," the database reported.

Teanna scratched her head. "Could he sneak on the flight somehow?"

"With handprint tech, DNA and iris scans, not likely," Ted said. "Even the terror networks haven't figured out a way to crack that code yet. Let me try: visual, row 6 Alpha-Bravo-Charlie-Delta; sweep forward, high speed." Ted's commands brought up a holographic display of Teanna swiftly loading her bags, sitting down, and intermittently turning her head toward an empty window seat. Both Ted and Rhianne snickered.

"You were served a number of drinks, Miss Kirkwood," she scoffed. "Couldn't you have 'imagined' that you were talking to him?"

"Yes, Rhianne, I imagined him," Teanna said sarcastically. She held the disk to the redhead's face. "He left me an imaginary card too. See it? Naw? Guess you can't, 'cause it don't exist."

"Do you believe this, Ted? C'mon. Someone dropped that in your seat, or it fell from your folio. It's not the first prank to be played on someone drunk."

Teanna reared back and removed her earrings. "Heifer, I will drop you."

Before the confrontation became more heated, Ted stepped between them. "It's all settled. Miss Kirkwood, it's time for us to exit the plane." He put a hand on Teanna's shoulder. "You may want to get something to eat before you head home."

"Sounds good." Rhianne positioned herself next to the captain. "The usual at the steakhouse?"

". . .is where I'm going." He eased away from the stewardess. "Alone."

Rhianne stomped up the ramp and out of the plane. A perfect gentleman, Ted allowed Teanna ahead of him. Inside, she wondered whether he did so to look at her body. She made sure her coat remained in her arms so he could get a good look.

Teanna did not particularly like steak, but she would go to the restaurant too. If it meant having male company, she would eat a 16-ounce porterhouse.

Though the two went to the same place at approximately the same time, Teanna missed the uniformed steward. She chose a stool at the bar, as waiting for a table during lunch rush would take far too long for someone who did not even like steak. The bartender droid did not give her the spiel about the hand cut beef or how good the Kobe burgers were, which she appreciated. Chicken breast in wine sauce, rice pilaf and asparagus with a glass of pinot noir would do it.

Halfway through her platter, Ted appeared, spinning a strong whiff of musk into her nostrils. "Do you mind if I have a seat next to you, Miss Kirkwood?"

"Please," she said, mouth half full. "And it's Teanna."

"Teanna, nice to meet you." He set down a monstrous plate of chicken and steak nachos smothered in cheese before signaling the bartender. "My friends call me Ted. My family calls me Tiny."

"Pleasure," she said with pomp. "Aww, why Tiny?"

"I weighed three pounds at birth," he admitted. "Obviously, it has no bearing on where I am now. Have we met before? I think we have."

"I know. I look familiar; must got one of them faces."

"Bottled Yuengling? Thanks." Ted said to the droid before finishing a few nachos. "I guess we haven't met then," he said, still chewing. "Sorry to talk with my mouth full, but I'm starving."

She ate when he ate and, when he spoke, she finished

chewing so that she could answer him or provide a retort. "Nice to have you join me."

"Yours was my last flight for the week and I'm not in a rush." He came closer to her ear. "If I'm being honest, I'm trying to avoid Rhianne, too. She's been after me for the longest. Employees can't date, but most do it anyway. It's a good job with decent pay and I like the benefits. Not trying to lose my job doing something stupid. That's why I showered before I came down here. It's the once place she can't follow me."

*He showered. That's why I ain't find him. But he sure talks a lot.*

"So, this Chu guy?" He shoved a few more nachos in his mouth – gracefully, but with obvious importance. "What's his deal?"

Teanna retrieved the die and placed it on the table, explaining Chu's lecture from beginning to end using the same scenario that he did; a human life. Ted listened intently to each detail, though he devoured food from his plate at the same time. She finished with her question and Chu's dilemma. *If you go back in time, change somethin', how'll you know you changed it?*

Ted drank his beer and did not answer, but the recognition and interest in his face piqued Teanna's interest. "You look like you know what I'm talkin' about."

"Hold on a minute." He eased back, signaled the droid and pointed to his empty bottle. The machine raised its artificial thumb and rolled to a nearby refrigerator. "Chu's talking simple chaos theory."

"It's *not simple*," she argued. "What do you know about it?"

"So, one day in the college library, I'm bored senseless and I pick up this book. . .changed my life. It was religious, almost, like an epiphany. I understood it all. Kind of scary, really."

"Uh huh." She sounded skeptical. "Chaos theory, huh?"

Ted took two cocktail straws and laid them parallel on the bar ledge. "Let's say these two straws represent different versions of your life. The first straw is what we're living right now. You married, divorced, got kids?"

Teanna chuckled. "Marriage and babies? Never in the plans."

"If you went back in time and had a kid, Chu is saying that you create a different reality than the one you currently live in. Say instead of being single, you got married to a guy named Ted and had a son named Luke."

"I'd never marry a Ted," she smiled. "Don't sound like the tied-down type."

He laughed and picked up the second straw. "*If* you went back in time right now, found a Ted and married him, you think you'd have a Luke?"

"No. *Yes.* I don't know!"

"Chu said he could fix the odds? How? What's more likely is you screw something else up. Messing with time is different than we think. Maybe you have a girl, twins, a miscarriage. You get divorced, he abuses you."

Though Ted ate with vigor, the negative possibilities stopped her from chewing "Does it gotta be bad?"

Nacho crumbs dropped from his mouth. "It's chaos — unpredictable, violent, chaotic. That's the point. It could be good, I guess, depending on your point-of-view."

"Do you even know the answer to the question?"

He drank enough to wash down his food because Teanna grew more impatient with his long-winded explanations. "I think so, but I don't care what scientists say, it's not humanly possible."

"What is it?" she interrupted. *If he don't give me a straight answer!* Teanna gulped down the last of her wine, but clung to her glass.

"Assuming it's possible, someone's sent back in time and they make a decision changing the past – the only way they would ever know that they had altered anything is if they were told."

Slowly, Teanna's eyes opened with realization.

"Someone with knowledge of the original timeline and the altered one would have to tell them – God, in other words, or someone like Him."

Teanna's glass slipped from her hand to the ground and shattered into a dozen fragments. She knew the answer, and must contact Doctor Chu.

# CHAPTER SEVENTEEN

*January 28, 2050*

"Where is she?" Harper's surprise translated well across the three-way hologram.

Damario checked the time. "Landed at Metro Airport an hour ago."

"Metro's an hour from here with good traffic." Quinne fidgeted in the bathroom: the one soundproofed room in the apartment and the lone place where Troy would not disturb her. "Sound the alarm and go get her!"

"You don't get it. If I do that, she might run."

"How you figure?'

"She pays with printed marks, doesn't own a registered holophone, and largely stays away from public places. If she wanted to vanish, she could. . .and we need her."

"Got an idea." Quinne's face brightened. "You a cop, but *we* ain't."

Harper caught on. "And instead of driving, I have a hybrid helicopter at my disposal that will get us there twice as fast, if not more. Just say the word."

"I'll pick up Quinne. Meet you in 15." Damario disconnected and dressed in plain sight, so that his wife would know the nature of his business. Though his vacation had ended, that did not mean Robinne would not fuss. She walked into the room and immediately stiffened.

"Nope. Not tonight." Damario accidentally dropped his

armament belt and she grabbed it. "You can't go without this."

"That's not funny."

She stuck her finger into his chest. "You promised me some alone time today, again, remember? Burgers on the grill, movie, Sweet Georgia Brown. . .any of this sound familiar?"

"I caught a break in the James case. I have to go. I'll be back."

"I know how this goes. You won't be back for dinner, or maybe even breakfast tomorrow. What were you talking on the holophone about?"

He sighed. "I don't have time for this."

She pulled him by the shirt and led him through the foyer into the kitchen. "Then make time, Negro. Something's not sitting right about this case. You've been obsessive and weird. It's like you're hiding something."

He wanted to tell her the truth, about Harper, Quinne, Teanna – all of it. It sounded like a foreign language inside his head only Harper and Quinne understood. "I can't tell you why. I'm not cheating, if that's what you thought."

"I never thought you were cheating!" she said, more irritated than angry. "But you're hiding something, and sometimes, that's even worse than if you were."

Damario tenderly laid his hands on hers. "I need you to trust me. I can't tell you now because I don't know everything." He reclaimed his belt. "That's the truth. I will be back – maybe not for burgers, but definitely breakfast."

"Kiss me goodbye," she said, crossing her arms.

Damario did so passionately, quickly stepping into the front room and flying out of the door. He mapped a mental shortcut to Quinne's apartment before starting the transport. With his emergency lights on, he could make up the time he spent halfway explaining things to Robinne.

He arrived at Quinne's home minutes ahead of schedule. Before he could open the transport's suicide door, Quinne bolted from the building, angrily yelling in Spanish mixed with English obscenities. When the passenger door did not open, she cut her eyes at Damario, who readily unlocked it. With one last outburst directed at the man standing in the doorway, she dropped the bag slung over her shoulder into the foot space and plopped onto the seat.

"I don't get why guys gotta be possessive. I mean, he act like I'm gonna see another guy. You've got to be like what, twice my age?"

Damario chuckled. "Something like that."

"I'm not into older guys. . .at least not that much older."

He swung into a sharp left turn to the highway. "Is there a point to this?"

"I left him. I'm gonna need help gettin' the rest of my stuff later."

"I don't do domestic calls."

"Ain't that serious," she said, clicking her teeth. "Just stay there while I get the rest of my clothes. Everything else's his."

"Stay there with my Ordnance? Sounds serious to me."

"Then forget it," she huffed. "I'll do it when he's not home, with my Ordnance."

He dialed Harper's direct line from the transport's communication module inside the dashboard. She did not answer. Instead, she sent him directions to the home's landing pad and a guest code to the security system. "Depending on how this goes, you might not be back for a while anyway."

When Damario and Quinne pulled through the gates, a charcoal grey helicopter/jet hybrid idled on a small landing pad. Though they shouted over the rotating propeller, its sound made it impossible to hear. The trio entered the cabin and strapped themselves in. Soon, they were airborne.

"Right on time," Harper mused. "I usually run late, myself."

"So, how will we catch her?" Quinne stared directly at

Damario. "We'll land, what, almost two hours after her? She could've already left."

"She's still there. My security scan updates every five minutes. Teanna's been there for an hour now and she just ordered her meal not too long ago. I have eyes at the entrance and he'll get her if he tries to leave. I told him I need some time with her before we bring her in."

"Do you think she knows Micah's whereabouts?"

"I don't know what she knows, but I'm interested in finding out." Damario unfolded a digital notepad and accessed everything the women described from their dreams. He juxtaposed theirs with his, one over the other, and would ask Teanna for any information she could offer.

After nearly a half-hour of flying, the pilot radioed for permission to land. They landed at the west side of the airport. The steakhouse where Teanna ate was located in the east branch. Once inside, Damario identified himself to an airport official and commandeered a transport normally used for handicapped passengers and their baggage. The official insisted on driving, but promised to do so as fast as reasonable to get them there.

It took ten minutes to reach the eatery section of the airport, where the trio disembarked. Damario rushed inside, with Quinne and Harper in tow. He sprung into the restaurant and breathlessly described Teanna to the bartender droid, who pointed to the barstools. *None of the women were wearing a red suit! Where is she?* Quinne and Harper stood behind him and looked at one another. The women checked both bathrooms without being asked. Damario phoned Justin Rochester, whom he had stationed at the airport's exit.

"Easy, D, I know what you're going to say."

"What am I going to say, J? You lost her?"

"I'm just forensics, dude. If you want it done better, get it on the books and not somebody off-duty."

Damario cursed. "Look, you got anything for me?"

"She got into a public serve Crown Alice with a steward named Mitchell. They're stuck in traffic headed east. Can I call it in now? At least let me call Shenk. You're freaking me out a little. Cap's going to bust a brain vessel, if he finds out what you've been doing off-hours."

*West?* "Back to the city? Can you find out where they're going?"

Damario's friend smiled. "The Exodus Foundation. You're welcome."

Though she visibly perspired, Teanna kept her jacket on, surprising Ted. If hiding her visible cleavage was her intent, she failed. After their meal, he insisted on seeing her to wherever she intended to go. She had been drinking from the plane to the steakhouse, dropped a wineglass, and gone into a trance. He assured her that anyone decent would have seen her home too.

But the address she gave to the droid was west, in the city's industrial district. *She doesn't want me to see where she lives.* He did not know of a way to look up the address in front of her without Teanna realizing his motives.

"Burning the midnight oil, huh?"

Teanna snapped free of her thoughts. "Sorry, what?"

"You're going to work after a half-day flight?"

"You do what you have to. Somebody's gotta pay the bills."

"Yeah." He eyed the colored soles of her pumps and her jeweled clutch. "What's your occupation? You never told me."

She sucked her teeth. "What's with the questions, Ted? Seriously."

Ted pointed to the trail of tail lights ahead. "We're going to be here for a while, that's all. Making conversation, just being friendly."

"Weather's crazy. The mark is up. Did you see the Dodgers game last night? That's small talk. You askin' particulars 'bout my life, and all I want is a quiet ride."

*Somebody's defensive. Maybe it's the alcohol?* Ted gestured surrender. "Just a conversation, honest."

Teanna overreacted, but it ticked her off that his tone suggested it. She did not want an honest conversation, and did not want to put forth the effort to lie. *What's he after, anyway?* She hated persistent men, especially annoying ones who talked a lot. His concern also irked her, for she did not know the reasons for it. "I work, Ted. I'm good at it and I makes money. Really, that's all you need to know. What 'bout you? Who you goin' home to, your wife? Baby momma?"

"Nobody." Ted crossed his arms and turned to the window. He stared at the picturesque landscape outside. The setting sun lit the sky with violet and tangerine undertones. Watching the reflection of the light painting the sky during flights gave him inner peace.

As he watched the panoramic view and the sun descended into the horizon, the Crown Alice began to move faster. Finally, the traffic broke and they traveled at a normal rate of speed. When he looked back at his traveling partner, Teanna gently snored. A thumb-sized, gold disk protruded from her slightly closed left hand. Ted plucked it free and read it. *We're stopping at the Exodus Foundation? She must be after that Chu character.*

"We will reach our destination in approximately five minutes," said the droid in a calm male voice. The change in volume roused Teanna. Ted flipped Chu's disk close enough to her hand that it looked like she had put it there.

Teanna blinked her eyes. "This is a luxury Crown Alice? Caribou Coffee endorsed?"

"Yes," said the droid. "That is correct."

"Large raspberry mocha, extra whip." Teanna placed her

hand over a panel and a steaming cup of light red liquid with a fluffy white crown rose to meet her palm. She blew the whipped cream back and sipped. "Mmm, sex in a cup."

"And for you, sir?"

"No thanks." He held up a hand. "Caffeine makes me jittery." He pointed to his top lip.

Teanna had relished her coffee so much that she neglected to clean the whipped cream from her lips. Before an offer to "do it for her" came from Ted, Teanna used a napkin to blot out the mess. "Thanks."

"Given current traffic conditions and our present traveling speed, we will arrive at our destination in two minutes."

"Enough, Teanna. What's with the Exodus Foundation?"

Startled with realization, she looked at the disk by her thigh. "Snoop much, Ted? God, I can't even catch sleep without you botherin' me. You really gotta know?"

"Yes," he hissed. "I really do."

Teanna punched a code into her holophone and set it to replay a downloaded news video. A small display emerged and rotated to face Ted. *This is Nora Hunter. In tonight's news, inventor, mathematician and former Exodus Foundation CEO Dr. Miles Chu is dead. Chu, whose foundation had its state funding revoked in last year's final Congressional session, was found in his home, victim to a single gunshot wound to the head. Police investigations have ruled it a homicide.*

Ted's eyes bulged. "But. . ."

"There's more." She held up a finger. "Look at the time and date stamp."

He focused his eyes on the lower right corner of the display. *Chu has been dead for days!* "I don't understand."

"That's why we're here," she said.

The transport slowed. "We have approached our destination." A thumb plate appeared on the interior of Teanna's and Ted's doors. "Your fee is 18,342 marks. Verify a funds transfer with your fingerprint. Thank you for this opportunity to service you this evening." The droid paused briefly. "Your transfer, in the amount of 18,342 marks, is complete. Thank you, Mister Adharma."

Teanna looked at Ted, whose hands rested on his knees. "You usin' fake names now? Who's Add-harm-ya?"

"What are you talking about? I didn't touch a thing."

Teanna's door raised open. The austere looking European exposed an impeccable set of teeth and reached underneath his left arm.

Ted reached across the seat and covered Teanna, shielding her from the ensuing Ordnance shots.

Upon hearing Ordnance fire, Damario raced from the ground floor area near the air tubes to where the firing originated. In front of the building, he saw a Crown Alice with one door lifted open and a smashed payment panel. Inside, a large man slumped over a woman in a red business suit.

"Officer Damario Coley, badge number 086114. Notify emergency channels," he said to the driving droid before checking the man's pulse. *Dead.* After he withdrew his hand, he touched the woman's wrist. *Alive.*

Harper and Quinne stood clear, but they were close enough to interpret the morbid scene, noticing the immediacy with which a quartet of flashing lights and blaring sirens approached. They stepped aside, quickly establishing themselves as bystanders, not witnesses.

Two black-and-white Capers parked neatly at the curb. Two droids exited the first vehicle and secured the area as a crime scene, with Madison close behind. Soon thereafter, medical droids from an ambulance converged on the bodies. Damario ducked beneath the erected laser markers with Madison following him.

"I'd expect nothing less from you on a night off." Madison smiled at him. "Couch's uncomfortable, but you can have it whenever Robbie kicks you out."

"I stumbled into this one, Maddie," he said to his partner. "Honest."

"However you want to play it. What do we got?"

"Print scans identify him as Theodore Mitchell, 37, commercial steward, no record. Shot inside the transport, while trying to shield Teanna Kirkwood."

"Wait, let me guess, that's the girl from your dreams; the Boricua in the sweats?"

He nodded.

"Surveillance?"

"Off-line in the transport. No witnesses and the record of payment's already been scrubbed. Fast and clean, for a hack job."

Madison scoped the area. Cameras inside the traffic signals had a 100-yard rotating diameter focus. Using a palm-sized surveillance device, she made a three-point figure with her thumb, index and middle finger to indicate direction. All three cameras had been disabled. "What are you doing here?"

"I needed to check something out. . .playing a wild hunch."

"If you hadn't drawn duty for that government thing, I'd put marks on you getting benched. You'd be sitting in a chair getting scanned and poked."

*No thanks,* he thought. "Forensics, got what you need?"

A droid head swiveled all the way around to face Damario. "Medical Examiner Rochester will be in touch with you, detectives." The droids filed into their Caper and drove away. The ambulance followed. The machines pronounced Ted dead at the scene, while they declared Teanna to be in critical condition.

"D, let's go. If she makes it, we'll have to question her."

"Yeah." He paused. "Harper and Quinne – they need to come with us."

Clearly, her partner had a plan. "Alright. Let's go."

Within five minutes, the solemn caravan of two ambulances and a Caper screeched to a stop in front of the hospital's emergency bay doors. Damario and Madison rushed inside behind the stretchers, validating their identity as admission tickets. Harper and Quinne remained. Nothing the officers did indicated that they should do otherwise.

"We just s'posed to sit here, Harper?" Quinne unwrapped a piece of chewing gum and folded it inside her mouth.

"Caper doors don't open from the inside – at least the ones in the back don't. So yes, Quinne, we sit here and wait." Harper folded her hands and exhaled a deep breath. "Tell me about yourself."

"Uh uh. You first."

"What do you want to know?"

Quinne loudly chomped for a few seconds. "Harper's a weird name for a chick."

"My grandfather loved this old book, *To Kill a Mockingbird*, so he named my daddy after its author. Daddy thought I'd be a boy, so he decided I'd be his junior, and couldn't be talked out of it. Harper was his name, Charlotte is hers. My middle name is Charlotte."

"Got any kids?"

"No." Her answer rang with hints of sadness. "How old are you? Planning to go to college?"

Quinne stared at the glistening condensation on the transport window. "I'll be 20 this May. Ain't goin' to nobody's college. Too expensive and pointless."

"What will you do, then?"

She clicked her teeth. "You think I'm on assistance, eatin' up your hard earned marks? When I worked, they took it outta my check, so I take it when I got to."

Harper turned her head toward the window, away from her fellow prisoner. She had never known the difficulty of juggling bills, nor would she.

Madison's shadow and the approaching taps of her work shoes against the pavement broke through the silence. A gust of cold air whisked into the transport when she opened the driver's side door and closed it after settling down onto the leather seat. This was the last place she wanted to be – babysitting Damario's merry band of amnesiacs. If he did not return in 10 minutes, she would go in. After all these years, death still did not sit right with him.

"She's in critical condition and in intensive care," said Madison with gravity.

"That don't sound good."

"It's not good, Quinne," Madison replied. "The medical droids don't expect her to survive the night."

# CHAPTER EIGHTEEN

Teanna stirred, opening her eyes to white. Any sound she might hear would be drowned out by nothingness. She stood, though no pressure or weight reported to her back, legs, or feet. The bright atmosphere yielded no sun or source of light to illuminate it. It smelled of nothing – no freshness, stale or distinctive odor. She was alone and not breathing.

"Hello?" The sound of her voice flowed from her brain, drowned in her throat, and resurfaced into the space as a gentle, unintelligible whisper. Her lips failed to move. *Am I dead?* A dozen small burns needled her skin, like a group of smokers had smudged cigarette butts onto her body. She wasn't dead, at least, not the way she imagined death to be.

Suddenly, a hand touched her skin. Stripped of the ability to move beyond the impulse to blink, she looked ahead. A handsome gentleman in a police uniform appeared in her peripheral vision. The man said something to her, but the voice rumbled like it was underwater. Whatever he said, it carried importance – like lives depended on it. He soon disappeared. In his place came an ethnic mutt of a man who looked to be of Asian ancestry. Worry lined his face in the form of crow's feet and wrinkled cheeks. Whatever concerns he had clearly brought him deep sadness.

"You've done a terrible thing," he said with compunction.

Teanna understood. His voice resonated in her ears and mind, but she could not directly provide an answer. *What I gone an' done?*

"The strongest human impulse is self-preservation." His weathered face animated with grief. "We would do anything to save ourselves, to preserve our way of life; others, not so much. You made one such decision."

Two things came to mind, both of which she regularly reminded herself to forget by burying them inside of a glass. A tinge of regret shot into her heart each time she thought about it, but she knew the risks. Without those incidents, Teanna had a shot of living a normal, healthy, productive life. Her throat and eyes swelled, sending her into a pit of swallowing blackness.

"I am Stan Witmore, of the pilot medical droid program." The mechanical head raised and adjusted so that its optical lenses were level with Damario's eyes. "Teanna Kirkwood's condition has worsened. A reaction to her anesthesia led to angioedema in her throat and eyes. We performed an emergency cricothyrotomy to give her the ability to breathe and we relieved the swelling in her eyes. She still cannot breathe on her own."

Damario hung his head. Whatever information Teanna possessed, including the identity of her assailant, would likely die with her. "Does she have a living will on record, Stan?"

"Yes, Detective. We have received it, and it will be executed according to her wishes."

"Its orders?"

"Do Not Resuscitate."

Damario held his breath. Stan rolled to the side of Teanna's bed where the ventilator and machines monitoring her vital signs were located. He imagined the android would perform a complicated operation. Instead, Stan used a mechanical digit to touch an infrared sensor to disconnect the ventilator.

The Asian man, now a shade older than he previously appeared, opened Teanna's eyes with his fingers. "You do not have much time left."

*For what? What ain't I got time for? Who are you?*

"You do not know me because I was never born. But I have my father's eyes. I had a sister once."

A slender-but-curvy girl appeared beside the man; a female young enough to be his granddaughter. The golden streaks in her hair reminded Teanna of the most beautiful sunrise she had ever seen in Japan. Tears burst from the corners of Teanna's eyes.

"Do not cry for us, dear one. You are forgiven."

Teanna regained her mobility. She tightly embraced her children. Gradually, a luminous aura surrounded the trio.

Thirty seconds after Stan deactivated Teanna's ventilator, her bandage-patched body exhaled like a deflated balloon. She lay still. The heart monitor abruptly jumped to a flatline.

Damario dropped his head in defeat and turned away. He'd lost her.

"Easy, D," said Madison, her arm wrapped around his waist. "There's nothing you could've done. Someone got to her before we did."

"I thought. . ."

"Yeah, but I thought you might need me here." *He's taking this too hard.*

Years of closely working together had endeared her to his habits following the loss of a victim. Madison was a good partner and an even better friend. "Thanks, Shenk."

"I've already requisitioned her personal effects." She clung to a clear bag and scoped it at eye level. "Nothing worth noting; a Hristoff clutch it would take me decades to afford, the usual. Makeup, birth control. . .wait." A gold, thumb-sized disk rolled down the bag's bottom seam to a corner.

Madison handed Teanna's belongings to Damario, who donned a pair of plastic gloves. He reached into the bag for the disk and held it between his right thumb and index finger. *Dr. Miles Chu/CEO Exodus Foundation.* He could not risk placing the disk into evidence and losing it via clerical error. Pocketing it would contaminate evidence and place the investigation in peril. "Jupiter's back at the James' house. Give me a lift?"

"Of course." Madison led Damario from the room and out to her Caper, where both Harper and Quinne dozed off. The sudden temperature change and the sound of the lifting and closing of doors roused them both.

"What happened?" Harper read their expressions, as did Quinne.

"Tell me you got something?" Quinne waited for an affirmative answer.

Damario thought back to the disk. "No. Nothing."

Madison witnessed her partner's dismissive face. *Why did he lie?*

En route to Harper's home, about 20 minutes away from the centrally-located hospital, Madison and Damario did not exchange words, but listened to the police scanner. *Quiet.* In their experience, peace preceded storms of relative chaos and anarchy. The white noise lulled Harper and Quinne to sleep in the backseat.

Meanwhile, Madison thought the lack of action had a chance to stick. US President Mateo scheduled a week-long talk with Italy Prime Minister Nandor Adharma. All senior officers were given some sort of street duty starting in less than 48 hours. Open cases would be moved to an "as needed" basis or, in an emergency, be handed to officers of lesser rank. If she and Damario pleaded to continue their investigations, it would have to come on the heels of concrete evidence. They had none.

In front of the entrance to the James home, Damario stirred the sleeping passengers with a gentle hand. "Harper, Quinne, we're here."

"Pull closer, Detective," Harper mumbled, while waving her hand. "The gate's sensor won't pick up my DNA markers this far away."

Quinne squinted her eyes. "This ain't my side of town."

Damario slowly directed the transport past the opening gates and around the property to where he parked. "It's Harper's. You're the next stop."

Realization evolved into panic. "I can't go back, not after today."

Harper yawned and stretched out her arms. "You don't have to. Get your things. You can stay with me tonight. Figure the rest out later."

"Why you bein' nice to me? You don't even know me."

She brushed off Quinne's suspicion. "Someone once did the same thing for me."

Madison released the safety locks on the rear doors and turned her head to face them. "Call us if you remember anything at all. We'll be in touch."

Harper and Quinne exited the vehicle. Damario moved to do the same, but Madison tugged at his jacket. "Wait, Damario. Wait a second."

He looked back. She rarely called him by name. "What?"

*You're keeping that disk? What aren't you telling me? Why won't you be honest with me?* "Headed home?"

"I need to," he said with resignation. "It'll be 11:00 by the time I get there. You said it yourself. Robinne's a good woman."

"Good night."

Madison shifted over to the driver's seat. She watched Damario hand Quinne her belongings from his transport and then she followed him as he drove through the James manse's side exit. Tempted to trail him all the way home and confront him over the missing piece of evidence, she split from him when the location of her apartment required her to take a different route.

"Why's he contaminating evidence?" she thought aloud. In all the time she had known Damario — dating back to the academy — she did not know him to act like this. He was unbalanced, distracted, and a little unpredictable. He customarily did everything by the rules and refused to turn a blind eye to misappropriations and missteps by others. *Wouldn't he want me to hold him to the same standard?*

She trusted him, unlike any other man she had ever met in her life. Damario's presence and encouragement at the academy helped convince her that she did the right thing in choosing public service over a real estate career. Besides, she could always invest or flip properties on the side.

*Whatever's he doing, I have to know.* She made a U-turn.

Damario inhaled and held his breath, but Robinne did not occupy her customary squawking perch: the cold and empty front room. Even in the midst of their worst fights, she retained a measure of composure and hospitality by piling bed sheets and a pillow on the worn armrest. Not any longer.

"Hall dim," Damario whispered. If he tripped, Robinne might wake up. But the closer he drew to the top of the staircase, he noticed a growing triangle of light. He cursed and placed his hand on the wall access panel. The bedroom door retracted. His rolling suitcase faced him on the neatly-made bed.

Robinne emerged from the bathroom with his grooming bag. "I didn't think you'd be home before midnight."

"Am I going somewhere?" he deadpanned.

"I packed enough to get you through the next few days."

"It's my house, too, Robinne. I'm not going anywhere."

Robinne's shoulders dropped. "You want to try and talk me out of my decision? We've been through this."

Damario approached the bed and lifted the envelope. "What does it say?"

"Nothing new," she shot back.

*You're a workaholic. Great with the kids. You avoid everything. Emotionally cold.* Damario sat next to the suitcase. *This won't be an easy fix,* he thought. "Listen. . ."

"Stay at a hotel on the other side of town. We can afford it."

His eyes widened. *She knows about the investment account.* "I can explain. . ."

"You've stashed away a small fortune. I knew you didn't buy those fancy shoes with overtime pay," she said, arms crossed. "After all these years, you're dirty? What've you been spending it on, strippers? Prostitutes? Another family?"

Damario licked his lips, rubbed his hands on his legs and exhaled. *I have to tell her the truth, although she won't believe it.* "I've been having dreams – the same dream – for a week. They're like intense repressed memories that I can't shake."

Intrigued, Robinne tossed the grooming bag onto the closest side of the bed and pulled up the sleeves of her white wool sweater. "Go on."

"I'm inside a round room, surrounded by equipment – like I've had an operation. I saw something like it inside a condemned building downtown, but I'd never been inside that building before in my life. But I wasn't alone. Three women were there. One of them was Harper James, and another one died tonight."

The development complicated the quick break she had planned. It explained his behavior as of late, including his obsession with the missing person case.

"The money," he said, stopping when Robinne sat down next to him and moved closer. "I play the stocks. I knew you wouldn't approve, so I borrowed some marks."

The air between them constricted. Robinne bit her lip and eyed the ceiling. *Madison.*

"Why are you always like this about her?"

Robinne faced her oblivious husband. "She's single, skinny, her butt's tight with boobs that don't sag. She flirts with you all the time, and you like it."

"Robbie."

"Robbie what?" She stood to her feet. "Look me in the eye and deny it."

In college, she and Damario were inseparable. He turned down the one threat to their relationship – a paid internship offer at G.R. Cooper – years ago. He graduated with honors and a business administration degree, while she completed her studies and the certification process for early childhood education.

Years in a dead end job and the pressure of Christian's impending birth sent Damario toward the financial steadiness and thrill of a civil service position. For the most part, Robinne dealt with the constant possibility her husband might be killed. But every once in a while, she cried in fits and experienced insomnia.

"Madison's my partner."

"I'm your partner!" she shouted back, pointing at her chest.

He knew Madison's continued presence in his life hurt his marriage more than helped it. When they met, Madison had a husband, whose chain she yanked until he divorced her. "Alright. I'll do it."

"Do what?"

"I'll request a transfer first thing in the morning," he said in a monotone.

"Don't do me any favors." Robinne leveled the suitcase to the floor. "Leave."

Believing space to be the best option, he slightly bent to kiss his wife goodbye, but she turned away from him. Irritated, he snatched the bag by the handle and left the room, pausing at the hand plate to shut the door behind him. He purposely stomped his feet down each stair and exited the home.

On the first concrete step, he deeply inhaled the crisp midnight air until his lungs burned. He could purchase a few days at the deluxe hotel where the Coleys spent their first year anniversary. He could also stay at the Four Seasons – another designer hotel where celebrities stayed – or the budget options; a Red Roof Inn, Howard Johnsons, or Microtel. He had money to burn.

Opening his holophone, he thought about calling Robinne and giving a conciliatory speech; about how he was wrong to allow Shenk to be so close to him, their flirtatious partnership bordered on adultery, and he was sorry. He'd apologize for things she regularly accused him of doing, but he did not notice himself. Closing the hidden accounts would help, and he would no longer trade.

Midway into dialing his own home number, a pair of red taillights and a trail of exhaust smoke caught his eye. He ventured down the street until the familiar license plate came into view. Smiling, he entered the street. The passenger lock clicked open and he opened the transport's suicide door. He needed a friend.

"Blinds, open 50 percent."

Gears whirred and parted the Venetian blinds enough for Robinne to watch her husband safely get into his transport. He'd sit inside of it, turn on the engine, and think about things. Then, he'd call her in a few minutes and issue a blanket apology. She'd try to play hard to get when he did and then give him the Sweet Georgia Brown. In the morning, he would request a transfer out of the precinct and all would be well.

Whenever they fought, he left their station wagon so she could shuttle the kids around without hassle. He had his police vehicle and the department did not mind him using it for personal travel, as long as he stayed inside city limits. Robinne smiled and readied herself for the house holophone to ring when a blue glow lit up the palm of his hand. Her handheld lay on the dresser. Either way, she prepared herself to hear what he had to say.

When he closed it, Robinne stopped. *Is he coming inside?* No, he headed to her left. *But why?* She rumbled down the stairs, opened the front door, and scuttled down one step from the pavement. There, she saw her husband's silhouette open a passenger side door, toss his bag into the back, and get into the transport. When it pulled onto the street, Robinne recognized the municipal license plate and cursed.

She could not get into the house fast enough. Inside, she compulsively brushed her hands through her hair and paced. *I should call him. But he's sitting next to her!*

Mind scrambling, Robinne dismissed the idea of a drink. One would smooth the edges off of her anxiety; two could put her better at ease. It had been five years. She and Damario downed shots after their graduation, and followed it with marijuana – at her suggestion. Robinne's former reputation when it came to hallucinogenic substances preceded her. But, she kicked the habit during her first pregnancy and had not sipped alcohol since.

She hated scotch, but Damario's Oban represented the only alcohol in the house. Without the kids to cling to, Robinne hurried to the kitchen before she changed her mind and poured herself a glass. The brown liquor gushed into the tumbler. She sniffed it at a last attempt to deter herself, but it failed. It burned going down her throat and warmed her stomach. A distinct, pleasantly distasteful residue remained on her tongue.

Robinne refilled her glass and drank it faster than the first. *I hate you.*

She placed the glass onto the counter and swallowed a generous swig straight from the bottle itself. *You made me do this.*

Tears burst from her eyes as she dropped to her knees, still drinking. The scotch sloppily dribbled down the sides of her cheeks, down her chin, and onto her sweater, staining it. *They've been sleeping together, probably this whole time.* She used the edge of her sleeves to blot her face and clean off the wetness from her face.

Seething with anger, Robinne screamed and collapsed into a sobbing heap on the black-and-white tiled floor.

# CHAPTER NINETEEN

*January 29, 2050*

Micah James kept the ragged sweatshirt hood pulled low over his forehead. This way, he could be unidentifiable from all distances. If anyone broached his periphery, he balled up his fists to strike first and ask questions later. The tactic served him well against the aggressive vagrants who attacked for the sake of doing it. He lost his watch and tuxedo jacket the first night he spent sleeping on the street, but gained a sweatshirt and a trenchcoat a couple of days later.

He hoped Harper had not given up on him. He lived. Sending word in any form – a holophone call or personal appearance – threatened that status. Micah suspected the police force worked to find him, but that the people after Doctor Chu would get to him first. Once he figured out what to do, he would move on it.

Each morning, he walked the streets, asking for food only when his stomach rumbled. Guilt plagued him. He and Harper possessed enough money to feed every homeless person for the next three counties. But he had to stay under the radar – not just for his sake, but for those counting on him.

At six o' clock each morning, he patronized a rescue mission on Market Street with an antique neon *Jesus Saves* sign hanging outside of it. The place served breakfast without scanning identification. Micah had cased it for days, unsure whether or not he could partake of it without being recognized or questioned.

On his first day, a cheery blonde filed past the masses and made it a point to welcome him. "Hi! My name's Crystal, but my friends call me Cee Cee."

Micah paused and stuttered until she laughed and clapped her hands.

"You don't have to tell me your name. You looked new, and I know all the regulars. Welcome to the Market Street Mission. If you need anything, ask for me."

This morning, he looked for her to ask if she could protect his lone valuable. Gradually, the line moved inside and he noticed a tuft of teased yellow hair bobbing back and forth behind the service line. Crystal smiled at Micah, and when he did not return it, she removed her gloved hands, dropped her spoon in the grits, and left. Soon, a man replaced her and did not break stride serving the men, women and children. Micah accepted hominy grits from him, but they would taste different now that Crystal no longer served them.

At the end of the line, Micah looked at his pancakes, pork link sausages, eggs, grits, and toast. He eyed a seat at his customary table and started that way until Crystal arrested him with a hand on the arm and motioned with her head that he should come with her to the back.

Micah followed her through the kitchen, around the cooks and service workers, and out the other side into a carpeted area with offices. She laid a hand on a plate outside the one labeled, *C. Cantrell.*

"Come on in," she said. "My desk is a mess, but as long as you don't mind eating on your lap, the seats are comfortable. You look like you could use a break."

Micah settled against the warm red leather and relaxed for a second before voraciously digging into his food.

Crystal folded her hands together. "Sorry to interrupt, but do you mind if I say a blessing over your food? It's something I like to do."

"Knock yourself out," he said, with a mouth full of pancake and sausage.

"Father, thank you for this food that he's about to receive. Bless Mister James that he may be fruitful, multiply, fill and subdue the earth with the gifts you have given him. In Christ's name we ask all of these things. Amen."

Micah choked at them mention of his last name. "You know who I am?"

She glanced at a framed picture on the wall. In it, Doctor Chu shook hands with a man, Micah assumed, pastored the mission. They stood beside a large ribbon in celebration of the building's opening. Crystal posed at the pastor's left side; Micah stood to Chu's right. "I never forget a face. I was so sorry to hear about his death."

"What? Doctor Chu is dead?"

"It's been all over the news. He was murdered."

His appetite quickly gave way to paralyzing fear. It started in the knot formed in his stomach and spread through his limbs. The objects in his right pants' pocket grew more burdensome by the second. *Whoever got to him might be looking for me!* "This is crazy," he managed to utter. "I don't know who to trust, or what to do."

"Maybe I can help."

"I don't see how. No prayer is going to save my life this time."

Crystal chuckled. "Close your eyes. You've trusted me this far."

Though it violated all his beliefs and scientific training, Micah complied. He listened to Crystal call out to God on his behalf. She called Him at least three different Arabic names, asked for Micah's protection and salvation, that his faith would increase, and she invoked the name of Jesus at the end.

"Amen," she said, with finality.

"Amen," he repeated. Micah's body tingled, though he had not washed his body to a large extent since Tuesday night. He shoved his right hand into his pants' pocket and lifted his plate from Crystal's desk. His appetite had returned to full strength. The knot in his stomach dissolved, though he refused to credit it to God or prayer.

"Would you call yourself an atheist, Mister James, or an agnostic?"

"Agnostic," he replied. He finished off the pancakes and moved onto the eggs. "I have doubts just like everybody else, but the questions I have, no one can answer."

"Scientists usually do," she admitted. "Doctor Chu was different. He's the only person I ever met who believed science explained acts of God instead of refuting them. Mister James, faith is all about belief without proof you can see. Most times, the proof you want doesn't exist. You have to believe, anyway. Sometimes, that's all you get."

Up for the theological challenge, Micah puffed out his chest. "That's supposed to be good enough, huh? Tell me – do you believe in time travel, Crystal?"

"I never think about it. And please, call me Cee Cee."

He ignored her. "If it was possible, would you go back to your past?"

"Uh uh." She sipped long from a cup. "The past is the *past*. No regrets."

He laughed. "You don't regret anything you've ever done?"

"I regret a lot," Crystal said. She paused and blinked hard. "But I wouldn't change it. Mister James, every day, people count on me to do what I'm called to do. If I went to my past and changed my life, I might not have been around to change theirs."

"I never thought of it that way." Micah heard a faint beeping in the room and cocked his head. His eyes scanned the room.

"I hear it, too," she said, staring at his legs. "It's coming from you."

Without pulling out both items, Micah palmed the golden thumb-segment sized disk that Doctor Chu gave him shortly before he left the Exodus Foundation a week ago. To his surprise, the sound stopped and a holographic map popped out. It highlighted an address on the other side of town. He thought the disk to be a business card or a storage device, not a homing beacon.

"I have a transport outside." Crystal gathered her belongings.

Even half asleep, Damario recognized the plush atmosphere beneath him meant Robinne had kicked him out. Their sofa was a homey-but-hardly-comfortable hand-me-down and the queen-sized mattress in their room needed replacing. He should have purchased one and taken the lecture on frivolity. Robinne preached sacrificing luxury for necessity. He respected that, but respectfully disagreed. A game-changing amount of marks collected in their account. *Shouldn't we use it?*

He cracked his eyelid open enough to see the display on his watch. *Eight o' clock?* He jerked up and checked his holophone. His wife had not called, so he dialed the house and her handheld. *No answer.* Damario shook his head. *Not yet.*

"Good morning." Madison trolled around in the kitchen. "Sorry, D. Nothing but coffee. You know how I do it."

"Yeah. That's fine." Sitting up, he folded the bedcovers she had given him and retrieved his uniform shirt from the armchair.

"Don't worry," she said, without turning around. "She's fine. She'll call."

"It's different this time." He reached his arms through the

sleeves and buttoned the shirt close to the top.

"Really? How so?"

"It's one thing about the money. The dreams were something else."

He did not mention Robinne's distaste for his and Madison's inappropriate deportment. To Madison, it was enjoyable and safe. Damario didn't expect sex after buying her a meal. He did not lobby sleazy pickup lines at her. Their partnership boiled with sexual tension. They did not need to have sex to alleviate it, though it sure tempted her. She slept on the bed's right side last night just in case.

Damario slipped on his shoes and entered the kitchen, but he stayed back from Madison and the coffeemaker. After the pot filled, she handed it over. He filled the mugs she had set aside. While he returned the glass container to its warming cradle, Madison put cream and a measured amount of sugar into one, stirred it with a spoon, and passed it to him. They stood about five feet apart and silently drank.

Madison gathered up courage. "I have to ask you something," she spat out.

"Shoot."

"Ten years, and I've never known you to contaminate a scene."

Sooner or later, he guessed Madison would bring it up. He reached into his pocket and held the disk between his thumb and middle finger. "Look at it."

Curious, Madison slid over to him and carefully plucked it away. From a distance, it appeared to be a business card or a storage device. Upon closer inspection, Madison noticed a difference in size and its uncharacteristically-warm temperature.

Damario pointed at the device. "It's a trace, Maddie. Someone's looking for Teanna Kirkwood and it wasn't her killer."

*He's right. The shots were intentionally sloppy.* "The shooter didn't remove it. . ."

". . .because he didn't know it was there," they said in tandem.

*Madison's brain sparked with realization.* "But what if you're wrong?"

The doorbell rang.

The partners looked at each other – Madison quietly back to her bedroom and Damario snuck behind the couch. She reappeared with her Ordnance. Armed with his, Damario gestured toward the door. Madison hid behind a nearby support pillar. She tapped her ear and mouthed the word *beeping.* Even a makeshift bomb would kill them both at this distance.

The doorbell chimed again.

Madison calmed herself to level the stress in her voice; the built-in safety feature would trip, if the computer sensed a threat. She trained her weapon high. Damario aimed his low. "Open front door."

The door retracted into the ceiling. A hooded vagabond froze at the threshold.

"To your knees!" Damario shouted. "Hands behind your head."

He complied, kneeling on the hallway carpet. Madison noticed his balled up right fist. "Open your right hand," she commanded. *"Slowly."*

The man moved his hand forward and produced a gold disk, similar to that of the one Damario had shown her.

Madison yanked back the hood, revealing his face. "Who are you?"

Before he could answer, Damario spoke. "Micah James."

Shocked, Madison stepped back. Damario helped Micah to his feet, escorted him inside the apartment, and closed the door. "I'm Detective Damario Coley and this is Detective Shenk. Mind if we ask you a few questions, Mister James?"

"No, not at all." Before he sat down on the white leather couch, he checked Madison's eyes for approval. "Please, call me Micah," he said after sitting down. Damario took to the armchair, while Madison stood in front of the HTV.

"Micah," said Damario. "How did you get here?"

"My former boss, Doctor Chu, gave me this." He scratched his growing mustache and produced the disk. "He asked me to keep it for him. I had no idea what else it could do until it started beeping this morning. It showed me this address."

Damario dug into his pocket and palmed the other disk. "Were you looking for Teanna Kirkwood?"

"No, but she's one of the seven."

*The seven? Me, Quinne, Harper, Teanna, and Micah — that's five. Who are the other two?* "Start from the beginning."

Just as he did with Doctor Chu, Micah played the audio from the inauguration dinner and narrated it — from Prime Minister Adharma's death to Kareza Noor reanimating the dead body. Micah stopped and waited for reactions. Both officers were struck dumb. Neither could articulate cogent thoughts. Following a few minutes of silence, he continued his explanation.

"I went back to the Exodus Foundation and Doctor Chu showed me something." Micah pulled a pair of thick-looking eyeglasses from his pocket. "When I saw it, he told me to protect myself until I could get to safety. I didn't understand. Now, I do."

"What's that?" Madison managed, pointing at the glasses.

"Doctor Chu called it a Geometric Occipital Demonstrative Symbiotic Interface."

Damario repeated the words to himself. "G-O-D-S-I. A God's eye?"

Micah dismissed the acronym. "It's retrofit to the genetic markers of seven people. I'm one of them, so is Harper. I imagine that Teanna Kirkwood's another."

"What does this God's eye show you?" asked Damario.

"It's hard-to-explain." Micah muttered. He remembered what he had seen of himself and his life with Harper, or lack thereof. "Can I use your holophone, Officer Shenk? I'd like to call my wife and let her know I'm alive."

"Sure." She pointed around the corner. "Go into the study for some privacy."

"Thank you." He got up and disappeared around the corner. Madison waited until Micah could no longer hear them talk.

"I thought you'd be relieved. Micah James is alive."

"But it doesn't solve anything. A zombie assassin running Italy?"

"D, listen. . ." Madison noticed that Micah left the God's eye and his homing device next to her on the couch's cushion.

". . .masquerades as a transient and reappears with a . . . whatever it does?"

"Here." She placed the glasses and disk onto Damario's lap. "On each arm, look: a circular groove. Try fitting the disks in them. That might be how it works. He needed both to make it work. Chu gave him one and Teanna got the other."

Damario fiddled with the objects until they slid into place and the power activated. He glanced at his partner, who gave him a nod of approval. After a small hesitation, he put the arms behind his ears and rested the device on his nose's bridge.

In what seemed like seconds later to Damario, a firm hand shook his right shoulder. He jolted with a start and removed the God's eye.

"D," Madison said with caution. "You're alright. You were out for 45 minutes. I was about to call the hospital, but Micah insisted that you would be fine."

Damario flexed his right arm before gently fingering his right eyelid. Madison looked the same, except her hair measured considerably longer than what he had just seen. His wedding ring was plain yellow gold, not diamond-studded platinum, and he was a policeman, not a budding financier. Though now, his stock success made sense. He looked over at Micah James, who wore a knowing expression.

"No, Officer Coley, you didn't see an alternate reality. You're living in one."

When Damario returned home, he halfway expected his children to mob him, thrust themselves upon his legs, and insist that he hoist them into his arms. Christian and Gabriel's presence calmed both him and his wife following the heat of battle, and the couple tended to more readily compromise and agree once their tempers cooled. This one was different. The children were still with their grandparents.

"Robbie?" From the bottom of the staircase, he noticed the light from their bedroom and detected the scent of liquor. *Worse than I thought.* "Robbie?"

He treasured every drop of that blended scotch, and intended it to last him at least until the end of this year. Before now, it could have happened; Robinne stopped drinking altogether in '45. To that point, the home-schooling mom handled sobriety like a professional, and though Damario shunned drinking beer in her company, she waved it off. "I can handle it," she'd say, and she did.

Damario searched the old hiding places. If he found another bottle underneath the sink, she wanted to get caught. Liquor stored in washed-out cleanser containers equaled *trouble.* He searched the pantry, refrigerator, cabinets, laundry room and trash and found nothing but his empty scotch bottle rinsed clean in the recycling bin. As he journeyed up the stairs, Damario improvised his story. If he told her about time travel and alternate realities, it could push her over the proverbial cliff.

"Robbie?" From the doorway, she appeared an absolute wreck. On the edge of their bed in a white cloth bathrobe, Robinne hung her head down to her chest. A white bucket sat between her legs. A bird's nest of uncombed hair exploded from her head and her chocolate skin glistened with beads of sweat.

"Hey stranger," she weakly responded. Talking increased the pounding and spinning.

He tiptoed closer. "Need water?"

"No," she said, steadily breathing. "Got some."

He eased onto the mattress, so it did not bounce. "So. . ."

"No steps, alright? Sponsor's been called."

He thought back to the irony of the 100-year-old Christmas gift from Madison. So that he could keep it, he lied and told Robinne that Justin Rochester from forensics pulled him in Secret Santa. Rochester sampled alcohol almost as often as he picked up one-night stands. Another secret he and Shenk shared played a part in this. "I should've gone with my first mind and given it back."

Robinne licked her dry lips. "I called Madison last night."

Damario's heartbeat quickened. *Did she call her drunk? What did Madison tell her?* He said nothing. The scotch lie was the least of his worries.

Robinne lifted her red eyes and looked at her husband. "I told her our take on things. You're transferring. You need a different partner. She was a woman about it."

*Our take?* "About what?" His voice rocketed in pitch.

"Her feelings for you."

His body stiffened with panic. "I didn't sleep with her. . .ever."

"She said you're best friends. You'd never transfer. Not even if I begged you."

That much was probably true, but Damario gave his wife room to further explain. "We're in the middle of a big case, Robbie, a game changer."

Robinne tenderly scratched her head. "That'll always happen.

Something has to die, Damario. If I start drinking again. . .the doctors said it'll be me."

Damario remembered the grim diagnosis after her C-section to deliver Gabriel. Years of indulgence in foreign substances stressed her body to the brink of organ failure. "We can get through this, Robbie. Just give me a week. One week."

"No," she forced out. "I need a divorce."

# CHAPTER TWENTY

Harper's insides leapt with joy when Micah called that morning. *He's alive!* Happy to be wrong, she packed him a change of clothes, deodorant, a blade and shaving cream, toothbrush and a travel-size of toothpaste. She immediately alerted a still-sleeping Quinne to the development. "Quinne, *Micah is alive.* Get up and get dressed."

"Huh? Yeah." Her head stayed underneath the heavy 800-thread count quilt.

"What do you want for breakfast? Order anything you want."

"Huevos rancheros," Quinne blurted, finally pulling the cover down. "Anything?"

Harper shook her head and rolled her eyes. "Just tell the service droid and be downstairs in 15 minutes. It'll take us awhile to get across town."

As she descended the winding staircase, Harper thought that Quinne may take her time. Each guest room connected to an in-suite bathroom and the deluxe showerheads sprayed streams from multiple directions. The shiatsu setting would massage the sore leg muscles Quinne pulled during her run yesterday.

"Good morning, Missus James," said the female droid. "What will you have?"

"Eight-ounce Blue Mountain, black with sugar. Two slices of light toast, buttered; two poached eggs and a turkey sausage link."

"As you wish."

Harper trailed the droid into the kitchen, where the breakfast nook bathed in natural morning sunlight. She chose to sit in her customary chair across from Micah's, which faced the holovision. No need to see depressing news reports. *Micah's safe.*

Minutes later, when breakfast had finished cooking, Harper spent extra time saying grace. "Thank you for saving my husband," she prayed. "Thank you for keeping him safe. Thank you for our life together. Thank you for how You've blessed us. Thank you for this food, and may You be blessed in our eating and drinking. Give peace to the Kirkwood and Mitchell families in their time of mourning. In Jesus name, I pray. Amen."

Harper started eating, and she had finished about half of her plate when Quinne entered the kitchen, unloaded her duffle bag from her shoulder, and sat in Micah's chair. Bare-faced and wearing a black rock t-shirt and tight jeans, Quinne looked young enough to pass as a preteen.

"Good morning, Quinne."

"Good morning." She stretched out her arms and folded them down when the droid approached with a plate of food. "Huevos rancheros, a four-ounce Kobe steak, and hash browns. Coffee with cream and sugar and freshly-squeezed orange juice."

Quinne blushed at her order and now felt compelled to eat it all in a hurry. Being at the James' house certainly beat life with her paranoid ex-boyfriend.

"Kobe beef? We have an ambitious one here."

"Sorry. You said anything."

Harper giggled. "It's fine. Everybody does that the first time. Did you rest well?"

The quip put Quinne at ease. "Best in years."

"Good. Eat up. We have a busy day ahead of us."

Madison tried to distance herself from the insanity surrounding her partner, but found herself sucked into it. Though they had solved one case by finding Micah James, two more cases – the

Kirkwood/Mitchell double murder and the Noor death/ transference – unraveled. Damario put on the God's eye, passed out for 45 minutes, and had recently awakened. Now, he looked at her, as if something about her had changed.

"To understand what I'm about to tell you both, you have to accept two things." Micah leaned forward on the chair's cushion. "One: time travel is possible."

*Scientists had been trying.* "Alright," Damario relented. "What's the other?"

"Two: five people were sent back in time and you were one of them. I'm not one of them, which is why I know the world, as we know it, never existed as it is right now."

Madison interrupted. "What happened to change it?"

"Doctor Chu worked on a hypothesis called the Sixth Equation. He theorized that the traveler had a one-way ticket back in time. Whatever he changed about his world, he would live through it in an alternate quantum reality – a world of his own creation."

Damario wrung his hands. "So, Chu's responsible for all of this?"

"No. His theory lacked method. There's something else you should know."

Madison's doorbell rang. She kept her Ordnance at her side and held her finger to her lips. She carefully approached the front of the apartment and eyed the peephole. Quinne and a jittery Harper waited on the other side. Madison opened the front door, and Harper almost knocked her down while running to her husband. Though Micah smelled terribly, she jumped into his lap and smothered him with kisses.

"I can't believe it," she said between smooches. "You're alive! Where have you been? Why didn't you come home?"

"It's a long story, Harp, but I'm here." He pushed back a little. "Officer Shenk, if you don't mind, I'd like to. . ."

"Come with me; I'll get you a towel and a washcloth." Micah accepted the bag of clothes and toiletries from his wife and followed Madison to the guest bathroom.

Harper watched Micah go and wanted to join him, just to be in his presence again. She brightly smiled at Damario, who she credited with the reunion. "Thank you, Officer Coley, for whatever you did to get him back. I can't ever repay you."

Damario's countenance fell. "I didn't do anything, Harper."

"But you did. You pushed through, even when it looked like he might not ever come back, and there were no clues to where he'd gone. I don't know what I would've done without him, Officer. So, you see, I'm in your debt and owe you gratitude."

"Excuse me." Damario walked over to Madison. "I need to go home and talk to Robbie, catch a shower, and get some breakfast."

Harper's eyes widened. "Seriously, now? You can't wait an hour?"

"I gotta clear my head, Maddie. All this is too much."

She sighed. "Go outside then. Get some air. Call the station and check in, then hit up Robinne, patch things up, and come back inside. I'll order food."

"Alright," he relented. Madison watched him go until he reached the elevator tubes. Damario casually saluted her before dropping out of sight.

After securing the door, Madison returned to the living room. A laughing Harper pushed Quinne's shoulder.

"Your husband – he smells like old meatloaf and hot trash."

"You see," she cackled. "He'll come out a new man."

Madison skirted the two and sat next to the God's eye. She handled the glasses with care and set them on her lap. *I wonder if I can see through them?* While the two joked, she put them on her face. A flurry of images flashed before her eyes.

"Stop!" Micah shouted. Groomed and dressed in a maroon

sweater, black dress slacks and loafers, he reclaimed the God's eye from Madison, who blinked a few times to allow her eyes time to adjust to the light.

"Easy, honey." Harper watched Madison's face for signs of trouble. "It looks like she's okay. Besides, she wasn't asleep for long. Are you alright, Officer Shenk?"

"Y-yes. I'm fine."

"This isn't a toy, Officer Shenk. It's DNA-specific technology!" Micah shook the glasses. "It's only coded for seven people. You could've been seriously hurt, or killed."

"Take it easy, man," Quinne interjected. "She ain't worse for wear."

Micah reared around, ready to launch into Quinne, but stopped short. "Sorry. . .I just didn't know if Doctor Chu programmed a trap into the code. Did you see anything?"

She definitely shook her head and averted her eyes. "Nothing but a bunch of images I didn't understand. Tell them what you started telling us, Micah."

He explained the absolutes they had to accept: the Sixth Equation and the alternate lives they now led. Harper volunteered to be the next to go. Micah reluctantly handed her the God's eye, settled down on the couch next to her, and held her hand.

Damario fought the temptation to start Madison's police transport and drive straight home. Rather, he dialed the home number and waited. Robinne's voice interrupted the automated voicemail message. "Hello," she slurred.

"Robbie? Are you alright?"

"Fine. Tired. What's up?"

The long pauses between words put him on guard. "You never called your sponsor and got into the Oban again?"

"Mmm. . .not much gets past you, Detective."

Apparently, his wife's bend toward addictive substances extended to both realities. She skipped anesthesia during childbirth, shunned caffeine, and barely took aspirin because of it.

"Come home," she implored from beneath a frazzled mess of scattered hair. "Take care of me."

Understanding time travel posed a problem to the sober, much less than the inebriated. "Wish I could, but I can't right now. I'm on the job. I'll be home later."

Robinne edged her body to the end of the mattress and belched. "Enjoy it?"

"I didn't sleep with Madison, Robbie."

"Might as well."

Frustrated, Damario breathed deeply and counted down from five. "You have the kids?"

"Mom and Dad's." Robinne retched and threw up into whatever receptacle she stationed underneath her head. Before she did so a second time, Damario disconnected the line.

He couldn't tell her what he had seen. *Back in college, I received my internship offer, accepted it, and went east. We broke up. I became a successful executive at G.R. Cooper and married Madison. You'd be a strung out drug addict. Madison would've cheated on me with Justin and I lose an arm and an eye in a crash.*

He imagined a coherent Robinne dismissing the explanation as an insult to her intelligence. An affair, switch of sexual orientation, or a drug-running operation would be an easier sell. She'd accuse him of making up an excuse to skirt around the truth.

*I really married Madison?* Since they met at the academy, they carried an underlying attraction for one another. *But enough for marriage?* He doubted it. A lack of substance to build a foundation beneath the chemistry explained why he divorced her; that, and the fact she cheated on him multiple times. This Madison possessed a healthy libido of which she had a tendency to share too much about, but she did not crave it. *Why did that marriage fail? Why did this marriage fail?*

After a quick check-in phone call to the precinct captain, Damario left the transport in the parking lot and walked back into the building. By the time he exited the elevator tubes and Madison let him in, he assumed they all had used the God's eye. Harper cried uncontrollably and Micah consoled her. Quinne had been crying, but stifled any more tears by blinking and swiping tissue underneath her nose. Madison appeared affected by the somber scene – sympathy and not empathy. Damario would never tell her that they had been married in another timeline.

No one compared notes, but merely processed their alternate lives. Harper leaned on Micah's shoulder for strength. *This life is something. We dodged a lot of pain by choosing it. But you don't play God without consequences.*

Quinne sniffled. *They got the American Dream. E'erythin' you could possibly want and, if they ain't got it, they can buy it. That's power. Can't believe I lost Troy and our baby, and here I am. Can't hardly stand him.*

Harper swooned when her husband touched her face. *I'd trade all the money we have for the one thing I can't have. Girls, women get pregnant every day accidentally on purpose. No matter what I do, my child is stuck in that world and my money in this one. A child from my body, and from his. Our son.*

Damario stared at Madison, whose eyes gazed back with quiet tenderness. *We were married. Robinne got addicted to drugs, and I lost my arm and eye. You cheated on me with Justin. Why? Could we have made it work? Did I give up too soon?*

Madison looked away, unable to sustain the connection. *It's me. Something's wrong with me – not Robinne, not Damario, but me.*

"Why'd you show me this, man? Huh? My current life ain't screwed up enough without somebody tellin' me how screwed up it was somewhere else?" Quinne visibly trembled and cursed.

"Who did this to me? And what we gonna do 'bout it?"

"Do you have a computer, Detective?"

Madison retrieved it from her bookshelf. "Who doesn't?"

"Everyone, one-by-one, tell me what you saw. We'll compare notes."

The trio told the less personal aspects of their stories. Micah scribed them on a stand-alone holographic display, and interpolated images from the God's eye. All of them had memories of the round room. Through the interface with the police department's facial recognition software, Micah discovered the identity of the woman that all of them mentioned; a far younger version of Kareza Noor. She strongly resembled the woman Damario kissed, Quinne's public defender advocate, the CEO of the Genesis Institute where Harper worked, and the guest host on the forum talk show he'd seen

"Kareza Noor is the key?" Harper's brow furrowed. "But she's dead."

"No," said Damario. "Not necessarily."

# CHAPTER TWENTY-ONE

Aboard Air Force One en route to the west coast, Nandor Adharma celebrated by drinking a flute of 1907 Heidsieck. Little about the human experience pleased him besides culinary pleasures. He relished the tenderness of a medium rare prime rib cut wading in a cesspool of au jus and blood. Prior to his indoctrination into mortal culture, he brutally killed to see it.

After all, the former manner dictated animal sacrifice. Following the completion of the old order, however, such offerings were deemed unnecessary – and the blood of his replacement did nothing to satisfy that appetite.

Sitting adjacent to Adharma, Ramsey Mateo, the newly-elected President of the United States, anticipated a return to his home state for a few days. There, he and Adharma would broker Palestinian and Israeli peace talks over a centuries-old problem: the restoration of Israel's Biblical borders. Adharma convinced the two to momentarily stand down, long enough to join him and Mateo on neutral ground away from the White House. In two days, the conference would take place at Camp Bradley, a presidential retreat near the White Mountain range. Adharma promised him that a peace treaty of no shorter than seven years would "revolutionize the world, as you know it."

Mateo powered down his projection computer and tapped his fingers against the arm rest. Adharma sipped his champagne and hummed an upbeat tune. The president cleared his throat and the head of state still ignored him. "Nandor?"

"What?"

"Preach about goodwill and the advantages of foreign policy, if you want, but the Palestinians will never go for this."

"We've been over this, Ramsey. They can't afford to keep killing each other; isn't that why your government cut off aid? Swift, decisive action brings definitive, measurable results. Flip-flopping gets you nowhere."

The foreigner made sense. America's conversion to marks and its reluctance to aid Israel brought the countries to the table in the first place. The terms were simple; declare a seven-year armistice, during which both countries must switch to the mark and restore Israel to its pre-partition boundaries.

Palestinians and Israelis would share the land and live in peace. In turn, Italy and the United States agreed to pump billions into the area over a decade and fund research methods to make the desert land arable. The reunited Israel nation would then grant drilling rights to its benefactors.

On paper, Adharma's proposal heavily favored the Israelis, but he insisted the parties would sign. Among his more ridiculous assertions: the Arabs would permit a ceremonial rebuilding of King Solomon's temple northeast of the Dome of the Rock.

"Mark my words," Adharma claimed with assurance, touting his maternal Jewish heritage. "It'll happen."

Mateo disagreed. Religious fundamentalists were serious about their beliefs. They battled hard against his campaign of unity, and they planned to do so for his '51 reelection campaign. The fiftieth sitting chief executive and the first full-blooded Hispanic was also the first avowed atheist in the nearly 300-hundred-year-old country.

"If this deal goes down, you will be remembered in the annals of history, Ramsey." Adharma swished the alcohol around in his mouth and swallowed.

"What about you, Nandor? What's your motivation?"

He smiled. "All I want for this world is the right leadership."

Since late that afternoon, when she and Micah returned from Detective Shenk's apartment, Harper soundproofed the bedroom. With her room stationed at the back of the palatial second floor, Quinne did not have a prayer of hearing them no matter what the couple did. Still, she did not want their reluctant houseguest to be mortified by intimate sounds of passion, should she stop by for any reason.

In truth, she and Micah spent a handful of time being physical with one another. Even during their lovemaking, she could tell his thoughts preoccupied him. Whenever he and Doctor Chu worked on a project – which he finally revealed as the Sixth Equation – she could tell. Two-thirds of his attention went to involuntarily calculations. Whatever he did at the moment occupied the free third. He wanted to figure a way out of this alternate reality mess. Micah thought he could do the same with Harper's infertility. But, the problem with no clear mathematical answer had odds stacked in the wrong direction.

After dinner, the Jameses retired to their room and Quinne to hers. Harper slipped into a comfortable peach nightgown. Micah wore cozy, wool grey pajamas. He crawled into bed beside Harper and kissed the pillows. "Oh, I missed you!"

Harper's giggles waned into curiosity. "What's it like – living on the street?"

Micah's eyes rolled back, as if the memories were distant. "Hell."

"Mike. I'm so sorry."

He snuggled up to her shoulder and laid his head down. "How was it, with me gone?"

"Same." She kissed his forehead. "There's one thing I keep wondering, though."

"What?"

"Why us? There's trillions people on the earth to send back. Why me? Why Quinne, and Teanna, and Officer Coley?"

"I'm not sure."

His voice trailed off, which meant Harper had a third of his attention. "What's on your mind?"

"Harp, I met someone at the shelter, and something she said stuck with me. She said maybe science does not refute God, but supports God. That's interesting."

Stunned that her husband said the word, "God," Harper perked up. "Continue."

"Micah played us an audio recording of Kareza Noor killing the Prime Minister of Italy and then inhabiting his body. If humans have a sort of invisible essence, it makes scientific sense that two essences cannot occupy one space. But if she can transfer her essence to someone else, she's clearly inhuman."

*Is he talking about spirits?* "Okay."

"Time travel is impossible and God doesn't exist. I believed that a week ago."

Harper stifled her building excitement. "And now?"

Micah turned contemplative. "I'm not so sure. What am I supposed to do when the proof I'm looking for doesn't exist?"

"Sometimes, baby, you have to believe anyway."

Crystal told him the exact same thing. *Had they talked?* "You miss them, don't you?"

"Who?"

"Gabrielle and Christian."

Harper bit her lip and stared at her stomach. "It didn't escape my attention that Officer Coley's children have almost the same names, if that's what you mean."

"It's not your fault, Harp, or mine. It's just the cards we were dealt."

The explosion of the abortion clinic played over again in her mind. "No, Mike, it's not. I traded in my hand, remember? Now, I can't have children."

"We discussed this. We can adopt, get a surrogate. . ."

Harper shook her head. "It's not the same. I wanted our baby – in my body."

"And you think we can't because you presumably went back in time?"

"You don't play God without some kind of consequence, Mike. We have to fix this."

Set to disturb the married couple, whom she imagined were carrying on like newlyweds behind closed doors, Quinne hesitated. *It can wait.* She padded down the carpeting back to her assigned room and laid face down on the bed. The luxurious life of comfortable mattresses and service droids suited her, but she could not stay forever. If Anibel welcomed her back home, could she tolerate the signs of the cross and routine dousing of holy water?

It beat the alternative. Troy monitored her coming and going unless she snuck out while he slept. Without prior approval for an excursion, she anticipated a shouting match or, at worst, a punch into the drywall. She promised to leave him for good if he did, but didn't.

Unaware of how the others processed their alternate lives, Quinne genuflected before hers. She did not believe in God's will and mandate over her life; that meant she did not control her life. She liked the idea of destiny knitted with the law of attraction. Attract positive things to yourself with good thoughts. Weave enough optimistic vibes together to form a desirable destiny. In either world, she failed. Troy and their baby died in one reality and he threatened the baby out of her in this alternative version.

The painful, messy miscarriage passed without further incident. He never knew.

The thought of joining the military arose before, but Troy pushed it out of her mind. She needed to be there for him, and whatever he intended to do as an "entrepreneur." He never sold anything after drugs, which he quit after another dealer got shot on Troy's run. His death rattled Troy's core enough for him to drop the drug game. Afterwards, he did nothing but piecemeal jobs that paid under the table, sleeping when he did not work or harass Quinne.

As Harper granted Quinne voice authorization to use the house's amenities, she put up a soundproof barrier. The last thing she wanted was for her hosts to hear a mix of yelling and cursing. Troy deserved the piece of her Puerto-Rican mind she reserved for special occasions.

On the fifth ring, Troy answered the call on audio only. "Who's this?"

"Q."

His surroundings audibly shifted. "Where you at?"

Though she trembled inside, Quinne gathered up courage. "Out. Across town."

"Across town? When you comin' back?"

"Never," she said with extra emphasis on the word's second syllable.

"Catch you at Anibel's, then."

The gusto in his assurance appalled her. If he did come after her, she had packed something in her bag for him. "Ain't goin' there neither." Troy cussed her without pause until Quinne interjected. "Why I gotta be all that?"

"What you gonna do without me, Q? Join the army?"

*I'm a good enough shot for it.* "Wasn't doin' nothing with you. Can't be too bad off without you."

He huffed. "So, why call – 'less you thinkin' 'bout comin' back?"

She thought for a second. "Somethin' you need to hear."

Suddenly, the holograph of Troy popped up. He stared into Quinne's eyes. "What'chu gotta say?"

"I'm better than this, better than you."

He wagged his index finger back and forth. "No you ain't and you know you ain't. You sayin' that 'cause you think that's what you're supposed to say."

"Troy, you. . ."

"Forget all that, Q. Army. . .it ain't for you to do. Come back here, where you belong, with me."

"Stop it. Just. . ."

"Won't hit you again, promise. We belong together."

Whatever happened, she did not belong to Troy in two different realities. Her composure faltered. "You owe me your life! That's s'posed to be you in the ground, not your boy. I saved you."

Opposition brimmed at Troy's lips, but Quinne cut him short. "I saved you and you did this. You killed the one good thing to come outta us. You did that, Troilus, and he ain't do nothin' to you but be conceived.

"One night, you did runs. Never came home." Quinne's voice wavered. "Right there, on the kitchen floor. . .by myself. You ain't care, couldn't care. All that mattered to you's-you, and what you ain't got or couldn't get. It ain't always 'bout you, Matter-of-fact, it ain't never 'bout you."

Troy's thumb blotted a tear before it passed far down his cheek. Quinne was always outspoken, but more foot-high soapbox than cresting mountaintop of fury.

"However you got another chance, you got it. Do somethin' with it."

"Sound like you been hangin' out with Anibel. You got religion now?"

Quinne's face softened. "Purpose."

Early Sunday morning, still reeling from his wife's emotional disintegration, Damario arrived at the downtown precinct. The California king bed inside the hotel room offered unlimited comforts; adjustable softness, 800-thread-count sheets.

When he did shut his eyes, frames of the altered past slid past his consciousness. Like an outsider, he bore witness to the best days of his post-graduate career in finance. He married Madison and never remembered seeing her so finely coiffed. *Why would I leave a past like this?*

He woke up and remembered the reasons. Though partially detached to the experiences – believing it as truth based on evidence he could not verify – he had definite opinions on the subject of marital infidelity. *How do you erase intimacy – intentional, raw, naked intimacy?*

Of course, he faced temptation like any other red-blooded married man. Robinne knew of his appreciation for women of different ethnicities and she did not attack the quiet fascination when he saw one. He operated respectively; glancing, not staring, no touching or verbal comments. Merely a wisp of recognition and the lingering memory of beauty. A mental, emotional, or spiritual barrier existed between him and adultery. Madison did not have that block; in that reality or this one. He divorced her because of it, and her other husband – in this world – did the same.

Damario stood at the corner of her desk until she moved a chipped Superman relic of a mug with a light brown drink in it toward him.

Madison's hands glided over her desk console. "I question your sexuality every time I buy this drink for you. Don't worry, it's nuclear hot."

He smirked. "Perfectly acceptable for a grown man, heterosexual or not, to enjoy a latte made with two-percent milk and no whipped cream." He sniffed the hot liquid. "Let's talk, Shenk. . ."

"Nothing to talk about."

They would talk about it, but not *now*.

"We've been assigned to the Camp Bradley motorcade."

Escorting four heads-of-state, which included President Mateo and the heads of two warring Middle-East factions, was an honor. Though Mateo invited the parties together, Italian Prime Minister Nandor Adharma would grease the wheels toward reuniting Israel and brokering peace. Damario, however, viewed it as political posturing.

"I'm supposed to think this is a big deal, aren't I?"

Madison eyeballed him. "Forgot. You've been stuck on another planet."

"Reality, not planet."

"Whatever. I know Mateo is hosting this thing at Camp Bradley, but if you ask me, and pretty much anybody with a pulse, the Italian guy's coming out roses in all this."

"You know he's not really Italian – not a full one, at least. He's Moroccan, and part Jewish, or something."

"His reputation stands the most to gain. And you, the mark is going to go up a couple hundred percent, at least. You have to like that."

The thought dropped weight in his heart. He understood it from a perspective; slashing the federal deficit by cutting foreign aid in exchange for drilling rights without the risk of armed conflict. Something indistinct about the business unsettled him. "I guess. I don't trust politicians. Never did."

"Well, like them, you're not stuck in the lower 75 percent tax bracket with us peons. Lose your job tomorrow and you're good. It's a 90 minute drive, tops; three hours round-trip. No sweat."

Damario rounded Madison's desk for his own adjacent to it and placed his coffee on the tempered glass corner reserved for it. With a swipe of his hand, he opened his official orders. Each assigned officer would be paired with a droid and join a 25-transport processional from Metro airport to an area surrounding Camp Bradley. Only the pilot vehicle possessed point-to-point direction, and the president's private detail handled that.

He sat down in his desk chair and gulped. "No sweat. Just fending off terrorist threats, assassins, random crazies. . ."

"Hasn't been an attempt at that in 30 years. You won't lose a limb, I promise."

Damario coughed. "What'd you say?"

Madison looked confused. "What? The last assassination attempt?"

"No. After that."

"What's the big deal?" she covered.

"Nothing," he said, with her response fresh in his mind. "Nothing at all."

She hopped up, grabbed Damario's hand, and dragged him to an empty interrogation room. After darkening the one-way window and disabling the sound and recording devices, Madison cornered him against the wall. "Talk."

He pointed at her face. "You saw through the God's eye. Why'd you lie?"

"Didn't like what I saw," she said, backing away. Madison wanted so badly to question him about his emotions. He possessed them, on *some* level. Otherwise, why would he have married her in a different reality? *Why didn't you tell me?*

He read her darting eyes. "I didn't see the point," he said under his breath.

She thought if she had not cheated on him in the other reality, in a warped way, he would have been hers in this one, too. She chewed her lip to keep from saying something that she would later regret. "Has Micah figured out a way back?"

"Don't know. Don't care."

"Why not?"

His look said it all. "Whenever you go back to something, it's never the same."

"I get it. Leave your wife for the woman who cheated on you in an alternate reality? I get it. I wouldn't do it, either." Madison's voice quavered.

"It's not like that, Maddie. . .not really."

"Then, what's it like, Damario? Spell it out for me. What's it like?"

He knew what he wanted to say. "It's not that you're unattractive."

She knew that, as she found him staring at her on a number of occasions – especially in casual clothes. It did not give her hope, but merely attention that she liked. Madison wanted him to continue and say the things she always hoped to hear from a man. Desire was never the problem. Plenty of men desired her. But none wanted her heart. Damario had the capability to do so. She knew it.

"You're more to me than a partner, a friend. You're my *best friend.*" Damario stepped to the side.

"Do you love me, or even like me D? Make my life and tell me that you do."

"You don't get it, Shenk." Damario's handheld holophone rang from his pants' pocket. It was an alarming ringtone he assigned to all members of their little group. To Madison's behest, he answered the call. "Micah?"

"Officer Coley, Officer Shenk." The holograph of the man saluted them with eye contact. "I accessed everything viewed on the Geometric Occipital Demonstrative Symbiotic Interface."

"Go on." Madison blinked away the extra moisture at her eyes.

"I think I know why Kareza Noor sent us back."

# CHAPTER TWENTY-TWO

*January 30, 2012*

Damario hushed all talk of the altered present until he and Madison could join Micah, Harper, and Quinne at the James homestead. Separated by a couple of feet, the partners filed paperwork, answered questions, and handled routine tedium from their desks.

When Damario shut down, Madison used the silence to think. Years ago, she pursued, arguing her perspective point-by-point. Damario ignored her, or did a convincing job faking amnesia. If she unraveled all of her confusing emotions, he'd never hear them. Ignorance scored far worse on her card than apathy or rejection.

Following four hours of intense concentration to avoid his partner at all turns, Damario eyed the time. "Shenk."

Madison's hands rummaged across her desk. "Meet you outside." She watched him exit the precinct. *What do I do?* Happily or unhappily, Damario and Robinne had been together for the better part of a decade. People control what attracts them and who they love; she believed that. But she did not care to control it. Robinne always knew, and Madison regretted playing a part in driving Missus Coley out of sobriety. Hiding her eyes behind fancy sunglasses, Madison exited the building and entered Damario's police transport at the front curb.

Once she closed the passenger door, Damario pulled away. Several times, he stopped short of saying anything because it would not improve the situation. Lust or love – he could not validate or return it. They shared a spark. Properly kindled and flush with fuel, sparks ignite into fire. He owed it to God and his wife to give the marriage another chance, didn't he?

He considered that Robinne kicked him out under mental and emotional duress, and she mentioned divorce. She sounded resolute. Could she be serious? Resolution did not equal filing. And even without contest, the process would take months. Space to reassess and time apart afforded Damario the opportunity to handle this time travel/alternate-reality nonsense, uninterrupted.

*Would I go back?* He gave it a second thought. Sacrifice his right arm and eye to become a divorcé and a quarter-machine? He enjoyed his life here and, though his level of income did not touch that of his former self, he could continue to trade. Unlike there, the problems he and Robinne had were mountable obstacles. On the other hand, could he forgive Madison for sleeping with Rochester? It took all Damario's resolve not to hit the man this morning when Rochester brought up the score of last night's Lakers game.

"Penny for your thoughts?" Madison expected him to ignore her offer.

"The future, the past, the alternate – why us? Why Teanna and Harper. Why Quinne?"

"I don't know."

He turned the wheel right and stopped in front of the house's main gate. "Out of ten billion people on earth, Maddie. I just don't get it."

"Micah will clue us in."

The two parked in front of the mansion and were welcomed inside by Harper before they had the opportunity to ring the doorbell. She escorted them to a sprawling living room with a taupe leather sectional couch and a hand-knit maroon throw rug on the ebony hardwood floors. Thick golden curtains prevented the mid-afternoon sunlight from entering the soundproofed room. Damario chose to sit next to Quinne, and Madison did so across from him next to Harper. Quinne observed the awkwardness between the two and watched them both for clues as to what it could be.

Wearing specialized gloves, Micah pulled up a three-dimensional holographic screen and accessed a file folder marked *GODSI*. "Last night, I reverse engineered the Geometric Occipital Demonstrative Symbiotic Interface enough to access its residual memory. It stored our realities, including Teanna's, which she did not live to see."

Curious, Madison waved her hand. "How does it work?"

"It accesses part of your brain, converts the electrical impulses and plays it as a series of quick-moving images. Doctor Chu designed it to go hand-in-hand with a pill you ingest before using the G.O.D.S.I.

"The drug is an analgesic, anesthetic and stimulator. The stimulator allows you to process the information at that rate and the analgesic and anesthetic prevent the pain. Without it, the G.O.D.S.I. renders the user unconscious for an undetermined amount of time." Micah kept the other potential side effects to himself; without everyone's participation, the truth would never be known.

"You said you know why we were sent back, and you have a plan?"

"Yes, Officer Coley." Micah switched displays with a twitch of his hand. "However she did it, Kareza Noor sent us back to different points in time. Officer Coley, you went back 13 years, to 2037. Harper, 15 years, to 2035. Teanna went to 2033, and Quinne, you went back to 2048.

"That's almost 50 years altogether and then some – which may be the age difference between the Kareza Noor of our former reality and the one who just died. I'm guessing she was near death, which explains why she jumped bodies."

Quinne shook her head after hearing the explanation another time. "Still don't make no sense."

"But why did she do it?" Damario's legs and hands tensed.

"Tomorrow, Nandor Adharma, President Mateo, the acting prime minister of Israel and the president of Palestine will meet to discuss a landmark peace treaty."

"Yeah," Madison assented. "We know that. We're on duty for it."

"Good." Micah smiled with pleasure. "Then you can help."

Harper knew what her husband said thus far, but this revelatory announcement caught her off-guard. "Help do what?"

"Kill Nandor Adharma."

Damario paused, his hand on the butt of his Ordnance. "Stop right there, Micah, before you say something you might regret and we'll have to arrest you."

"One of us will kill him tomorrow. If you won't, I will."

Damario pulled his Ordnance and trained it at Micah. "Hands behind your head. You're under arrest."

"Wait, man!" Quinne yelled. "Let him finish!"

Harper rushed to her husband's side, unaware that the "surprise" he had in store for her was plotting international murder. "Have you lost your mind?"

"In reality one, you are married to Officer Shenk and work for G.R. Cooper," said Micah in desperation.

Damario handcuffed him. ". . .for conspiracy to commit murder. . ."

"Your research helps sway enough House votes to block passage of the mark."

"You have the right to remain silent. . ."

"When you were sent back, you turn down the internship at G.R. Cooper and never attend Stern."

". . .anything you say may be used against you in a court of law. . ."

"Here, the mark passes, which is why you were sent back. . .to make sure it did!"

"D, stop." Madison unhooked Micah's handcuffs. "Did you hear what he said?"

Damario mentally inventoried the information. In February of 2034, he received recruitment correspondence from G.R. Cooper, offering him a paid internship with the promise of employment consideration at its conclusion. He disregarded it and all follow up electronic mails. If he had attended Stern, he might have met the native New Yorker; Madison still spent major holidays in Flushing.

Micah rolled his wrists and exhaled. "Teanna's son, Teiji, starts a grassroots petition in support of alternative fuel sources. It gets a groundswell of support and the president puts a 15-year ban on all drilling. When Teanna goes back, she aborts Teiji."

The word sucked the air out of Harper. She dropped into her seat and stared into open space. Her children might as well have been aborted; her choice to return exposed her to experimental environments that made her barren. She had to help fix this.

"Quinne saved the life of her boyfriend. In her original reality, she cleans up, becomes a marine, and shoots Kareza Noor dead. None of this ever happens."

The weight of her mistake hit Quinne like a giant weight. *Me?*

"Harper dropped her Applied Physics course in college and finished her degree in psychiatry. In two years, she would have counseled the scientist responsible for the arable land cure Adharma will give to Israel and Palestine. Without her, he decides to do it despite its damaging long-term effects." He swallowed hard. "I'm alive and I shouldn't be. I died in an explosion there."

"That's hardly a doomsday scenario."

"We live in a delicate balance, Officer Shenk. Six realities were altered with a specific end game in mind, and we're living in it.

Noor did not do that for sport. I'm willing to bet my life that the end game is destructive."

Damario stared at him. "If Kareza Noor killed a man and assumed his identity by absorbing into him, who's to say he can even be killed?"

Micah grew reflective. "The proof that we can make a difference doesn't exist, Detective. You have to believe, anyway."

The answer did little to assuage their fears, but inspired hope. Damario knew he should arrest this lunatic, but Madison appeared less disturbed than intrigued. Quinne pretended that the fate of the earth had not been in her hands and she dropped it. Harper cursed, and wondered out loud what her husband thought. *Assassination? Treason? Murder?*

"We had to be of one mind to get here. We'll have to be of similar mind going forward. Either you arrest me, or you stay."

The detectives exchanged looks. Madison played the heavy in instances where they deadlocked, and she said nothing.

"Harper, Quinne, same goes for you. Leave or stay – right here and now."

Though his viewpoint made less logical sense to her, Harper did not consider bailing out on him. She believed his story, or enough of it not to throw it all to the wolves. If this being – Kareza Noor, incarnate – was supernatural, shucking it from its human shell was not murder per se, but exposing its true nature. *They had to fix this.* "I'm in."

"Me, too," Quinne responded. The entire thing was wild; killing a prime minister to save the world based on events occurring in an alternate reality. If only she fired the kill shot in this reality, too! It would be too poetic for words; a badge of honor in the theater of war. She would not receive a medal, and may not survive, but she'd do it for the good of mankind.

"Arrest him, Shenk."

Madison stared at him. "I can't do that. Not until I hear the whole story."

"Can't or won't?"

"Neither."

Damario asserted himself. "Fine. I will. Hands behind your head, Micah. To your knees."

Harper moved to her husband's side. "If you arrest him, you'll have to arrest me, too."

Quinne joined in and flanked Micah's other side. "Yeah, me, too."

Madison banded together with the trio and gave her partner a look of expectation. *Join us or not.*

Ignoring the pull inside of his gut, Damario docked the handcuffs on his armament belt. Whatever convinced Madison, it strengthened his resolve. He did not want to see her die, nor did he desire to turn her in for going rogue. He showed his palms to the group in surrender, and walked out an unwilling accomplice, but not an active participant. Outside this situation, he considered silence different than acquiescence. Within his decision, he thought of it as a kind of self-preservation.

After entering Madison's Caper, he noticed a blinking message indicator from the precinct. He entered the security code and played the message. The man in question, Nandor Adharma, appeared on the holographic screen. Finely-dressed, Adharma smirked and trained his eyes ahead, as if somehow watching Damario.

"Officer Damario Coley," he said in the message. "At your convenience, please join me at the Royal Gentry hotel in the presidential suite. I have an urgent need to see you."

Damario started the engine and turned on his emergency lights. He would be there by 3:30 – about ten minutes. *What does he want with me?* Fear entered his heart, as he did not know the extent to which this being wielded supernatural powers. For a man who faced death in one form or another every day, this particular challenge terrified him. Beneath his shirt, he wore a cross. He wished it meant more to him than a piece of jewelry he rarely removed. Church was an afterthought for him and Robinne did not pressure the family to adhere to one particular faith. She believed in God, but thought Allah could be his name, too. The Koran, the New King James Bible, and several texts on Zen Buddhist philosophies and Confucianism lined her digital shelves. She read her daily horoscopes and preferred natural herbs to medicinal practices.

To Damario, God existed, and he did not debate another name for Him. But it was not Allah. He invoked Hebrew names for God; *El Elyon, El Shaddai, Jehovah-Raah* – in times of trouble. He did not "live for Jesus," but he believed in Him. He grew up in church, got baptized at 13, and regularly attended services until college work and a part-time job got in the way. Then, he met Robinne, who convinced him that Sunday mornings in bed with her could be a religious experience, too.

"Father," he said, exasperated. "This is a nightmare I can't wake up from. Why am I living this life? What am I supposed to do?"

At exactly 3:30, Damario pulled in front of the hotel and greeted the valet, who could not park the official vehicle. En route from the parking lot to the hotel entrance, he continued his prayer. "Protect me, please. I don't know what I'm walking into and I'm afraid."

As he entered, a thought popped into his head. *Do not lie.*

With all four heads-of-state staying in the luxury hotel, all personnel, official or not, had to surrender weapons, armament belts, shoes and holographic phones. Damario did so and passed the scanning without incident. The security detail afforded him comfortable sandals and escorted him to the elevator tubes. Damario braced himself for the propulsion to the presidential suite.

On the top floor, he was scanned once more and led to the penthouse by a droid. When the door opened, Adharma rose from a throne-like chair to greet him.

"Greetings!" He offered his hands and firmly clenched Damario's. "Come in, won't you?"

"Prime Minister Adharma. . ."

"Please," he implored. "Call me, Nandor. I hate lofty formal titles. Though others find them necessary, I find them pretentious."

Damario's armpits were moist with sweat. "Why did you ask to see me?"

"I greatly respect the office of a policeman, Detective. I need a favor from you."

"W-what could you possibly want from me?"

Adharma poured himself a tumbler of scotch. "Do you drink Irish scotch, Detective?" He drank a healthy amount before refilling the tumbler to a higher level. "This is 120-year-old Macallan. This little bit costs three months of your salary. Personally, I believe you're underpaid. You face all sorts of dangers every day. Have a dram with me. It'll be our little secret."

Reluctantly, Damario reached out his hand and accepted some. He relished the taste. It was much better than the bottle of Oban Madison bought for him. When he finished, Adharma offered him more, but he declined, still holding the glass.

"No, Detective, this is not a social call. You must know this insistence on tight security is Ramsey Mateo's doing and not my own. I see no need for it."

*No need for security?* "You're a world-renown politician. People want you dead."

"Death is not something I concern myself with, Detective." *Not anymore.* "I would like you to drive me to Camp Bradley tomorrow. Alone."

"Why me?"

"I suspect there's an American sleeper cell plotting to sabotage the talks. Are you aware of such a machination?"

Compelled to tell the truth, Damario nodded. "Yes."

Adharma guzzled his third tumbler of scotch. By now, he should be a bumbling drunk, but his alcohol tolerance proved to be astronomical. "You will be my shield. She will not shoot if she believes you to be in mortal danger. And you will be."

Damario's lip trembled. *How did he know?* "I won't do it."

On cue, Robinne entered into their view, bound at the hands and feet and gagged. Adharma flashed an ominous smile and physically restrained Damario from going to her with one hand. He raised an Ordnance with the other and shot Robinne dead without hesitation. Paralyzed with shock, Damario dropped the glass. His vision blurred and his shallow breathing bottomed out into hyperventilation.

Adharma placed his arm around Damario and whispered into his ear. "Tomorrow, at 6:15 in the morning, you and I will arrive at Camp Bradley. If I fail to get there, your in-laws and children will also die. This is a small taste of what I can do."

Through his haze, Damario did not doubt the sincerity of the killer's words. His thoughts translated into incoherent mumbling.

"You and your friends helped me solve a problem. In turn, I provided you the opportunity to reboot your lives, so to speak. And you granted me godhood. Thank you."

Suddenly, Damario snapped back to normal consciousness inside Madison's Caper at the James mansion. His right hand cradled a thumb-segment sized blood red disk with the Italian flag and crest emblazoned on it. *Did I dream it? A half-hour has passed!* He dialed Robinne at home, and received no answer. Immediately, he tried Adharma's penthouse at the Royal Gentry. He answered on the first ring.

"Hello, Officer Coley. How may I help you?"

"So, you do know me?"

"Of course," said Adharma in a convincing tone. "We spoke not too long ago."

Damario cursed at the man. "You killed my wife."

"I don't know what you mean, Detective. I did no such thing."

At that, his holophone rang. The caller identification said it originated from his home. Without announcing so, he muted the transport line and picked up. "Robbie, are you okay? Where were you?"

"Hey Damario," said his father-in-law. "I brought the kids home because her mom has the stomach flu and I can't pull double-duty. Robbie told us what's going on."

He paused. "Is she okay?"

"Robbie? Yeah, she's at our house."

"Do you know that for sure?"

"Sure as a half-hour ago. Don't worry. I'll stick around to see them off to school tomorrow. The school transport gets here at a quarter after 6:00, right?"

Damario froze. *It did.* "Thanks, Dad. I'll talk to you later." He un-muted Adharma.

"So, are we done here, Officer Coley? I have a four o' clock."

Still confused, he backtracked. "Why did you ask to see me again?"

Adharma pointed to the thumb-segment sized, blood red disk. "The arrangements for driving me tomorrow. Please be prompt, as we must arrive no later than 6:15 a.m.. You understand – timeliness will throw off the criminal element."

"I understand what must happen, Mister Prime Minister."

"Good," he uttered. "I will see you then."

Damario dragged himself from the vehicle toward the mansion's entrance. Quinne, Micah, Harper and Madison – who crossed her arms and frowned – gathered and met him outside. "You can't kill Adharma, Maddie." His voice broke.

Her glare melted into tender compassion. "D, where have you been?"

"If you shoot him, he'll kill Robbie, her parents, and my kids. He showed me he would."

Micah grew alarmed. *He knows about us, what we want to do.* Among the quintet, Madison was the best shooter. "You went to see him?"

"He called me, Micah. Asked me to be his driver to Camp Bradley tomorrow. If I don't, he'll do it. He said Maddie won't shoot him, if I'm in the way."

*He's right.* "What's the play?"

Damario cleared his throat. "We kill him first."

# CHAPTER TWENTY-THREE

*January 31, 2050*

Early Monday morning, Damario used his name at each security checkpoint en route to the Royal Gentry hotel and glided through them without issue. He maintained a steady driving pace and minded the delicate package on the passenger seat.

"Prime Minister Adharma is expecting you," the human guards said with a hint of jealousy. Adharma's reputation as a peacemaker, worldwide financial icon, social media maven, and political strategist preceded him. President Mateo rode shotgun on this deal. The conference revolved around Adharma and what he alone could do.

He left his transport at the hotel and entered another; a black stretch with tinted windows, flying the Italian flag. Damario wished for coffee. The two lattes he drank after his 2:00 a.m. alarm woke him up and stimulated him for now, but the unmapped road to Camp Bradley was dark, wide, straight and poorly lit. He and Madison knew this and shared it with the group the night before, suggesting the cover might mask a getaway on foot.

According to the orders handed to him by Adharma, they were the first stretch Bentley of three. Eight police motorcyclists and Capers preceded them. Without a distraction or unforeseen obstacle, the motorcade would travel too fast for anyone but an Olympic-class marksman or professional sniper to successfully shoot it. The Bentley's tinted glass was standard issue and not bulletproof.

"Good morning, Detective." A cheery Adharma slid into the backseat. "What a wonderful day to change the course of the world as we know it!"

He tipped his uniform cap in deference. "May I ask you a question, Mister Prime Minister?"

"Teanna Kirkwood? Theodore Mitchell? Yes, I killed them both," he said matter-of-factly. "You were never going to figure that out. I destroyed the Ordnance, disabled the cameras and erased the transfer. Now, let's get going. We don't want to be late."

When Adharma clapped his hands, Damario started the engine and turned up the heat. *I should turn around and kill him now.* His Ordnance weighed heavily against his hip. Micah warned him not to give into his anger – especially with no guarantees for his safety, or that of his children. Now, in the man's presence, he could care less and wanted the evil presence to suffer and die miserably. But he stuck with the plan.

Minutes later, the caravan pulled off and Damario fell in line. Helicopter/jet hybrids followed overhead, shining spotlights down ahead of them.

Adharma closed the solid barrier between Bentley's cab and its rear. God only knows what he's doing back there, Damario thought. Though a frost warning had been declared, the road had slickness in some spots. He did his best not to skid much, though he'd gladly trade an arm and eye in a crash, if it meant destroying Adharma.

Pressured with the second most important task – the distraction – Harper completed it to the best of her ability using household switches and common chemicals. It unnerved her, as she violated her government contract and at least three or four national and international laws doing it. Thankfully, chemistry was her specialty in college; fellow students came to her for study notes and advice. Applied Physics was where she struggled, and the fact she chose psychiatry in another life was not surprising. Micah supervised her and stepped in when she trembled too much to handle mixing volatile substances. In all, she assembled two modes of destruction.

To avoid suspicion, Madison donned her uniform and handcuffed them both. She would drive.

Quinne heard Madison call her five minutes ago. Waves of adrenaline and nerves kept her vigilant. She did not need a lengthy explanation to do her part. She looked at it as her first official order as a soldier. She mused on her artificial future and the different battles she figured to have. The glory of war did not outshine its ugliness – like how it broke her uncle into flawed mental and physical fragments. Her bones might have been powdered in places, like his, and she would relive the horrific smell of death into her golden years.

*If I make it that far.*

If not, glory awaited her on the other side. She believed in God and Jesus, and even "got saved" years ago. She just did not pay obeisance to the Jesus that Anibel worshipped. The battles of the Bible interested her most; where kings of ancient times killed everything moving. The only one to die in battle that she remembered was Saul. He could not follow orders – something she would never fail at doing.

To keep himself awake, Damario thought back to the last time he had seen his children; another day he left without spending time with them. He choked up, thinking about his boy's chubby legs and Christian's recent developmental strides. There were no guarantees that he'd return to them, but if he did not do anything, they might as well be dead. Nothing about Adharma indicated a tendency to keep his word.

Madison involuntarily popped into his head. On Sunday night, before he left for the hotel room in one of Micah's Cougars, he received a passionate kiss from Madison. He did not pull back as fast as he should have. Worse, he enjoyed it. The touch felt familiar and touched off a heated chemical reaction in his body. *What was I supposed to do?* Under the threat of death, she indulged a desire. Robinne would never understand it, in any form.

*Whenever you go back to something, it's never the same,* he thought.

Without warning, the caravan slowed. Damario panicked, as any setback advanced time closer to 6:15, and he was the only one in a rush. Adharma retracted the sliding partition and glowered through the opening. "You have a schedule to keep, Officer Coley. Find out what's going on."

Damario hurriedly called the emergency channel. It didn't work! He pounded his fists into the steering wheel until the horn burped. "My orders are not to leave you, Mister Prime Minister."

"Find out what's going on. Get out and do it!"

He exited the Bentley. The other officers did the same, as their communications had been shut down, as well. As they neared the lead Caper, a dead deer and two of its young came into view. The animals, who slipped in running across the road, had downed three policemen and their cycles.

Damario tapped one of his superiors on the shoulder. "We're gonna keep going soon, right? We can drive around that."

"Get back to the Prime Minister, Coley. Now!"

He jogged back to his Bentley and noticed a rustling in the

bushes. Thinking it to be another animal, Damario entered the transport seconds before an explosion shattered the windows, igniting billowing clouds of flame and smoke.

Madison covered her mouth to muffle her cries. With the plan broken by the deer, each person on the team had to improvise. The overhead spotlights shined on her, and the reflective snow banks illuminated her position to the policeman searching for an assailant.

"Freeze!" they yelled.

Instead, she ran, darting through tree branches, zig-zagging to avoid Ordnance fire. To her left was a dangerous slope. She steered away from it, but inadvertently led the chase to the original rendezvous point. To throw them off and to warn the others, Madison drew her weapon, turned, and haphazardly fired in her pursuers' direction. They split into two groups; those who continued after her, and the marksmen who set up to return fire.

When she resumed running, several shots embedded into her back, causing her stumble and roll down the mountainside of jagged rocks.

Without evidence to the contrary, Micah knew both he and Harper would be in jail for the rest of their lives, or worse. He still carried the bigger explosive. Though Quinne could not be found, they would not run. It was not part of the plan.

"God, forgive me," he said. "I love you. I never said that enough." Bright lights had exposed their position. As policemen closed in on them, he kissed the tears away from Harper's face.

"I love you too," she muttered. "And I'm sorry for passing physics."

He smiled. "This is the life we were meant to have, Harp."

"Hands behind your heads." Obeying the simple command could set off the timing mechanism, which Harper set at five seconds.

She looked at Micah, incredulously. "What life? Well-organized suicide?"

"Purpose."

The phalanx of officers led them down the embankment, where they would summon reinforcements. Micah looked over at his wife, who smiled when the officers removed the package hidden underneath his jacket and opened it. Together, they quietly counted to five.

The second, larger explosion drew all remaining human attention away from the conflagration burning in Adharma's luxury transport. Quinne gripped the Ordnance with her hands and skulked behind the smoldering vehicle, ducking behind it whenever the lights got too close. *Something's moving inside.*

When a break in surveillance provided itself, she poked the barrel through the busted windows and squeezed off a few rounds. The passenger seats were empty.

Whirling around, Quinne searched the darkness and its depths for him. Emergency sirens faintly roared miles away. At that distance, she had – at best – two or three minutes to complete her mission. The stench of death filled the air. Quinne refused to search the Bentley further for fear of seeing Damario. *Where is he?* She circled the vehicle and found a coughing Adharma on bended knee.

Blood flowed down his nose and from his ears. *"You. . ."*

Quinne pulled the trigger three times at point blank range. The projectiles penetrated Adharma's skull and dropped him to the macadam.

She watched him die, celebrating when he breathed his last.

When they came to arrest her, she laid the Ordnance down, fell prostrate on the highway, and placed her hands behind her back. *I did my part.* Her compatriots paid the ultimate price so she should pay hers. They had saved the world, and no one would believe the tale if she told it.

# EPILOGUE

Throughout the trial, Quinne admitted complicity in the assassination plot. She passed every psychological test. Her lack of remorse heightened the American public's outcry for blood. Protesters lined the court steps, calling for the teenager to receive the maximum penalty. Not even the Hispanic political groups who opposed the death penalty came to her aid.

Guillermo and Anibel did not visit their daughter during her imprisonment, nor did they attend her sentencing. However, Damario's widow, Robinne, flew to the prison once with her children. So did Charlotte Lowe, Laverne James, Gene and Hilary Shenk, and a girl named Crystal who had helped Micah. All asked to know why their loved ones participated in propaganda of the deed. Quinne's unspectacular, dissatisfying answer echoed her response to the media.

"We did what we was meant to do. . .to make things right again."

Adharma's death forced the mark down to a fraction of its former glory and incurred a financial crisis across four continents. Israel and Palestine resumed fighting in the most bloody of manners, decimating the Dome of the Rock and the Wailing Wall. The ten-mark nations suffered from skyrocketing poverty.

Now, two weeks away from lethal injection, Quinne paced in her cell until a guard escorted her to an open meeting area. There, Channel Zero personality Nora Hunter would conduct the first one-on-one interview with the most infamous living criminal in recent history.

Dressed in a black and white Hristoff pantsuit, Nora warmly smiled. "Try to relax, be honest and open. Think of it as an opportunity to tell your side of the story."

She nodded and closed her eyes, as a makeup artist dusted her dry skin with powder.

Nora paused until the droid-operated camera glowed red. "Good evening. I'm Nora Hunter with Channel Zero, reporting live from the women's federal penitentiary. Quinne Marybeth Ruiz, the 19-year-old convicted of murdering Italian Prime Minister, Nandor Adharma, is speaking for the first time weeks before her execution by lethal injection.

"Quinne, your co-conspirators perished. You've claimed guilt from the get-go and declined to appeal your conviction. Why not try to save your life?"

She licked her lips. "My friends died for what we believed. I ain't no better than them. Ain't no different than a soldier on a mission's the way I see it."

"Who gave you that mission? *God?*"

Quinne remembered the Geometric Occipital Demonstrative Symbiotic Interface's nickname and smirked. *Things look different through God's eyes.* "I guess."

"Members of the religious community hail you four for saving the world from damnation, but media outlets have branded you 'anarchists'. Your thoughts?

She said nothing.

It's how they would be remembered.

**THE END**

# The Anarchists

Book Club Study Guide

After I finish a novel, I love thinking about what entertained or saddened me, and discussing the psychology behind the characters' behaviors with people who have read the same book. I sincerely hope these questions spark your group to have lively thoughts and conversations about the themes, issues, and conflicts at the heart of *The Anarchists.*

If you would like me to sit in on your group's discussion of *The Anarchists,* (in person, by webcam, or by phone) feel free to e-mail me at brian@authorbrianthompson.com

## GENERAL QUESTIONS

1. Which moments caught you by surprise?

2. What is the book's strongest theme?

3. Put yourself in the writer's chair. How would you have ended the book?

# CHARACTER SPECIFIC QUESTIONS

## *Micah*

1. Micah came from a rich spiritual heritage, but he shunned the faith. Why do you think he did this?

2. Gabrielle was Micah's daughter from a previous relationship. Explain the difficulties of nurturing a relationship or marriage with this type of situation.

3. What events turned Micah's mind in regards to the possibility of God?

## *Harper:*

1. What appears to be Harper's main issue with Micah: the fact that he's unemployed and they have money struggles or that he's reluctant to marry her?

2. Charlotte Lowe, Harper's mother, is affluent, yet refuses to help her daughter out financially. Discuss reasons why a parent may make this decision regarding their child.

3. Harper's decision to change her profession to something more lucrative also rendered her infertile. Is it a myth that a career woman can also successfully balance a family without one or the other suffering? Discuss.

## *Damario:*

1. After discovering Madison's marital infidelities, Damario did not divorce her. What do you think was his motivation for staying married to her?

2. Damario had marriages fail in two different instances. What do you think was the common denominator of them both?

3. Whom do you think Damario loved more, Robinne or Madison? Why?

## Quinne:

1. Troy's death sends Quinne on a downward spiral into alcohol and drugs. How do you think she could have been saved from this abusive behavior?

2. Crystal Cantrell, or "Cee Cee," was Quinne's best friend and roommate, but Quinne viewed her as judgmental, which is often a criticism of Christians. Could Cee Cee have demonstrated her faith in a different way to make it attractive to Quinne? If so, how?

3. Kareza states in the first reality that Quinne shoots her to death. In the second reality, Quinne kills Kareza by shooting her and receives the death penalty. In your opinion, did she fail to fulfill her destiny? Why or why not?

## Teanna:

1. Explain what you believe is the motivating factor behind Teanna's substance abuse.

2. Teanna involves herself in a destructive relationship with Tiny. Why do you think a single mother in Teanna's position would continue to date a man like him?

3. Teanna's decision to sever ties with Teiji's father leads to her aborting her son, never conceiving Meleasa and preventing her physical problems. She never knows the full effects of her choices until she dies. Explain what sort of insight you think you will have into your life choices at the end.

## Discover more by Brian Thompson:

Seers foretell the birth of a legendary king destined to enter a mysterious gate and end his people's oppression. Whether or not this passageway exists, nobody knows.

Following a brutal infanticide, the people give up hope, until a man with unbreakable bones emerges from the wilderness.

*Five out of five stars, "This blend of prophecies and Scripture will truly inspire everyone who reads it. I loved it! –Michelle Sutton, author of more than a dozen novels*

ISBN: 978-0-615-44374-4 * Paperback * 216 pages
Available in all electronic formats

www.greatnationpublishing.com

His personal life ruined, an ousted pastor flees south to start over, but is interrupted by a woman with a hideous scar and a secret. She passes him her life's work. Now, following her murder, it's up to him to spread the message she fought to protect, battle violent enemies, and face an uncertain destiny.

*"With suspense, humor, realism, and integrity, Thompson's The Lost Testatement is a worthy read that holds its own." — Stephanie Perry Moore, author of the Alec London series.*

ISBN: 978-0-578-05549-7 * Paperback * 264 pages
Available in all electronic formats

www.greatnationpublishing.com

www.ingramcontent.com/pod-product-compliance
Lightning Source LLC
Chambersburg PA
CBHW071130170626
46809CB00002B/558